ANY SECOND CHANCE

BOOK 2 OF THE TIME WRECKER TRILOGY

....

ELLEN SMITH

ESW BOOKS

WASHINGTON, DC

ESW Books
Washington, DC

Editing: Shayla Raquel, ShaylaRaquel.com
Cover Design: Monica Haynes, TheThatchery.com
Book Layout ©2020 BookDesignTemplates.com

Any Second Chance/ Ellen Smith. -- 1st ed.
ISBN 978-0-9961999-4-0

For my husband,
A.B.S.
and our children,
G.B.S., R.N.S., and V.M.S.

ANY SECOND CHANCE

Chapter One

WILL

He had been waiting too long.

Will Sterling shifted from one foot to the other, peering up and down the busy sidewalk. It was almost six in the evening, and the city showed no signs of slowing down. Will stood only steps away from the restaurant entrance, but he might as well have been invisible to the people who hurried by.

Across the street, at least a dozen people were knotted tightly around an earnest-looking speaker. Protestors, probably. Will took off his glasses, breathed on them, and untucked his dress shirt enough to wipe the lenses. He probably should have changed after the graduation ceremony, but his other dress shirt hadn't been clean and Will only had one sport coat. He pushed his glasses back on his nose and wondered if he looked as ridiculous as he felt, wearing a suit in the stifling heat.

Will could clearly see the gathering across the street now. Definitely protestors. Some of them were wearing white T-shirts with handwritten slogans scrawled across them. One had a poster board sign that read:

One Life, One Time

Make Justice STICK in 2006

That was something Will could count on about life in Washington, DC: There was always something to protest. In the last four years at Adams Morgan University, Will had probably seen hundreds of fliers for marches and sit-ins. AMU prided itself on social activism. Nearly every class broke into small-group discussions about the issues and ended in passionate arguments about American values.

Now that he was a newly minted college graduate, he hoped he'd never get roped into debating like that again.

Evidently, the growing crowd across the street didn't share Will's reluctance for activism. They were starting to get louder now, and the speaker in the center was even more animated.

"Do the crime, do the time!" shouted the speaker. The protestors nodded and murmured their agreement. They were talking about timeline rectification, Will guessed. Sending criminals back in time to right their wrongs.

The back of Will's neck prickled, and he reached up to wipe the sweat that had gathered under his collar.

"Do the crime, do the time!" the speaker said again,

insistently. The crowd tried to pick up the chant. They were quiet at first. Off tempo. Like a beginner picking out their first rhythm on a snare drum. Then their voices grew stronger, and a few linked arms.

Will turned away from the scene just as someone tackled him from behind.

"Hey, bachelor." Mara turned him around, laughing, and at the sight of her wide brown eyes, Will forgot everything else.

"Hey yourself," Will said. "And you won't be able to call me that for too much longer."

He leaned down and kissed her, lifting her chin up as he did. Mara usually shied away from public displays of affection, but today she threw her arms around his neck and kissed him back as if no one was watching. Will held her closer and marveled, again, at how perfectly they fit together.

"I was talking about your shiny new bachelor's degree, thank you very much," Mara said. The diamond on her left hand caught the light as she swiped back a strand of her long, dark hair.

"You got one too," Will said. "And yours was summa cum laude."

Mara shrugged. "Only registrars care about that," she said. "The degree is what gets you places. And . . . is this weird? I honestly feel like an adult now. It's just a piece of paper, but I actually feel a little older."

"You should feel a lot older," Will said. "We listened to

'Pomp and Circumstance' for a hundred years."

Mara suddenly turned, and Will realized the chant across the street had grown louder. "How long has that been going on?"

"Just since I got here," Will said. "Not long."

"That's going to put Dad in a great mood." Mara was quiet for a minute. "I think something's going on with his campaign. Dad's been super tense lately."

"What else is new?" Will asked. On an average day, Congressman Gaines exuded the kind of pressure that could turn coal into a diamond.

Mara didn't laugh. "I mean more than usual. He introduced that bill on Thursday—the one about outlawing time wrecks. I guess he thought it would save his reelection campaign, but . . . it hasn't. Dad's never had this much trouble in an election year."

Even the year he was accused of embezzlement? Will knew better than to say that out loud. Mara's smile had already disappeared, replaced by a little crease in her forehead. Will wanted to wipe away that crease and all the worries that came with it.

"Then maybe the little rally over there will cheer him up. They sound like they're on his side."

Mara's lips curved up, but her eyes weren't smiling. "Eh. They're probably not from his district."

"Okay," Will said. He took the opportunity to put his arm around Mara's shoulder and turn them both toward the restaurant. "How about this. In two days, my apartment will be *our* apartment. And in two weeks—"

"I get to be your wife," Mara finished. The crease in her forehead had vanished, and she laced her fingers through his. They walked up the stairs and into the restaurant together, leaving the loud, hot night behind them.

◆◆◆◆◆

Their families had been talking. Will could tell by the way his brother and sister leaped up and greeted them with high voices and extra-bright smiles. Will looked from face to face around the table, trying to guess what had happened while he was waiting for Mara outside. *Please not another argument about the wedding. Anything but that.*

Will's mother stood up to hug them both—"There's my graduate!"—and Mara's grandmother reached out to squeeze both their hands. Only Mara's parents stayed seated. Congressman Gaines nodded a greeting, and Mrs. Gaines said, "I was beginning to worry. Were you lost?"

"Traffic," Mara said lightly.

Will cast a wary eye at a low-hanging chandelier and made his way carefully around the table. Being over six feet tall had its advantages, but navigating fancy light fixtures was not one of them. Restaurants like this made Will feel like he was always just about to do something stupid, like knock over someone's water glass or catch his shirt sleeve on one of the little votive candles.

Will remembered just in time to pull out Mara's chair for her, but Congressman Gaines didn't appear to notice. Chris did, though. Will's two-years-younger brother gave him a sarcastic thumbs up and mouthed a single word—"whipped"—followed by a smile to show he was only teasing. Probably.

"Mara!" Becca said from across the table. "My prom pictures came yesterday. The dress was perfect. I can't wait to wear it again." She started to dig in her purse, but Bonnie Sterling held out a hand to stop her.

"Not now," their mother whispered. "Tonight is about Mara and Will's graduation. You can tell her about prom later."

"No, I asked her to bring them," Mara insisted, which was all the encouragement Becca needed to slide three photos across the table. Will recognized the woman in the pictures as his baby sister. He knew she'd bought her bridesmaid dress early so she could wear it to prom too. But now, seeing pictures of Becca dressed in a floor-length gold gown, with her hair all done up, she looked an awful lot like an adult.

"You look stunning," Mara said. "And is this . . . ?" Mara tapped the slick-haired boy posing with her in one picture, and Becca blushed. She was probably grateful when Mara's mother cut in.

"Mara, what's that paint on your fingernails? Is that blue? I thought you were getting a French manicure." Mrs. Gaines lowered her chin and glared at Mara over her bifocals.

"I did get a French manicure," Mara said. "In blue."

"Well, it looks awful. Make sure you get all of that off before next week. I have errands for you to run before the wedding."

"It'll be fine, Mom," Mara said.

Will watched the conversation like a tennis match. It was always a little startling for him to see Mara and her mother together, if only because they looked so much alike. "I'm halfanese," Mara used to say, flippantly, whenever anyone at college asked about her ethnicity. "But I guess the Japanese genes ran stronger." That was an understatement. Aside from the thirty-year age difference, Mara and Mrs. Gaines were identical. Physically, anyway.

"The blue matches your dress today. Very pretty," Mara's grandmother chimed in. Unlike Mara and her mother, Congressman Gaines and his mother barely looked related at all. Mary Gaines—or Grandmary, as Mara called her—was a tall, willowy woman with light brown hair barely frosted with white. She always seemed relaxed, as if she were just sitting down to tea. In contrast, Congressman Gaines was short, dark-haired, and perpetually in a hurry.

Grandmary smiled at Mara with genuine affection. "Mara, I can't tell you how proud I was to see you walking across that stage. All of your hard work has paid off."

"She's made progress," Mrs. Gaines allowed. "But of course, there's med school in the fall. That's when the real work begins. My first year of law school made college look like kindergarten."

Will's stomach clenched. *Here we go.*

His mother, Bonnie Sterling, cleared her throat. "I'm proud of both of them." Her helmet of blond hair, no doubt sprayed in place with layers of Aqua Net, quivered as she bit off each word. "Will has worked hard to get where he is today. He has a teaching job already lined up too."

"Of course," Mrs. Gaines said hastily. "Yes, they've both worked very hard."

Becca had gone completely still, while Chris balled his napkin up in his hand. They weren't going to college. Chris hadn't had the grades. He'd spent the last two years working in the stock room at Lowry's drug store, with the none-too-secret hope that someday he would work his way up to assistant manager. Becca was just about to graduate high school with a decent grade point average, but she hadn't been able to get a scholarship. Will had been the first of the Sterling family to go to college, and it looked like he would be the last one for a while.

I earned that scholarship. I deserved my chance. But Will couldn't quite make the pang of guilt go away.

"Although, it is a shame you'll be working up here," said Bonnie Sterling. "I really wish y'all would consider moving down to North Carolina. I know you want to stay up here while Mara finishes her schooling, but maybe afterward, you could move a little closer to home."

"You never know," Mara said smoothly.

Not on your life, Will thought.

Bonnie continued. "It's not like there's going to be a shortage of jobs for either of you. With Will being a music teacher and Mara going to be a nurse—"

"Doctor," Mara and Will said at the same time.

"Well, anyway." Bonnie sighed. "I just hope you'll consider it."

Will heard Chris coughing, the way he did when he was trying to cover up a laugh. It never worked as well as he thought it did. Out of the corner of his eye, Will could see that Chris and Becca were both hunched over their menus as if they were seriously considering the options.

Whatever. Chris always ordered the same thing. Steak and potatoes if they were somewhere classy, chicken tenders and fries if they weren't. Will guessed Becca would get a salad. According to their mother, Becca had given up the Atkins diet and decided to be a vegetarian instead.

Chris's little coughing fit drew a scathing glare from Bonnie across the table. Even though it wasn't directed at him, Will felt the weight of her scrutiny and looked away.

Congressman Gaines was staring intently at his BlackBerry, tapping out a message with both thumbs. It buzzed suddenly, the way Mara's did when she got an email, and the congressman frowned deeper.

Mrs. Gaines pursed her lips and nudged her husband. "Dear," she whispered. "Dear."

"My apologies," Congressman Gaines said, without looking away from the phone. "Please, carry on without me."

"Some people are making trouble for his campaign," Mrs. Gaines explained. She offered a smile to the rest of the table that said, *Please excuse my husband.* "He's putting it away now."

They all tried not to watch as Congressman Gaines, oblivious to his wife's words, continued reading and tapping on the screen.

This was exactly what Mara had been dreading. Will slid a hand under the tablecloth and squeezed her knee. Mara closed her hand around his and squeezed back.

"Dear," Mrs. Gaines said again, at the same time Mara's grandmother said, "Joel!"

The congressman sighed and clipped the BlackBerry back onto his belt. "Apologies," he said again. "It seems something . . . has come up. However"—he cleared his throat—"nothing could be more important than our time together." Congressman Gaines lifted his sweating water glass, and everyone rushed to do the same. "To new beginnings."

"To new beginnings," they all mumbled in unison.

"To Will and Mara on their graduation. We couldn't be prouder of you!" Bonnie Sterling jumped in.

Everyone raised their glasses again.

Will could feel his future father-in-law eyeing him intently. Will held his stare, steeling himself to keep from flinching. The congressman looked over at Mara and then back at Will.

Someone—Will guessed Grandmary—cleared her throat.

"Yes. To Will and Mara," said the Congressman, and he lifted his glass as well.

Tensions Rise as Time Wrecker Bill Moves Forward

May 18, 2006

WASHINGTON, DC — If Congressman Gaines has anything to say about it, time travel could soon become a thing of the past.

Timeline rectifications are at the center of yet another House debate. Earlier this week, Congressman Joel Gaines of Virginia introduced HR 6437. Nicknamed the "Time Wrecker Bill," Gaines's proposal would dramatically increase restrictions on the parole-alternative program. Some fear the new regulations would make timeline rectifications too difficult to obtain.

Others feel the bill does not go far enough. They are still calling for an immediate end to the controversial practice of timeline rectification, or "time wrecking."

Since the technology was introduced in 2000, timeline rectification has required approval from both perpetrators and victims of the crime. Currently, convicts must undergo a rigorous six-month rehabilitation program before timeline rectification is considered. Victims and witnesses of the crime must also consent to allow the criminal the chance to "undo" their actions. Their agreement must be vetted by a psychiatrist and a social worker before the case goes before a judge.

HR 6437 would increase these requirements for both convicts and the victims of their crimes. Under Gaines's plan, criminals would be required to complete a two-year rehabilitation program that incorporates growth opportunities and job training should their application for a timeline rectification be denied. Victims and witnesses would also be required to attend counseling sessions for two years to ensure they have been given the tools to deal with their trauma. Additionally, the burden of proof would be shared by criminals and victims alike to explain why the effects of the crime were "unusually difficult to overcome through other means."

Nelson Hart, lobbyist and cofounder of the prison outreach program Hart to Heart, was quick to voice his objections to HR 6437. "This bill is designed to strangle timeline rectification entirely," said Hart. "Rehabilitation takes time, healing takes time, but it also requires action. An extra eighteen months of thumb-twiddling is going to increase the likelihood that criminals and victims become entrenched in those roles, rather than acting to change them . . . [the timeline rectification] system we have now is working. We have less crowded prisons than we had six years ago, less people in halfway houses and reentry programs, less crime, because the system works."

Timeline rectification does work—perhaps too well. Since no one retains memory of the original crime after a rectification, it's hard to determine just how much of an impact time wrecking has had on society. However, data released in annual reports from the Timeline Rectification Division shows that former criminals have a low recidivism rate. Prior crime victims who received timeline rectifications reportedly enjoy higher education, employment, and income levels than crime victims who did not. States are spending far less on prisons and supervised release programs than they were prior to 2000 as well. While the Department of Timeline Rectification stops short of providing a number of completed rectifications—claiming "the logistics of providing an up-to-the-minute number in this field would be impossible"—estimates frequently number in the tens of thousands.

Although many have heralded HR 6437 as a step in the right

direction, not all are pleased. Anti-time wrecking organization One Life, One Time has publicly separated themselves from Congressman Gaines. Although once a staunch supporter of the congressman, the organization acted quickly to denounce HR 6437.

"There is no moral or ethical way to justify changing the past," said Alicia Barnes, founder and CEO of One Life, One Time. "Although the crime may only directly affect the criminals and victims, time affects us all. We are continuing to call on our legislators to immediately and permanently halt timeline rectifications."

Congressman Joel Gaines defended his bill and his position in a brief statement to the press. "No, we aren't trying to shut down timeline rectifications. I've come to realize that doing so would be unnecessarily harsh. We're simply trying to limit its use to situations where there is truly no reasonable or decent alternative. We want to make sure that offenders and victims have every opportunity to get their lives back on track before we resort to altering time."

Although HR 6437 falls short of outlawing timeline rectifications, the stringent requirements could make them nearly impossible to obtain. Could HR 6437 spell the end of timeline rectification? Only time will tell.

COMMENTS

HeyNowLilSusie
Oh, hey, something's actually helping to reduce crime. Surprised it took a politician this long to put a stop to it.

> **Starzzz**
> And not just any politician. Do you know anything about Joel

Gaines? Look up his background. It's . . . illuminating.

Dinomyte

Hold the phone. So the Department of Timeline Rectification literally releases data on the effectiveness of their program, and just sits on the names and criminal history of everyone who's ever been involved? Is anyone concerned about this? Any of us could be a criminal or a victim and not even know it. But Uncle Sam knows.

HHC559

Uncle Sam knows, and he's going to deny you a security clearance.

Dinomyte

Forget that. Uncle Sam knows, and he's going to make us pay.

No1ButME

Oh, my sweet summer child. Yes. The government knows more about us than we know about ourselves. It's 2006, and you're just now figuring this out?

Dinomyte

No need to be condescending. I wasn't trying to be argumentative, just thought-provoking.

No1ButME

And I think this happens a lot more than the average American realizes or cares. There you go. Thought provoked.

PrincessP

I wish the bill had a lot more restrictions, but I'm not going to turn up my nose at what's been proposed. Personally, I don't agree with timeline rectification at all, but at least I'm willing to listen to people who disagree with me and COMPROMISE. Reading these comments is like listening to a bunch of children! No need to argue about everything!

No1ButME

Welcome to the internet, PrincessP. I don't think you're going to like it here.

....

Chapter Two

MARA

Mara tapped a blue-painted fingernail on the steering wheel and sighed. It was only about ten miles from her parents' house in Alexandria to Will's apartment in DC. If traffic was light and luck was on her side, that meant a forty-minute drive.

Given the long parade of brake lights ahead of her on the George Washington Memorial Parkway, today was definitely not Mara's lucky day.

I should have waited. Mara knew as well as anyone what rush hour would be like at nine o'clock on a Monday morning. Only this time, Mara wasn't on her way to school. She was on her way to Will.

Mara's car was packed to the brim with the last of the belongings she'd kept at her parents' house. Books she hadn't had room for on campus, mostly, and winter clothes she hadn't worn for months. The rest of her things were already in Will's apartment.

Soon-to-be our apartment.

The question of where Mara would live for the two weeks between graduation and the wedding had rarely been discussed. Tristan, Will's roommate, had moved out just before commencement—hopefully taking his life-size Wookiee replica with him. Mara's parents hadn't had an opinion about her officially moving in with Will. At least, Mara assumed they didn't. They hadn't exactly asked, and she hadn't exactly volunteered.

Will's mother had an opinion, though. At the end of the graduation dinner, Bonnie Sterling had fixed her son with a look that spoke volumes.

"I'm sure you'll be lonely in that apartment now that Tristan's moved out," she said. "I'm sorry we have to go back on Sunday—you know if it wasn't for work, I'd love to stay longer."

"I'll be fine, Mom," Will had said. The tips of his ears always turned pink when he was embarrassed. Mara loved that. Even if she didn't love being lectured by proxy on chastity.

Bonnie had pursed her lips and nodded before turning to Mara. "I guess you'll be spending some time with your parents these next few weeks. Soaking in those last few minutes at home before you have to move out and be a wife. What all do you and your mom have planned?"

Mara was glad her parents and grandmother had already left before this little exchange. "Just wedding stuff," she'd mumbled before Will jumped in and changed the subject.

Technically, Mara had gone back to her parents' house that weekend, even though she was alone the whole time. Her father had stayed at his DC office, citing some kind of urgent situation. Something to do with his reelection campaign, Mara supposed. Her father had claimed so many "urgent situations" over the years that she'd stopped asking. Mara didn't know where her mother had been that weekend. Working, probably.

There was an ache somewhere Mara couldn't pinpoint whenever she started thinking about her parents. She pushed it down and focused on the traffic ahead of her instead. There was a little space in the right lane. Mara merged smoothly and pushed the accelerator up to twenty miles per hour before she had to slam on her brakes again. Still, she felt better. It was progress.

So her childhood hadn't been that great. So what? Mara was a college graduate now. A future doctor. A future *wife*.

Despite the almost-standstill traffic, Mara smiled.

◆◆◆◆◆

Tristan-less, the apartment seemed so large and bare it practically echoed. It wasn't just the giant Wookiee model missing from the corner of the living room, although Mara was relieved not to have it towering over the end of the couch anymore. For their entire senior year, this apartment had been full of people more often than not. There had always been a video game tournament in progress, a senior project spread out on the kitchen table, or somebody wandering around the apartment with their laptop, trying to get a wireless signal. It had been a little crazy and a lot of fun.

Now the apartment was mostly empty and, Mara noticed, freshly vacuumed. Actually, the whole place looked cleaner than she'd ever seen it. Other than a few stacks of paper and unopened mail on the counter, the only clutter to speak of was the pile of boxes Will had helped her carry up from the car.

Mara spun around in a slow circle, taking it all in. The living room still had the two matching desks under each window, the extra-long brown couch, Will's keyboard, and a black IKEA coffee table. To the right of the living room was the kitchen and dining area. To the left was a little hallway with the bathroom on one side and bedrooms on the other.

That was it. Eight hundred and twenty square feet of paradise.

Will must have been thinking the same thing because he leaned down to kiss her. A sweet kiss, followed by another longer one that promised more to come.

"Welcome home," Will said. He frowned. "Wait. Wasn't I supposed to carry you over the threshold or something?"

"That's after the wedding," Mara said.

Will had turned the air conditioning on full blast after their last trip up the stairs. It came on with such force that the plastic vertical blinds on the living-room windows swayed back and forth, clicking a little against the two desks underneath. Goosebumps erupted on Mara's arms.

Will took off his glasses, breathed steam on them, and wiped them with the edge of his T-shirt. Without his glasses, Will's light blue eyes and the freckles that dotted his nose stood out. Mara felt a rush of heat rising in her chest. It was no wonder she'd fallen in love with this man—this kind, brilliant, utterly adorable man. And somehow, he'd fallen in love with her too.

"What are you smiling about?" Will asked.

"Just happy," Mara said.

"Good," Will said. "You're definitely happier than the last time I saw you."

"What, when we were suffering death by a thousand paper cuts over dinner?"

Will laughed a little. "Yeah. Sorry about my family."

"And mine! But hey," Mara said, holding a finger up to his lips. "You don't have to apologize for your family as long as I don't have to apologize for mine, remember?"

Will kissed her finger before moving it away and pulling her in close. "What I meant was, I'm sorry you couldn't stay over this weekend," he murmured against her hair. "With my mom in town and Chris and Becca being here . . . you know."

"But your mom's not here now, right?"

"She's already back in North Carolina."

"And your brother and sister?"

"Same."

"And me?" Mara teased, leaning back so she could see his face.

"You," Will said, "are exactly where you belong."

♦♦♦♦♦

Time and privacy had been luxuries in college. Now, Will and Mara didn't even bother to move off the couch. Mara laid her cheek on Will's bare chest and ran her fingers, lightly, from his shoulders all the way down.

"Wait," Will breathed.

Mara froze. "I'm sorry," she said. "Is this too fast?"

"God, no," Will said. "Let me just . . . this damn phone is driving me crazy." He pulled away from her, long enough to kick his pants down the hall to the bathroom and slam the door. Mara hadn't even noticed the ringing of his cell phone until it was suddenly muted.

"Sorry," Will said, pulling her back to him. "Where were we?"

It had been five days since Mara had slept over. Too long. She closed her eyes. Now she was here, and she was never leaving Will again.

Dimly, Mara heard another phone ringing. Over and over until both she and Will had to stop kissing and turn to the source.

"That's mine," Mara said, feeling overwhelmingly

irritated. *Who is it, the sex police?* With one hand, she dug into her purse to find her BlackBerry. If only she could shut it off without getting up. No luck. The phone kept ringing insistently.

"Sorry," Mara grumbled, untangling herself from Will just as the ringing stopped. She located the phone and the power button just as the screen flashed.

Five missed calls.

"Are you okay?" Will asked, just as Mara started to scroll down the screen. Two missed calls from her mother, three from Robyn.

"Something's wrong," Mara said. Will sat up next to her on the floor and put a steady hand on her back.

"Answer it," Will said as the phone rang again. Robyn's number. "I'm right here. If something is wrong, we'll handle it together."

Fingers shaking, Mara pressed the speaker button.

"Are you okay?" Robyn asked.

"What happened? What's going on?" Now that Mara had picked up the phone, the spell was broken. She felt suddenly exposed. And cold. Will retrieved her shirt, and she held it over her chest.

"I've been worried to death about you today," Robyn said. "I can't even imagine. Just remember nothing's certain yet. We'll all be here for you, okay? You and Will. No matter what happens."

"Happens with what?"

"With the time wrecker leak." Robyn's voice trailed off, as if she expected Mara to chime in at any minute. "Whether they prove anything or not, I mean. I just wanted you to know I'm here for you guys, either way."

"Time wrecker," Mara repeated. "Is it something about Dad? What does he have to prove . . . ?" She looked at Will, who simply shrugged.

The pause that followed was profound. "You don't know yet," Robyn said. "Oh. Oh no. I'm so sorry, Mara. I thought your mom would've called you."

"She did. I have missed calls from her, and from you," Mara said. She could barely squeeze out the next words. "What happened to Dad?"

"Nothing! Nothing. There's been . . . a hacker or someone got into the Timeline Rectification database and released it online. It's the names of all the people who've had time wrecks and then a huge manifesto about how we deserve to know the truth."

"Oh," Mara said. "That's awful. Those poor people."

"Mara," said Robyn. The way she said it made Mara sit up. Will caught her wrist and didn't let go. "Mara. It's you and Will. You're both on the list."

Breaking News: "Time Wrecker Leak" Shocks Nation

May 22, 2006

An alleged leak of the Department of Timeline Rectification's classified database may have exposed over four million Americans as "time wreckers." At approximately 10:00 A.M. EST, an anonymous tipster, identifying him or herself only as "an inside source," released the information on the dark web. The spreadsheet supposedly contains the names of every participant in a timeline rectification (criminals, victims, and bystanders) since the technology's approval in 2000. The alleged list includes over four million names, raising questions based on the Department of Timeline Rectification's own reports that they average just shy of two thousand rectifications a year. If the leaked list is accurate, how many people were involved in these rectified crimes? Could the list include data from years beyond 2006?

The leak comes amid heated debates around the country and on Capitol Hill about the ethics and regulation of timeline rectification. The tipster has not yet been identified. Stay with us for live updates as this story unfolds.

11:45 A.M.

As the so-called time wrecker leak continues to circulate, politicians and religious leaders are weighing in. Here's what people are saying:

From Phillip Randall, economist: What people need to understand is that each timeline rectification already requires a great deal of preparation and goes through many, many checks and balances. The concept of four million Americans legally completing a timeline rectification is, if not impossible, then highly improbable. Even allowing for the possibility that this list would contain all the victims and bystanders, as well as criminals, my understanding is that each and every participant would have had to go through the rigamarole to complete a timeline rectification.

The Right Reverend Bill Connors: Modern life has given us many new twists and turns, but some things remain constant. These crimes are sins, whether remembered or not. Attempting to alter God's timeline, no matter how noble the purpose, is sin. What remains for us now, in light of this leak, is to follow our highest directive: to pray for the sinners, to pray for peace for those sinned against, and to pray that this will lead to the end of our government's sins against God and man by allowing these despicable modifications. That is our calling now: not to judge, not to condemn, but simply to pray.

From the Straight Shot with Neil Poindexter: I am making it my personal mission to find out who this hacker is—or who they are, if there's a group of them, I don't care, I'll find them—so I can thank them, profusely, for saving our country from the brink of disaster. This is our moment. This is the time to take back control and demand answers. The Department of Timeline Rectification has been justifying their secrecy for too long. That's what it is, secrecy . . . all these privacy rights arguments are ridiculous. The Time Wrecker Department has been saying that knowledge of prior life maps would cause severe psychological trauma. I think we're going to see that particular smoke screen disappear very quickly right about now. And when it does, we're going to find out what the true motivation was for keeping us in the dark all these years.

From Deirdre Collins, television personality: I was shocked and saddened to see my own name listed on the time wrecker leak this morning alongside many, many others. To all my fellow time wreckers, I just want to say: you are not alone. We are not alone. Speak up, reach out, and don't lose sight of the beautiful person you have worked to become.

1:30 P.M.

No word yet from the Department of Timeline Rectification surrounding the data leak. While some feel this is an indication that the leaked information is false, others remain wary.

Alicia Barnes, spokesperson for the anti-timeline rectification organization One Life, One Time, says, "This is exactly the situation many of us at OLOT have been warning against since time wrecks became legal in 1999. We're seeing today just how damaging it is when people learn that they have another lifetime they cannot recall. The psychological implications of this discovery are simply staggering."

OLOT and several community organizations around the nation are offering free counseling services to those who were named on the list. <u>Click here to see what services are available in your area.</u>

2:15 P.M.

The Department of Timeline Rectification has issued the following statement:

"The events of this morning have left us stunned and shocked. While we can neither confirm nor deny the veracity of the leaked reports, we are deeply concerned about the privacy and security of all Americans. We urge the public to remain calm and not form any premature conclusions."

Chapter Three

....

WILL

Will sat backward in his desk chair, lightly running his hands over Mara's rigid shoulders. After Robyn's call, they'd gotten dressed quickly—so quickly that Mara had mismatched the buttons on her shirt. Her thin beige bra strap peeked out from her neckline.

Will ran his hands across her shoulders again and cursed whoever was behind this time wrecker leak.

Mara was staring intently at her laptop. "Look at this," she said. She used her cursor to highlight a sentence on the screen. Will leaned in closer, resting his chin in the space between her neck and shoulder. "See what it says here? 'Early reports of the data leak have been conflicting, with some sources stating the leak came from inside the Department of Timeline Rectification, while others stated the server had been hacked.'"

"Uh-huh," Will said.

"That's what I'm saying. There's no proof of what happened, or who could have done it. For all anybody knows, this is a publicity stunt. Someone just trying to get their fifteen minutes of fame," Mara said.

"Anonymously?" Will asked and immediately wished he hadn't. Mara didn't seem to notice. Will knew that face, the way she tucked her chin and squinted a little when she concentrated. Mara always looked like that when she studied.

Except they weren't in college anymore and this wasn't just some research project. A terrible coldness was settling deep in Will's core. He sat back in his chair.

Mara clicked on the next tab, opening yet another news story.

"I think it's a hoax," Will mused. "Like you said. It's just some activist group trying to stir up controversy. They probably skimmed names out of the newspapers or something to make a fake database and get everyone worked up."

"They made up a list of four million names? Er, four and a half million? That's ridiculous."

"Even more reason to think it's all made up," Will said. "I bet when people actually try reading it, they'll find cartoon characters and I. C. Wiener listed on there to pad the numbers."

When he said it like that, Will almost believed it himself. Mara's shoulders relaxed a little, so he kept talking. "And even if they didn't make up names outright, anyone can claim to have a list of time wreckers. No one can deny it, because people who've had time wrecks don't remember, and no one can confirm it, either, unless the Justice Department wants to land in a bunch of hot water for breaking confidentiality. It's kind of genius, actually."

Mara tensed again. "I wouldn't exactly call it genius," she said. "Depraved, more like. Sadistic. Evil."

"Evil genius," Will concurred.

Mara nodded absently and pointed to an article she'd been scrolling through. "There." She had highlighted her own name in a screenshot of the leaked database. "That's what keeps bugging me. My name is listed as Mara Gaines Sterling."

"So?" Will asked.

"So? I'm still Mara Gaines," she said. "If they just skimmed the list from somewhere, why wouldn't they use my current name? It's freaky."

"Maybe it's not you," Will said. "There's got to be another Mara Gaines Sterling somewhere in the US. There was another William Sterling at our college. Remember him?"

That made Mara laugh a little. "I bet he remembers that voice mail I left him by accident."

"It probably made his day," Will said. "But seriously, let's stop looking at the database. It's probably nothing."

"I wish." Mara clicked back to the search engine window, where she had typed "timeline rectification leak."

"Three hundred sixty thousand hits," she said, pointing to the screen. "That's not nothing."

"I mean, there's probably no truth to it." Will gently spun her desk chair around until Mara was facing him, not the computer. "You know how the news is. Everyone's all worked up for a week or two, and then they get distracted by something else."

"I *do* know how the news is," Mara said. With a suddenness that startled Will, she stood up and walked over to the kitchen.

Should I follow her? Will started to get up, then decided against it. *Let her go. She'll come back when she's ready to talk.*

He could hear Mara getting a paper cup from the plastic sleeve. Turning on the faucet. She swallowed it in three deep gulps and refilled it before returning to the living room.

Mara wasn't meeting his eyes.

"When Dad was being investigated," Mara began, and Will froze, "the media never quit. It wasn't like the reporters went to a press conference and then politely went home. There were news vans parked outside our house. There were people who followed me to school."

She was quiet for a few moments, running a finger around the rim of her now-empty paper cup. Will waited.

"And it didn't end when he was cleared of the charges, either," she said. "The investigation wrapped up during the summer between eleventh and twelfth grade. You know what? By then, it didn't matter. Everyone had already decided that Dad was a thief smd that all our money was skimmed off everyone else's taxes. My parents bought me a class ring, and I would take it off before school so no one would ask how we *really* paid for it. I got early admission to

Adams Morgan University, and everyone said, 'Well, you knew *you* were going to get in.' And they didn't mean because I got straight As. I *still* feel like I'm constantly having to prove that my family isn't stealing or bribing or cheating. That what we have is really ours."

"That was six years ago," Will said. "Are you sure it was really about the embezzlement stuff? People are always kind of nasty about money. Maybe you're reading more into it."

Mara crumpled the empty cup and crossed her arms.

Oops.

"Will, you've never lived through this," she said. Now her eyes were locked on him. "You've never seen your name in the paper for anything except the honor roll. Nobody's ever taken your picture unless they knew you. You have no idea what this could be like for us."

"I really don't think the time wrecker stuff is going to blow up like that," Will said. "With the case against your dad, I mean . . ." He stumbled to find the right words. "There were some numbers to go on, at least. There was some . . ." *Don't say evidence. Don't say evidence.* "What I mean is, nobody can prove whether this is real or not. And no one can prove it's us and not some other Mara and Will Sterling. Mara *Gaines* Sterling," Will corrected himself.

"That's what I'm trying to tell you," Mara said. "It doesn't matter if it's real and it doesn't matter if anyone can prove it. Once the media decides you're guilty of something, you're guilty for life."

"So we'll be the Bonnie and Clyde of public opinion," Will said. "It doesn't matter what anyone else thinks. We'll get through it together."

He went to her and took the paper cup out of her hand before wrapping her in a hug. It took a minute before Mara relaxed enough to hug him back, two minutes before she softened enough to rest her head on his chest.

It was going to be okay. Will could feel it. As long as they had each other, they could handle anything.

Will's phone buzzed in his pocket, and they broke apart. *I never should have picked this stupid thing back up.* He fumbled for it, letting it buzz three, four, five times before he looked at the screen. It was his sister Becca, texting so fast he could barely read each message before it was bumped off the screen by another one.

Becca: Will r u ok?

Becca: We heard abt the list

Becca: Mom is having a fit

Becca: Don't pick up the phone if she calls

Becca: Let me calm her down first

Becca: Ok?

Becca: Will?

Becca's text string was interrupted by more texts, this

time from Will's brother:

Chris: You better call Mom back

Chris: U there?

Chris: Call Mom

"See what I mean?" Mara said, rubbing her forehead. She walked back to her desk chair. "It's already starting."

"It's just Becca and Chris," Will said, but his heart was hammering. He didn't have time to text either of them back before his phone was ringing too.

It was his mother.

Will hovered his finger over the button for only a few seconds before he clicked his phone to speaker.

"Jesus, Mary, and Joseph!" Bonnie Sterling came on so loudly that Mara jumped. "What kind of craziness is going on up there? Answer me!"

"Mom! I'm fine. Mara's fine. Everyone's fine. Calm down, please," Will said. Even though his mother couldn't see him, Will had automatically raised his hands in a "don't shoot me" gesture.

"Don't you tell me to calm down, William. I cannot believe this. No, I *refuse* to believe this."

"It's just a rumor, Mom," Will said. He tried to sound confident, but somehow, the words came out flippant. Irreverent.

I hope it's just a rumor.

"Don't you go acting like it's no big thing when someone's accusing my boy of being a time wrecker. Him and his fiancée . . ." She let out a perturbed sigh. "How's Mara holding up?"

"I'm fine," Mara said. "Please don't worry about Will and me. I know it's terrible what people are saying—"

"Mara? You're there with Will?"

"Yes." Mara slid her eyes over to Will, as if to say, *I'm not going to lie.*

"Where are you two? Is someone else there with you?"

Why did Will still feel a sting of shame, saying it out loud? *I'm a grown man. If I want to live with my fiancée, I can.* But he still felt his ears and neck burning when he said, "It's just Mara and me at the apartment, Mom."

"I see." By the sudden chill in her voice, Will guessed that she did. "I was assuming Mara's mother would be nearby, at least, since she called me about the wedding."

"My mother called you?" Mara asked. "What about the wedding?"

The sudden silence at the other end of the phone was profound.

"About postponing," Bonnie said slowly. "Why don't I let you go, in case Mara's mom is trying to reach you all."

♦♦♦♦♦

Will hated to see the way Mara's hands shook as she dialed the phone. She stopped just before the last number. "No matter what happens, I still want to marry you," Mara said.

"Of course," Will said. "We don't need a big wedding. We already have our marriage license, even. Just say the word, and we'll go to the courthouse and get married."

She put the BlackBerry down, as if it were suddenly heavy. "I'm so sorry my parents are being like this. I'm so sorry."

"Stop," Will said. "You don't have to apologize for your family if I don't have to apologize for mine, remember?" That made Mara smile. "And we don't even know that your mom said anything like that. Mom might have misunderstood. She was pretty shaken up."

Mara pressed her lips together. "It sounds an awful lot like something my mother would say. Mom did call me. Twice. Before Robyn did. But she didn't leave a voice mail."

"And we won't know for sure until we hear it from her. I'm right here." Will rested his cheek next to hers. "And even if your parents do call the wedding off, they can't call our marriage off. We'll handle it."

"But it's two weeks away. Robyn and Becca have already paid for their dresses, and you, Chris, and Tristan rented your tuxes . . . people have probably already reserved their hotel rooms . . ."

"Just call your mom and find out if that's really what she's planning. If that's how your parents want to handle it . . . I mean, they were paying for it so . . . okay. It's going to be hard. But nobody is going to blame you for what your parents do." Will couldn't stop himself from adding, "But if they do call it off, that's it. If we end up having to plan another wedding, I want to pay for all of it ourselves."

"We should have done that in the first place," Mara said.

"Don't get ahead of things. Let's find out what's really going on."

Mara took an audibly deep breath and hit the last number on her phone. Mrs. Gaines picked up on the second ring.

"Mara. Good." In contrast to Will's own mother, Mara's mom sounded businesslike and efficient in the face of a crisis.

"Mom, I . . ." Something in Mara seemed to go dark. "I'm so sorry."

"I was just about to try calling you again." Even over speakerphone, Mrs. Gaines's voice was so severe Will almost apologized too. *We've done nothing wrong. There's nothing to be sorry about.* "Are you at Will's? I'll need your help tomorrow morning, so be back at the house early. Eight o'clock at the latest. Seven would be better."

"Mom." Mara swallowed before continuing. "We were just talking to Will's mother, and she seemed to think you were planning to postpone the wedding."

"Of course we are," Mrs. Gaines said. If words could shrink a person, Mara and Will would have been two inches tall. Each. "You didn't really think we could proceed under the circumstances, did you?"

"Yes, Mom, I did." Mara was starting to get angry, much to Will's relief. Angry Mara was so much more like herself. "I can't believe you would just cancel our wedding without telling us. Without even asking. People have made plans. What are the guests supposed to do? What about—"

"We'll discuss it tomorrow," Mrs. Gaines said, her tone curt. "There is far too much to do to waste time listening to your moping."

"Mom," Mara breathed. "Don't cancel the wedding."

"It's canceled. *Think*, Mara. You of all people should know how to handle yourself at a time like this."

"This is our wedding." Red patches appeared all up and down Mara's neck and face, but her tone was pleading, conciliatory. "This isn't just another party. Will and I are supposed to be getting married."

"I'm well aware, Mara," Mrs. Gaines said. "And since your father and I have generously planned and funded this wedding, we will make the decision. I expect to see you at eight o'clock tomorrow to help handle the additional work this has created. An apology would be appropriate as well."

The line went dead.

✦✦✦✦✦

Their first night alone in the apartment was sleepless for

all the wrong reasons. Will and Mara went to bed at ten, more out of convention than tiredness. Mara shut down her computer, and Will turned off both their cell phones. Both of them checked the lock on the door before they went to bed.

Will watched the time pass on the glowing digital alarm clock. Eleven o'clock. Midnight. One in the morning. Beside him, Mara was still and silent. Sometimes Will thought she might be asleep and tried to match his breathing to hers. Then headlights from a passing car would shine through their bedroom window, or they'd hear footsteps in the apartment upstairs, and both Mara and Will would jolt all the way awake.

"Wanna talk?" Will asked after Mara turned and folded over her pillow. The alarm clock showed it was just after two.

"Yeah," Mara said quietly. "It all fell apart so quickly. This morning, we were moving in together and now . . ."

"Hey," Will said, reaching over in the dark. He found her hand and held it in his.

"Do you think this is what it was like for us the first time around?" Mara asked.

"How do you mean?"

"In our first lifetime, when we decided to have a time wreck. What do you think happened to us that we were willing to undo our whole lives to change it?"

"It's probably not true," Will said. "And even if it is, we shouldn't try to guess what happened. We decided to forget for a reason."

That made Mara sigh—a sad kind of sigh that made Will want to roll closer to her. But maybe now wasn't the right time for that. He stayed on his side of the bed.

"What are you going to tell your family?" Mara asked.

"About the wedding? Or about their opinion that time wreckers are all sinners for changing time?"

"You don't really believe it's a sin, do you?"

"I'm not sure," Will admitted. It was easier, somehow, saying these things aloud in the dark. "I don't love the idea of it, but I can also see where it would be a good thing. I don't really want to think about it."

"I don't think we have a choice." Through the dim light, Will could make out her silhouette. She was propped up on one elbow, hair falling to her pillow. "I think we need to prepare ourselves."

"For what? Can things really get any worse?"

"Don't ask that," Mara said. "It can always get worse. I think what's happened so far today is just a taste of what's coming."

♦♦♦♦♦

Will must have fallen asleep at some point in those bleary early-morning hours. He awoke to Mara's reflection in the mirror as she was getting dressed. She was wearing a pair of white capris and a silky light blue top. She was putting in her pearl earrings when she noticed him awake.

"Good morning," Mara said, even though it wasn't.

Will patted the empty spot next to him on the bed. "Where are you going?"

"I was thinking about it, and I figured I should probably go and meet my mom. I'm not going to apologize to her or anything, and I'm sure I can't change her mind, but if I don't go now . . ." Mara sighed, looking momentarily defeated. "I just don't want to make things worse with her."

"I don't think that's a good idea," Will said.

"You don't know my parents like I do," Mara said. "Believe me. If I don't show up this morning, Mom will never forgive me."

It was a terrible idea. Mara would be back by lunchtime, crying and exhausted, furious at something her mother had said to her. Again.

"At least let me go with you," Will said. He pulled her down next to him, and for a minute, Mara melted into him. Then she straightened up and gently moved his hands away.

"It's better if I go by myself," she said.

Because your parents don't like me. Will turned away. It was bound to happen eventually. Mara had brushed aside all the little comments her parents had made over the last two years. *Why don't you wait and establish your careers? Aren't you concerned about William's security?* Their raised eyebrows and pinched lips echoed the whispers that had crept into Will's thoughts throughout their relationship. Mara was a future doctor, the daughter of a congressman and a highly regarded attorney. Will was a scholarship kid from the sticks, lucky to land a job as a music teacher.

Mara could do better.

Mara kissed him then. "I won't be gone long," she said. "I'll probably be back by noon. You know how Mom is. Everything's got to get done right away." She rolled her eyes.

"So let's do it," Will said.

"Let's do what?"

"After you get back today. Let's get married."

"What?" Mara's eyes lit up.

"We already have the marriage license. We can use it anywhere in the great Commonwealth of Virginia. We don't *have* to wait until June third."

They were going to do it. Will could feel it, in the way Mara collapsed onto the bed, all relieved and laughing, like he'd just proposed all over again. So it wouldn't be the wedding they thought they'd have. But it would be *their* wedding—all theirs. No one could stop them from getting married.

"You have no idea how much I want to say yes," Mara said.

Will's heart sank. "But?"

"And," Mara corrected him. "*And* . . . I don't want our wedding to be about the news cycle. You know? I don't want to just elope because of some stupid rumor. We should celebrate. I don't want to sneak off like we're ashamed."

"Who said anything about sneaking off?" Will asked. "Seriously. If it were just the two of us in the room, and we just waited and told everyone about it later . . . why couldn't everyone just be happy for us?"

Mara sat up. "You know it's not that simple."

"It should be." She was right, but Will didn't want her to be. He had to fight to hold himself together.

Mara kissed him again and looked at the door. "I don't want to go when you're upset," she said.

"I'm not upset," Will managed.

"You are. We both are. But we're going to work things out."

"Just go," Will said. "Do what you have to do."

"I'll be back soon," Mara said, squeezing both his hands. She looked back twice before the bedroom door closed behind her. "I promise."

Everything You Wanted to Know about Timeline Rectification (But Were Afraid to Ask)

By Atticus Craven for *Irreverent Genius Online*
May 23, 2006

So yesterday was exciting, right? Not only did we learn how many people have twisted the fabric of time and space beyond all recognition, but—get this—the special news report actually got more viewers than <u>last week's series finale of *That '70s Show.*</u>

That's right, people are watching the news for once. What a time to be alive.

Maybe you're like us. Maybe yesterday you were planning a relaxing day of hangover recovery when the media suddenly blew up with the Time Wrecker Leak and speculation over The List and talking heads debating What This All Means. Fun stuff. Unless, of course, you're a touch behind on current events and aren't quite sure what the big fuss is all about.

We've got your back. Here are the most common questions about time wrecking, asked and answered.

What exactly is timeline rectification?

Wow, you really don't get out much, do you? It's okay. That's why we're here. Timeline rectification was invented by Dr. Charles E. Bennington in 1999. It was approved in 2000 to be used by the Justice Department to rehabilitate criminals as an alternative to parole. Rather than wasting taxpayer dollars by sitting in jail or doing 90 billion hours of community service, criminals and their victims are offered the chance to go back and undo the crime.

So, like time travel?

According to the <u>Department of Timeline Rectification website</u>, no. "Although humans process time as a linear progression of events, recent advancements in science show us that time is better viewed as a fabric wherein each event in a person's life has a distinct set of coordinates. A timeline rectification does not send participants 'back in time' in the sense that they progress backward to a moment in their past. Rather, a rectification allows us to temporarily move the participants' state of consciousness to the precise coordinates of the original event, allowing them to change what occurs by behaving differently."

But for us peons without a background in metaphysics or whatever, yes, it's basically time travel.

Are all the people on the time wrecker list criminals?

Supposedly, no. The hackers claim that the list includes all participants, which could include the criminals, victims, and even witnesses of the original offense. Which is no longer an offense. Because it's been rectified.

Whew. Excuse us while we give our tiny brains a rest for a minute here.

But what exactly were the original crimes? When did they happen?

Nobody knows . . . yet. Well, presumably the hacker(s) know, because he/she/they claim that more information will be released if their demands aren't met. At this point, all we have is a long list of names and a lot of assumptions.

So why is everybody so upset about this list of maybe-former-criminals/maybe-former-victims?

Because people don't like criminals, even if they've been "rehabilitated."

Also (since we've established you don't usually watch the news), there are several activist groups that think timeline rectifications are unethical and immoral and should be illegal. One Life, One Time is a well-known anti-time wrecking activist group. Whether the people on the list were criminals or victims of the original (but rectified!) crime, these people would view all the time wreckers as unethical.

What if my name is on the list?

Relax! There's no way to prove it's really you or that the data is real.

What if my spouse/friend/coworker/neighbor is on the list?

Ostracize and humiliate them, obviously. (Kidding.)

Chapter Four

MARA

"Keep your chin up," Mrs. Gaines said under her breath, keeping one arm linked through Mara's.

Mara leaned against the trolley of packages, accidentally setting off a long, whining squeak from the right wheel. Great. As if Mara and her mother hadn't already attracted enough attention rolling into the post office with all these boxes.

"I don't think we have to return all the wedding gifts today," Mara muttered. "I think people would understand if we waited for things to die down a bit."

That was exactly the wrong thing to say. Mrs. Gaines withdrew her arm and circled one hand around Mara's wrist instead. "After you cancel a wedding, you return the gifts," she said, her voice even lower. "We are going to show we do the right thing, the right way, every time."

Each word stung. *Mom believes that list is real,* Mara thought. *And she blames me for having a time wreck.*

A Gaines would not have a timeline rectification, whether

they were the criminal or the victim. A Gaines would own up to their wrongdoing or quietly accept their misfortune. A Gaines would find a way to spin the whole incident in a way that built character, inspired others, and showed leadership.

The line ahead of them shuffled forward. Mara used one foot to push the trolley a few inches and tried to ignore its protesting squeak. A cart like this wasn't built to hold so much weight, but Mrs. Gaines had insisted, pulling box after box out of the SUV.

"There's no time for that," Mrs. Gaines snapped back when Mara suggested making two trips. "We need to get in and get out. If you'd been at the house earlier, we could have been at the post office as soon as it opened. Please at least try to stay inconspicuous."

If you wanted to be inconspicuous, why not ship them from your office? That's where you mail everything else. The dark part of Mara's mind supplied the answer immediately. *To hurt me. To embarrass me. To punish me for having a time wreck.*

There had been plenty of that this morning. Each repackaged wedding gift included a handwritten note from Mara, following her mother's template:

Dear (Name),

Thank you for your kind and gracious gift in anticipation of my marriage to William. Unfortunately, due to unforeseen circumstances, our wedding cannot go on as planned. Please accept my gratitude for your thoughtfulness and my apologies for the change in plans.

Sincerely,

Mara Gaines

For the guests who hadn't sent gifts ahead of time, Mara's mother had printed up an announcement card on their home printer. With the swirly cursive font and thick cardstock, it looked almost as official as their wedding invitation had been.

> Congressman and Mrs. Joel Gaines
> regret to inform you that the marriage of their daughter
> Mara Elizabeth
> and
> William Sterling
> will not take place
> June 3, 2006
> as scheduled.

Which wasn't a lie. The marriage would take place, but definitely not as scheduled. Mara thought back to the hurt in Will's eyes when she'd left this morning, and her heart gave an agonizing twist.

Just get through this, and then I can go back and make things right with him.

The thought made her lift her chin and square her shoulders.

"That's the way," Mrs. Gaines said, apparently noticing Mara's shift in demeanor. She gave Mara's wrist a final squeeze and let go just as the next postal worker motioned them forward.

Please don't know who I am, Mara silently begged, but it was too late. The woman's eyes widened when she saw Mara and Mrs. Gaines approach. When Mara's mother thrust the stack of announcement envelopes across the counter, the Gaines family letterpress seal would have removed all doubt.

"These cards need to go out in this morning's mail," Mrs. Gaines said. "And all the packages should be delivered two-day express."

"Of course," the postal worker said, quickly sweeping the stack of cards into a nearby bin. "Anything perishable, liquid, or fragile in these packages?"

"These five are fragile," Mrs. Gaines said, motioning for Mara to put them onto the counter. Mara sneaked a look behind her as she leaned over to pick up each box. The line of waiting customers was even longer than she'd thought, and most people were watching her. Some of them just looked annoyed, while others were staring with narrow-eyed interest.

Mara resisted the urge to look behind her again as she waited for the postal worker to key in the address for each package and print out the labels. By the time the astronomical shipping total was charged to her mother's credit card, it was all Mara could do not to run straight out of the building.

The postal worker gave Mara and Mrs. Gaines one last appraising look. "Will there be anything else for you today? Stamps?"

"No," Mara said, turning on her heel and walking as quickly as she could out the door. Behind her, she heard the postal worker offer a compulsory "Have a nice day!"

If it were a nice day, I wouldn't be here.

The fresh air outside felt good on Mara's face. *One hard thing done. I just have to do one hard thing at a time.*

"That was a bit rude," Mrs. Gaines said, catching up to her. The outside door of the building was shielded from the rest of the shopping center by a wall of ivy-covered trellises. No place to turn, which made it easy for Mrs. Gaines to block Mara's path. Reluctantly, Mara stopped. "Mara. Listen to me. You can tell the measure of a person by how they treat waitstaff and service people. You might have at least said goodbye or thanked her for helping you."

Mara bit the inside of her cheek. She was going to get a sore there. It was already tender.

Mrs. Gaines continued. "Now, we need to be off to the country club to see Dianne. I already spoke with her over the phone this morning, but she was gracious enough to make time to meet with us in person."

"Fine," Mara said.

Mrs. Gaines raised her eyebrows. Mara met her gaze steadily, and for once, she didn't flinch. The expected, unspoken "Yes, ma'am," hung between them.

"Let's go," Mara said, emboldened. So this was what life could be like if she refused to be cowed. For a moment, Mara let herself imagine that she'd done even more. If she'd driven back instead of helping her mother with the packages. If she'd refused to write the thanks-but-no-thanks cards. If she had refused to show up in the first place. Mara could still be at the apartment with Will right now. They could be planning their elopement.

The fantasy wavered for a moment, then broke.

No. It would have made things worse. Mara had been right to come today. As long as she cooperated, her mother might cool down eventually. If she picked a fight now, her parents would never forgive her.

Mara ignored her shaking knees and walked around her mother, past the trellises, breaking into a sudden burst of light.

"There she is!" someone shouted, and it wasn't just sunlight on Mara's face anymore. In the parking lot, Mrs. Gaines's SUV was surrounded by reporters. Now they were all coming toward her, microphones out, shouting rapid-fire questions.

"Ms. Gaines, there's been speculation that you and your fiancé were involved in a time wreck to cover for your father's unethical political dealings. Can you comment?"

"We've been told that you were just in the post office returning your wedding gifts. Was your time wreck a factor in your breakup with William Sterling?"

Mrs. Gaines suddenly wrapped a strong arm around Mara's waist. "We have no comment on the rumored database leak," Mrs. Gaines said smoothly, escorting Mara to the car. The reporters had no choice but to step aside as Mrs. Gaines marched past. "Sit up straight, but keep your face down," she whispered as Mara entered the passenger's side door. The door slammed, and Mrs. Gaines walked around to the driver's side of the car.

Mara pulled her seatbelt across her chest, trying desperately to catch her breath. It wasn't just her knees that shook anymore. Her entire body trembled as she tried to block out the reporters who stood only steps away from the car. How had they known she was here? Why would anyone care so much? Even when her father had been in the news, there hadn't been that many reporters on the first day.

Mrs. Gaines started the car and fastened her own seatbelt. "I was afraid that would happen," she remarked as coolly as if she were observing a fallen soufflé.

Mara took a full breath in. "We're just going to go back to the house now, right? No point going to the club if we're going to be followed."

"It's gated. Nobody will be able to follow us in there, and Dianne will be discreet. We owe her a meeting, not an excuse." Mrs. Gaines barely looked over her shoulder before throwing the car into reverse.

To her right, Mara heard an explosive bang.

"What was that?" she screamed just as Mrs. Gaines snapped, "For God's sake, Mara, don't look!"

Another burst of lights erupted. It wasn't until they were miles away that Mara could piece together what happened.

It had been a soda can. Someone had thrown a soda can at the car to make her jump. And now the reporters would have had a perfect shot of Mara looking startled and afraid, staring backward out the window as the car zoomed away.

The perfect picture of a time wrecker.

◆◆◆◆◆

For two miles, the only sound in the car was from the radio, blaring traffic updates and weather reports in the district. Mrs. Gaines reached over and changed the station without comment as soon as a news story about the data leak began.

Maybe that meant her mother was as rattled as Mara was. Mara pushed her hands under her thighs, sitting on them to keep them still. Mrs. Gaines's hands clenched the steering wheel so tightly that each knuckle turned paper white.

Mara tried to think of something to say, but the words didn't come. A ditty for a car wash played off the last commercial.

"Are you ready . . . for a candidate who will move us forward?" demanded the radio. "Congressman Joel Gaines has represented Virginia's Eighth District for ten years.

When is he going to move us into the twenty-first century?" Mara felt as if her heart had stopped while the radio announcer paused dramatically. "He won't—but Conrad Gibbons will."

Mrs. Gaines jabbed at the radio knob with one finger and missed. The commercial continued. "Are you ready . . . for a candidate who will represent us with honesty and integrity?" Another dramatic pause. "Congressman Joel Gaines says he is against timeline rectification, but his own daughter is a time wrecker. How can we trust him to stay tough on crime?"

"He won't—but Conrad Gibbons will."

Mrs. Gaines pushed the knob again. The radio shut off abruptly, and the car was flooded in silence.

There was one rule in the Gaines family household that was never disobeyed: "Don't look for your name in the news." When she was little, Mara thought it was about modesty or something. Maybe her parents didn't want her to go bragging to her friends that her father was on TV, even if it was just a commercial for his campaign. Mara had been a little hurt by it, in fact. Why would her parents jump to change the channel or take away the newspaper at the mere mention of their last name? Did they think Mara was so awful that even a little notoriety would make her conceited?

But when her father's investigation happened, Mara realized it was much deeper than that. Words hurt. By then, Mara could look up the news on her own when she was at school, and she did. She had to know what people were saying about her father. And once Mara started to read, she couldn't stop. Even when the accusations against her father got wilder and wilder. Even when the words people used to describe her father sank down into the deepest part of her heart, only to resurface late at night. *Is that really what he is? Is that what I am?*

Mara had never told her parents what she'd read about the investigation—not back then, and certainly not after it was all over. She was sure they knew, in that piercing way her parents had of seeing straight through her, whenever they cared to look. Before Mara started college, her father had gifted her the BlackBerry along with two pieces of advice: "Don't look up anything you're not ready to see" and "If you aren't calm, you aren't ready."

Now that her name was on that time wrecker list, Mara doubted she'd ever be truly calm again. It wouldn't be good for Mara's mother to see her on her BlackBerry at a time like this, though. Stealthily, Mara worked her cell phone out from her purse and texted Will. He was probably still upset. Why shouldn't he be? But she needed him. Hopefully, he would understand.

Hopefully, he needs me too. Mara shook off the thought as disloyal. She could have stayed this morning. Or she could have let him come too—so what if her mother didn't like it? Mara typed out a quick text and sent it before she changed her mind.

Mara: It's worse than I thought

Will texted back immediately.

Will: What is?

"Mara." Mrs. Gaines's voice made her jump.

"Um," Mara said, scrambling to hide her BlackBerry again. "Sorry."

What am I apologizing for? Mara tried to hang on to her anger, let it give her the strength to stand up for herself instead of folding.

"I hope you aren't trying to look up the news on your phone." Mrs. Gaines pursed her lips as she merged off the highway and onto the long, narrow road that led to the country club. "Let's talk about what happened at the post office. I wasn't anticipating that there would be quite so much media attention on you so soon, and that was my fault. I'm sorry. With your father's anti-timeline rectification bill and your own name appearing on the list, I should have predicted how much you'd be up against." Mara's mother sighed, either from regret or irritation. Probably the latter. "That said: this list, this scandal, does not define who you are. You are still Mara Elizabeth Gaines. You are our daughter, you are a college graduate, and someday you are going to be a doctor. This moment in time is not the last word on what your life is about."

Mara's anger evaporated when she looked over at her mother. Mrs. Gaines was still looking straight ahead, but there might've been—maybe?—a little tenderness in her voice.

"But this scandal can ruin your life if you let it. It's entirely up to you how much this is going to affect your future. A little prudence now, a little thoughtfulness, will save you from a lot of damage in the long run."

Mara hated to admit that her mother was right. At least partly. Wasn't this exactly what she'd been telling Will yesterday? That it was so easy for things like this to spin out of control. That it was the right thing—the better thing—to slow down now instead of adding fuel to the media firestorm.

Still, Mara felt a little pull at her heart when they turned into the parking lot of the country club. It wasn't that she'd always dreamed of getting married there, exactly. Mara had lost control of the wedding planning as soon as she and Will announced their engagement. There were times when Mara had even dreaded the formal affair her parents had planned.

But it would have been nice to share the day with her family. She was going to miss having Grandmary help her get ready. Dancing with her father at the reception.

But the most important thing is Will. Lots of people didn't get fancy weddings with everyone they knew in attendance. And lots of people never even fell in love. Mara was still the lucky one because she had Will. Mara wrapped her fingers around her BlackBerry and allowed herself a small sigh of relief. Soon. She would be back with him soon.

"We're right on time. Good. Let's not keep Dianne waiting," Mrs. Gaines said. Mara felt strangely numb as they got out of the car and climbed the long wooden stairs up to the deck. From the highest point, the country club offered a beautiful view of the Potomac. One side of the deck had a gazebo, where she and Will would have had their first dance if the weather was nice. The room they would have used for the dinner had a long wall of windows overlooking the river. Mara had been to several weddings at the club, all for children of her parents' friends. Even if she hadn't really known the people getting married, the weddings themselves had been breathtaking.

Not here. Not on June third. But someday. Mara let the last word echo in her head with every footstep. *Someday. Someday. Someday.*

Dianne's office had a door at the far end of the upper deck. An office with a view must have been one of the perks of the job, even though Mara wasn't entirely sure what Dianne's job was. She was simply Dianne, the ginger-haired, middle-aged woman who appeared in the background at every event at the club. Smoothing the table linens. Greeting the important guests. Ensuring that everything went off without a hitch.

Today, Dianne looked as calm and collected as ever,

although she did rise to greet them at the door. "Augusta, hello. And Mara," Dianne embraced her and gave a pitying smile. "How are you holding up, dear?"

"Fine, thank you," Mara said, the way she was supposed to, but Dianne gave her shoulder an extra squeeze anyway.

"Please, sit," Dianne said, gesturing to the settee and two armchairs at one end of her office. "Can I offer you anything? A Perrier? Coffee? Tea?"

"No, thank you," Mrs. Gaines said just as Mara was about to ask for a cup of coffee. "We won't take up much of your time. Thank you again for meeting with us."

"Augusta, please," Dianne said. "It's the least we can do at such a difficult time."

"And of course, we understand how difficult it is for you to cancel an event at the last minute," Mrs. Gaines said. "It's almost impossible to find a way to fill the time slot on such short notice."

"Ah," Dianne said. "Well, yes. Unfortunately, per the limits of the contract, we can't offer you a refund on the venue space, since as you know, the club does depend on the monies raised from our events."

"Of course, of course," Mrs. Gaines said. "My office helped write your contract. I know the terms very well." She and Dianne both laughed, in that lilting way that was all business and no humor.

Mara turned toward the window and blinked hard. *That was all our wedding was to her. Just another event.*

But it would have been beautiful, no matter how her parents thought of it. Mara and Will would have had that first dance on the deck. They would have stood with their backs to the Potomac and said their vows. They would have—

Mrs. Gaines cleared her throat, and Mara turned back to the conversation. The flicker of anger that had gotten her this far was threatening to catch fire. Mara pushed it back down. She was not going to lose control. Not now.

"I do think there is a way to mitigate that issue," Mrs. Gaines said. Dianne's smile didn't falter, but Mara thought she saw the woman's back stiffen ever so slightly. "As you know, my husband has been campaigning for his reelection as the congressman for this district, and of course with his timeline rectification bill and this recent . . . incident . . . things have been a bit complicated. Joel and I were thinking that perhaps we could put the space to use by hosting a different event. We'd still like to have a dinner that evening, but we'll open the invitation to all Joel's supporters and some of the notable members of our district. It would be an opportunity for us to show that timeline rectification does hit close to home for many of us. Joel understands that, and that's why he's working so hard to try to prevent this sort of damage from happening again."

Mara concentrated on tensing each of her toes in order as her mother gave her little speech. *Don't say a word. Don't move. Don't drop your face even for a second.*

"I think that's a lovely idea," Dianne gushed. "So gracious of you. I'm honored that we could play even a small part in such a special event."

Count to ten. Mara tensed each of her toes again, and then relaxed them all at once.

Mrs. Gaines beamed. "We would simply need to change the decorations—a patriotic theme would be nice, as we usually do for Joel's dinners—but I thought we could keep the same menu for the caterer's sake. We'll have some speeches at the beginning. I'll introduce Joel, and then he'll speak, and of course I'm sure Mara would love to say a few words for her father, since timeline rectification has affected her so personally."

"Excuse me," Mara said. Her voice sounded foreign to her own ears. She stood up suddenly and realized that she had no idea where to go. "I just need to use the restroom. Through the back door and then down the hall to the right, isn't it?"

Pathetic. Mara counted it as a small victory that she didn't turn around when her mother called her name.

"I'm so sorry. I'm sure she didn't mean to be so abrupt," Mara heard Mrs. Gaines saying.

"Not at all. She's being so brave through all this," Dianne said back.

Once she was safely ensconced in the bathroom, Mara leaned hard against the wall. *I hate them. I hate them all.* A wild feeling started to come over her. *I can't believe I thought it would help to come here. I need Will. I should never have left.*

Mara felt in her purse for her BlackBerry. As soon as she saw the screen, she gasped.

How had she not heard her phone going off? There were hundreds of text messages. Another alert said her voice mail was full. Her heart started hammering as she scrolled through text after text, all unrecognizable numbers:

You goddamn selfish bitch. You'll get what's coming to you.

Criminals should be sterilized and left to rot in jail.

Spoiled little rich girl. Daddy can't save you now.

Who are these people? Mara felt dizzy. *How did they get my number?* She held on to the counter with one hand as she kept scrolling. Will. She needed Will. Finally, she managed to tap on his name in her contacts list and type out a text.

Mara: Will, this is bad. I can't.

With one hand, she felt for the sink and ran cold water. There. She splashed the cool stream of water over the back of her hand, then reached up and wiped her face.

Better.

Mara reached for one of the disposable towels in the basket on the counter. They were the nice kind that felt almost like cotton. Mara rubbed her eyes until the towels disintegrated into little pills of lint.

Text me back, Will. Please. Mara tried to delete all the texts from unknown numbers as she scrolled through.

Bitch.

Cunt.

Whore.

Time wrecker.

The sound of her mother's footsteps echoed down the hall. Before Mara could even turn around, the bathroom door slammed open and Mrs. Gaines stormed in.

"Just what I thought you'd be doing," Mrs. Gaines said. "Give me the phone."

"Hey!" Mara said, but Mrs. Gaines didn't even pause.

"I understand that it is tempting to find out what's being said about you. I do. But if you are going to be successful and get anywhere in this life, you will need to tune out the negativity. If you can't control the impulse, I will. Give me the phone."

"Mom, wait!"

But Mrs. Gaines was already wrenching the BlackBerry from her hand. Mara pulled back—"Stop!"—and then the phone slipped from both their grasps. It flew out behind Mara, skidding along the tile floor and landing against the wall with a sickening crack.

....

Chapter Five

WILL

10:25 A.M.

Mara: Will, this is bad. I can't.

Will: What's bad?

10:40 A.M.

Will: Mara? R U OK?

Will: Pls text me back

11:11 A.M.

Will: I saw your pic on the news.

Will: Pls don't worry.

Will: It's going to be ok.

Without Mara, the apartment was unbearably quiet. She had lived there for only one day, and already Will felt her absence in every room.

Mara must be freaking out. Never mind that she had spent all morning with her mother. That was bad enough.

She'd already had a run-in with one reporter at least. Will hoped Mara hadn't seen how far that picture had spread online. But that would be hoping too much.

Now Mara's name and face were inextricably linked to the scandal. Every news article posted online now had a thumbnail of Mara's shocked, horrified expression. The text underneath said:

Time wrecker Mara Gaines—daughter of Congressman Joel Gaines—after discovering her name in the database leak.

Will bristled when he read it, even though technically it wasn't a lie. Mara had seen her name in the data leak yesterday. Kind of. Her married name, anyway.

Why would we have had a time wreck after we got married?

Will shook that thought off as disloyal. There had been no time wreck. Not for him and Mara, anyway. It was a nasty rumor. No substance to it. Just a list of names.

But the effects were real. Will looked again at the picture that accompanied headlines like

The Rewind Effect

Good Seeds, Bad Fruit: How Time Wrecking Went Wrong

Who Are the Time Wreckers? Meet Mara Gaines, Daughter of Anti-Time Wreck Congressman Joel Gaines

That wasn't his Mara. Something must have happened today to make her pull a face like that. Something big.

Maybe the leak is real. Maybe we really did have a time wreck.

Maybe we did, and she knows why.

Will's phone vibrated once, then again and again. Mara. Will flipped open his phone, only to find a string of texts from numbers he didn't recognize. All North Carolina area codes.

Are u all right? Praying for u at this difficult time.

When the Devil sees a good thing he gets busy making mischief! Lifting you up in prayer.

Have known your sweet family for decades and so sorry for what you're all facing. Love and hugs.

Don't be discouraged! We believe in you.

Probably people from his mother's Bible study group or something. Great. So now all of Deer Hill, North Carolina, was abuzz with the rumor. Will supposed it was nice of them to reach out. Mara's phone was probably ringing off the hook too, with support from her parents' friends. Or the girls from college. Robyn had been texting with her last night, saying things such as, "It's not your fault" and "You don't have to help your mom screw you over" and "Stop apologizing! You didn't do anything wrong!"

Only Tristan had returned Will's voice mail so far. They'd

talked a little this morning. *Don't worry about the tux. How are you holding up? How's Mara?*

How *was* Mara? Will ran a hand through his hair, making it stand up on end. He wished she would text him back. Call him. Even better, if she would walk back through the door now, ready to fall into his arms.

He would make it better. Will wasn't sure how, but he would make it better for her.

◆◆◆◆◆

It was well past noon now. Almost one o'clock. Will had spent the last hour pacing from Mara's open laptop to the front window. Checking his cell phone and then looking through the peephole in the door to the hallway.

Will nearly jumped when his cell phone buzzed. *Mara.*

1:30 P.M.

Bonnie Sterling: Come home.

It was only his mother. Will sighed and peeked through the vertical blinds again. Nothing but the quiet parking lot below.

Bonnie: Sweetie, I don't like what I'm seeing on the news. Please get out of DC. Just come home.

Bonnie: Tell Mara to pack a suitcase and come too if she wants.

Bonnie: We love both of you.

Bonnie: I just worry about what's happening up there in the city with all this craziness.

Bonnie: Please come home.

Will had to admit that it wasn't a bad idea. An uneasiness had settled over him. Maybe Mara wasn't coming back. Maybe her parents had kidnapped her or something. No, even they wouldn't do that. But something was wrong. If the reporters had already found Mara once, who knew if she was able to get away? Maybe she wasn't coming back to the apartment because she didn't want to lead them here. Maybe she wasn't answering her phone because she couldn't.

That made more sense. She was probably at her parents' house, waiting for the news vans to disappear so she could slip away. Will pictured himself pulling up right in front of the house and striding up to the front step. He would go and get her and take her away from here. They'd drive until night fell, and then they'd check into a motel in the middle of nowhere under different names and ride out the storm together.

That was a plan. He took one last look out the peephole, still hoping to see Mara running up the stairs. Nothing. Will strode to the bedroom closet and pulled out their suitcases.

If Mara couldn't get to him, he would go to her.

Maybe Mara had changed her mind about eloping. Maybe

when she saw Will coming to her rescue, she'd be the one pointing him to the courthouse.

Will packed as quickly as he could. Filling his own suitcase was easy. He could fit a few weeks' worth of clothes, plus his shaving kit and shampoo bottle. He would need his cell phone charger. Their pillows from the bed, in case they stopped somewhere for the night. Will hauled them to the front door. What else?

Will's electric keyboard would have to stay here for now. His other instruments had been rented from the university, and he hadn't bought his own computer yet, either. Mara would want her laptop, though. He carefully closed it before sliding it into her laptop bag. She'd want the charger for her BlackBerry too. Plus some books. Will cleared out the top row of their bookcase and stood them all end to end in her suitcase.

There was not going to be enough room for anything else. Will took out all the books but two. She'd want the mystery novel she'd been reading along with her dog-eared copy of *The Hitchhiker's Guide to the Galaxy*. It was her favorite. She'd even lent it to Will when they first started going out.

"That's how I knew you guys were serious," Robyn had said at the time. "There's loving someone, and then there's loving someone enough to let them borrow your book."

Will slid their marriage certificate in between the two books. That would keep it flat, at least. Over top of that, he could fit all the clothes she'd put in his dresser last night.

The bottles she'd left on the bathroom counter could fit in the front zippered pocket.

That would have to be enough. The suitcase would barely zip closed as it was. Will slung Mara's laptop bag over his shoulder and grabbed a suitcase handle for his first trip to the car.

Don't panic, Mara, he said silently, hoping that God or the universe or something would carry the message to her. *I'm coming.*

♦♦♦♦♦

Will had driven to the Gaines family home exactly three times over the course of their relationship. The first time was when he came to dinner to meet Mara's parents after they'd been dating a year or so. The second time, it had been for a celebration of Grandmary's seventy-fifth birthday. The third time, it had been to ask Congressman Gaines's blessing before proposing.

Will tried not to think about how *that* had gone as he took the last turn into the Gaines's neighborhood.

The brick colonial stood tall and dark at one end of the long, tree-dotted street. It was midafternoon, but none of the light and warmth of the summer sun seemed to be reflected in the Gaines house. It was hard to tell whether anyone was home at all.

There weren't any news vans. That was something. Will's

heart sank when he realized Mara's car wasn't parked out front, either. If Mara wasn't at her parents' house, where was she?

Still, he'd come all this way. Will parallel parked with some difficulty and walked up the path to the house.

No one answered the doorbell.

Will knocked three times, hard, for good measure.

The door cracked open just enough to reveal Congressman Gaines.

Will was always startled to realize that Mara's father was shorter than him. Most people were. At six-foot-three, Will was rarely able to look anyone in the eye. It was just that the congressman was so imposing Will always felt like a small child in his presence.

The congressman blinked up at him now. "Yes?"

What was Mara's father doing here on a workday? To hear Mara tell it, he barely came home at all. "That's why my parents' marriage has lasted so long," she had said once. "They don't see each other enough to realize they're miserable."

But here he was, home, at three o'clock on a Tuesday. The media was probably camped outside his office, Will realized. He would have come home early. That made sense. The congressman was certainly dressed for work. He wore a pressed collared shirt with the sleeves rolled halfway up to his elbows. He wore a tie, but it had been loosened in order to undo the top collar button. Everything about Mara's father exuded the kind of casual power that so many men in Washington had. Will was not among them.

Congressman Gaines raised an eyebrow. "Can I help you?"

"Hello. Yes. Hi." Will licked his lips. He felt Mara's father was already losing patience with him, which only made him more nervous. "I was wondering if Mara was here."

"She is not," Congressman Gaines said.

Will's stomach sank. "Oh. Well."

The congressman sighed, slipped off his bifocals, and pinched the bridge of his nose. "Am I to assume that Mara left, and you don't know where she is?"

"I don't know—she said she was going to help her mom," Will said, feeling shorter and dumber by the minute.

"Come inside," said the congressman, pulling the door wider. It was a summons, not an invitation. Will wiped his sneakers on the mat and stepped in.

Mara's father closed the door and locked it behind them before leading the way to a room just down the hall. Will recognized it as the study. The walls were lined with leather-bound books on three sides. Their spines stood at attention, as if awaiting orders from the large, intricately carved desk in the back of the room. Will gingerly sat down in one of the burgundy leather club chairs opposite the desk, and the congressman took his accustomed seat.

"My wife would be very unhappy with me if she knew I was having this conversation with you," Congressman

Gaines said. He slipped off his glasses again and tapped them on the desk blotter.

That didn't seem like a good start to Will.

"Mara is a very special girl," the congressman said. "She may not feel that I've been as present in her life as she would have liked, and she may have a point. However, I am not blind to who my daughter is. She's been at the top of her class since preschool. Everything she attempts, she achieves. Horseback riding. Poetry. Violin. The one thing Mara has always sought is the one thing she can never be." Congressman Gaines looked pointedly at Will. "Average."

It hadn't been an insult, but it felt like one. Will tried to sit a little straighter.

The congressman continued. "Mara has always shied away from the spotlight. She doesn't enjoy awards ceremonies. She applied to Adams Morgan University on early decision, and I suspect it was to avoid the prestige of having to choose between multiple Ivy League schools. I'm not saying that Adams Morgan isn't a fine school"—he held up his hand as if to stop Will from protesting—"but anyone can see that Mara could have aimed higher.

"That brings us to yesterday," said the congressman. "Mara will struggle with the knowledge that she had a timeline rectification much more than anyone else will. It's a blow to her pride to know she gave herself a leg up by modifying anything from her past. Due to the controversy, it's also going to follow her."

"There's no evidence that the data leak is real," Will said boldly. "There's no reason to think it is unless we have some kind of proof."

The look on Congressman Gaines's face and the slight incline of his head told Will that there was.

How does he know? Will was working up the courage to ask when Congressman Gaines started speaking again.

"When you came to ask me for my blessing before you proposed, I said yes. I could have made an argument at that point that you were too young. That your goals in life seemed . . . mismatched. That perhaps in time, you two would grow to be quite different people. However, my wife and I have always made it a priority to support our daughter. I decided that if Mara accepted your proposal, we would as well.

"However, I suspect that at least in part, Mara was attracted to you because she felt you represented an opportunity to live a more average life. Even if she did become a doctor, she'd be married to a teacher. If you two chose to have children, she might have decided to cut her hours and eventually move to the suburbs. There is nothing wrong with that kind of life, but we both know that Mara is capable of greater things."

Will felt his cheeks turn hot. "I think it should be up to Mara to decide what she wants her life to look like."

"Exactly. Right now, she's finding out that she won't be able to avoid the spotlight, and she's fighting that. But eventually, she's going to accept that public attention is unavoidable. I suspect that when that happens, she will lose her reasons to hold herself back from the life she's capable of living."

A life that doesn't include someone like me.

"Now," the congressman said, "in light of this new . . . information . . . you may be reassessing your life as well. It seems that you and Mara were connected in the past, and one might take that as an assurance that your marriage is, in some way, inevitable. Or, one might consider that this is evidence that your separation is, in some way, for the best."

"Did she say that to you?" Will asked, getting to his feet. "Did Mara tell you she didn't want to be with me anymore?"

The congressman appeared to choose his words carefully. "Not in so many words. But it seems obvious to me that Mara is putting distance between you two, and I strongly encourage you to let her do so."

♦♦♦♦♦

Will felt as if the earth was crumbling under his feet as he walked back to the car. Mara's father was wrong. Will and Mara were solid. Will and Mara were partners.

Weren't they?

He pulled his phone out of his pocket again. Mara hadn't called him. Hadn't texted.

Will read the last text she'd sent, hours ago.

Will, this is bad. I can't.

And then he'd sent her message after message. Will's cheeks burned when he looked at his own desperation, scrolling through the text thread like a ticker-tape confessional.

She told me she needed space. I just didn't get it.

No, Mara wasn't like that. She had always come to him when she was scared or stressed. Mara wouldn't just take off now. She wouldn't leave him in a two-sentence text. She would call, at least. See him in person, tell him to his face that this was too much, that she needed time.

Before he could lose his nerve, Will pushed number 1 on his speed dial.

Please pick up. Please just pick up and show me I'm wrong.

The phone didn't even ring once. "The number you have dialed cannot be reached," said a prerecorded message. Will frowned down at the phone. That wasn't Mara's usual voice mail.

Her phone might have lost power. Or the voice mailbox could be full. Will tried again, pushing each digit of her phone number instead of hitting speed dial.

"The number you have dialed cannot be reached."

Will couldn't get through to her.

Maybe that was the message he needed to hear.

The data leak was real. Congressman Gaines had all but

confirmed it. And if Will and Mara really did have a timeline rectification, then it didn't take much imagination to figure out who the criminal was. Will briefly flirted with the idea that they were both innocent. Bystanders, maybe, who selflessly agreed to a time wreck in the name of justice.

No. Will had gotten in trouble somehow, and Mara had given up everything to help him get out of it. They'd been willing to sacrifice their marriage because another life—any other life—would be better than the mess Will had made of theirs.

Mara must have felt it, on some level. That's why she hadn't stayed with him at the apartment this morning. Why she was so eager to help her mother cancel the wedding. Mara had already seen what everyone else saw, what Will had been too clueless to see.

Will unlatched the trunk and pulled out Mara's packed suitcase and laptop bag. If she needed space, he would give it to her.

Of Course Time Wrecking Isn't Illegal But It Is a Crime against Nature

Opinion piece in the One Life, One Time blog

In light of the recent Time Wrecker leak, One Life, One Time has come under attack by a number of time wrecking apologists. Some seem to be under the impression that our organization seeks only to end timeline rectification, with no consideration or understanding of criminal justice issues or the very real suffering of crime victims. Nothing could be further from the truth.

Allow me to clarify (again) the stance of One Life, One Time:

Yes, timeline rectification is legally performed and protected in our country. "Time wreckers," whether criminal or victim, are not breaking the law by accepting a timeline rectification.

However, that still does not make it right.

It is the stance of our organization that changing time is immoral, unethical, and unnatural. Our long-term goal is to overturn the Supreme Court ruling that allows timeline rectifications. Our short-term goal is to inform the public of the very real dangers of timeline rectification, support victims from being pressured into agreeing to a rectification, and advocate for those who have been affected by completed rectifications.

Since the time wrecker leak, some of our worst fears are being realized. Four and a half million people have now discovered that they were directly involved in a timeline rectification. They're finding out that the lives they know are built on a lie. They're left with questions such as: What was the crime? Was I the criminal or the victim? What could be so bad that I was willing to turn back time?

In addition to the 4.5 million people directly named on the list, we also have countless friends, family members, and associates who are now wondering how well they really know the people they love. Some of these time wreckers hold positions of trust in their community, whether that trust is in the form of a relationship, a social position, or a place of employment. Those around them have every reason to feel hurt, angry, or even violated by these revelations.

Would you leave your child with a caregiver who committed a crime and covered it up? I wouldn't.

Would you trust a family member who hid their criminal past from you? I wouldn't.

Would you trust the word of someone who went out of their way to change their timeline—not just for their own lives, but for everyone else's too? I wouldn't.

Some are saying that the time wreckers are being unfairly persecuted, that the hackers have violated their privacy. They are suggesting that these hackers be brought to task, much as we would discipline those who share information from sealed juvenile records or confidential government documents.

I would argue that the hacktivists will be thanked for generations to come for this act of civil disobedience. While I don't personally agree with their methods, there's no denying that they've accomplished in one short day what One Life, One Time has struggled for years to achieve. They've brought the ethical and moral issues of timeline rectification into the forefront of public consciousness and raised awareness about how prevalent this issue really is in our country. With the privacy laws protecting information on completed timeline rectifications, our conversations have been overwhelmingly theoretical, not personal.

Those of us who stand against timeline rectification have a large task ahead of us. We have names and even faces for people who have earned our distrust but deserve our compassion. We should not be cruel, but neither should we shy away from the facts.

Now is the time to discuss how timeline rectifications have affected us all and take steps to keep this from ever happening again.

Chapter Six

MARA

It was past four o'clock when Mrs. Gaines finally pulled into the neighborhood. *I should probably feel hungry,* Mara realized. She'd skipped breakfast and only poked at the chicken salad sandwich Dianne had provided them for lunch. It had been a long afternoon, listening to her mother and Dianne going over the details of her father's fundraising dinner. Mara had refused to help, giving one-word answers and pointedly ignoring her mother's tight-lipped stares. It wasn't much of a rebellion, but it was something. She'd deal with the rest of it once she was home with Will. Once she was safe.

I should have let Will come with me today. At least Mara would have had an ally, someone she could have turned to for strength. Now that her BlackBerry, dead with a shattered screen, lay at the bottom of Mrs. Gaines's purse, it felt like Will was farther away somehow.

Mara chipped away at the blue polish on one fingernail as her parents' house came into view.

There weren't any news vans outside the house. Not yet,

anyway. It hadn't taken long for the reporters to set up camp back when her father had been in the news.

But Dad isn't the one under the magnifying glass now. I am.

One step at a time. Mara forced herself to breathe as she followed her mother into the house. All she had to focus on for now was getting her keys, getting in her own car, and driving back to Will.

Her father was already home. It looked like he was waiting for them even, standing in the hallway right as they came through the door.

As if this day couldn't get any weirder. Mara tagged behind her mother, wondering if she should ask for the broken phone back or leave without it.

"Augusta," Congressman Gaines said. "How did everything go?"

"Most of the arrangements have been taken care of," Mrs. Gaines said, putting down her purse and keys on the front table. "I was able to—"

She was cut off abruptly when the congressman appeared to notice Mara in the doorway. "Mara," he said. "William stopped by for you."

"He did?" Mara's breath caught. "He's here?"

"No, I'm afraid not," Congressman Gaines said. "It seems—"

And Mara saw it, in the corner by the front door. Her laptop bag and purple suitcase, which she had unpacked and left in Will's apartment only yesterday.

"Oh," Mrs. Gaines said, following her gaze. "I suspected something like this might happen when . . ."

Mara wasn't listening anymore. She was already unzipping the suitcase. Of course Will wouldn't have left her. Not like this. Not *here*, of all places. But here were all her clothes, her toothbrush, her books—and in between them . . .

Mara fell hard against the edge of the suitcase, banging her knee on a wheel. It was their marriage license.

Mara barely registered the feel of two cold hands on her shoulders, guiding her up to her feet. Was it possible that this was Mara's own mother, wrapping her in a hug, giving her a pat on the back before releasing her? "It was bound to happen," Mrs. Gaines said soothingly. "Sometimes young relationships simply can't survive this kind of stress."

"Perhaps we should discuss—" Congressman Gaines started to say, but Mrs. Gaines silenced him with a small shake of her head.

"It's a shame," Mara's mother said. "But these things do tend to work out for the best."

♦♦♦♦♦

"Enough," Mrs. Gaines commanded. "Mara. Stop what you're doing and think."

Mara hurled the suitcase into the trunk of her car and swung the laptop bag on top. *I'm not unpacking here. He can't send me back to my parents'. If Will has something to say to me, he's going to do it to my face.* She slammed the trunk closed.

"Mara, please. Haven't you humiliated yourself enough for one day?"

Mara pulled her keys out of her purse, but her mother was still standing there, blocking the way. For a minute, Mara considered going around to the passenger's side and crawling across to the driver's seat.

"I came here this morning," Mara said. "I did what you asked. Now I'm leaving."

"To go where?" Mrs. Gaines said. "To go crawling back to your ex-boyfriend?"

"He wasn't just a boyfriend." Her lip trembled. Mara tried to make it stop, but now the rest of her body shook too.

"Look what he's done to you," Mrs. Gaines said. "My bright, beautiful daughter. You have your whole life ahead of you." Her voice hardened, and she crossed her arms over her chest. "And here you are. Crying over a boy."

The first sob escaped Mara's throat. Then another. Mara shielded her face with both hands. She couldn't let her mother see her cry.

"Listen to me," Mrs. Gaines said. "You will get through this. Your father and I will help. The dinner at the club will help to repair your reputation, and we'll do some charity work over the summer. You know how these things go, Mara. You have to control the story."

Mara tried to clear her throat, as if that would help her catch her breath. It came out like a whimper instead.

"And you know why I say that." Mrs. Gaines walked a few steps forward, close enough that her perfume overpowered the gasoline-and-dust scent of the garage, close enough that Mara could almost reach out and touch her. If she dared. "One of my greatest sorrows is that my parents passed away before you were born, Mara. Maybe if you had met them in person, you would understand how serious this is." Mrs. Gaines leaned closer. "My parents were the most hardworking people you'd ever meet. The kindest people. They never hurt anyone. And at the end of the day, it meant nothing."

It meant something, Mara wanted to say. She pressed her palms close against her wet cheeks.

"My parents were only teenagers when they were sent to the Manzanar camp. Imagine that, Mara. Imagine that it was World War II, and you were taken away from your home, your school, your neighborhood, and shipped off to an internment camp. For *three years*. My parents were born in the US, just like you. It did not happen that long ago."

A terrible calm settled over Mara. Like she was pushing away her feelings, only this time, it wasn't her choice. Her tears dried up on their own.

"Neither of my parents ever spoke of it. Not unless I brought it up, and I learned not to talk about it, either. Your Oma and Papa taught me by example. They worked hard, they kept to themselves, they were polite even to the customers that called them 'Japs.' My parents knew the ugliest of this country's flaws, and they still believed in the good."

"Mom—"

Mrs. Gaines clutched Mara's shoulders in her hands. It hurt. Her voice rose, echoing throughout the garage. "You are lucky to have the chances you do, Mara. Do you know how many people on that list would love a chance to speak up for themselves right now? They have worked as hard as you have to build up their lives, and now they're going to lose it all because history needs a villain." Mara forced herself to peek through her fingers, just long enough to see the anger written on her mother's face. Then Mara closed her eyes again and let the shame wash over her. "You can still get out from under this. You can still be the hero of your story. But you have to play by the rules."

Mrs. Gaines was still staring at her. Mara could feel it. She looked up, and this time, she met her mother's eyes.

"Come back inside, Mara," Mrs. Gaines said.

They were so close. Mara could see her own face reflected in her mother's glasses and hear the soft hint of emotion in Mrs. Gaines's voice. For once, Mara knew exactly how to make her mother smile.

All she had to say was yes.

Mara imagined an invisible thread pulled taut between them—the connection she had always longed for. She could put down the keys. Follow her mother back into the house. Let her parents take the reins.

It would be so easy.

"No," Mara said.

The forcefulness of it shocked Mara almost as much as it did her mother. There was a kind of freedom in this empty feeling. Mara uncovered her face and pulled herself up straight.

Mrs. Gaines let go of her shoulders so fast it felt like a little shove. "Are you determined to ruin your life?" Mrs. Gaines asked. Her voice had changed again. Mara stepped backward and glanced toward the door, half wondering if her father would show up now. Who was she kidding? He never came.

"After how hard we've worked for you," her mother said. "After how much we've sacrificed. You're going to throw it all away for a boy."

Mara had to walk around her mother to open the driver's side door. She had almost managed to get it shut before Mrs. Gaines pulled the door open again. Mara flinched. But it was only the garage door opener her mother was reaching for, unclipping it from the visor and snatching her arm back out.

"I can't stop you from leaving," Mrs. Gaines said. "But know that if you leave here now, you will not be welcomed back." She hit the button to open the garage door herself, and it trundled open. Slowly. Too slowly.

Mara turned the key in the ignition—a sudden, defiant sound that filled Mara with resolve. She lifted her chin and glared back at her mother. "I don't want to come back," Mara said. "I will never come back."

Mara threw off the parking brake and backed down the driveway without a second glance. It wasn't until she got to the Beltway that the car's air conditioning kicked in and Mara realized how much she'd been sweating. The blast of cold air on her wet face brought her back to the immediate, to the most important thing of all.

I have to find Will.

♦♦♦♦♦

Mara climbed the stairs to Apartment 305 two at a time. She wouldn't knock. No. She had a key to this place—their place—and she was going to use it. There was going to be a conversation. Mara deserved answers.

I told you I was coming back. You knew I was with my mother. How dare you just—

Her key found its place and the door swung open.

Mara stumbled a little as the wall of cold air-conditioning hit her. The apartment was dark and silent. Clean. The vacuum marks from two days ago were still fresh on the carpet. Mara focused on that while she took deep, painful breaths.

Will was gone.

The door swung closed behind her. Mara made herself walk farther into the apartment, measuring his absence in excruciating detail. The refrigerator still had food. Will's TV was still plugged in and the furniture was still there. His piano keyboard was set up and binders of sheet music were stacked on the bench.

But Will's suitcase was missing. One full dresser drawer was empty. The medicine cabinet was missing his shaving kit, his toothbrush, the little green sample bottles of shampoo that he insisted on hoarding.

Not only had Will left her, but he'd *left*. Gone to North Carolina, probably. Will would be back, but not anytime soon.

The missing pillows and pulled-tight comforter made the bed look horribly empty. Mara collapsed on it, burying herself in Will's spot.

It still smelled like him.

Mara had never felt so conscious of the borders of her own body as she did now. She could almost imagine that Will *was* here. If only he was. He would hold her so tightly that she wouldn't be able to tell where he ended and she began, and finally, she would relax. She would feel safe the way she only did with him.

Now what?

Mara squeezed her eyes shut, as if doing so could somehow erase the question from her mind. But there it was. She couldn't live here, not in this shell of a home without Will. Going back to her parents' house was out of the question. Who else was there? Who would even want her, anyway?

Mara wasn't just *a* time wrecker. Not just one of the four million people in the database. No. Now that her picture was out there, she was *the* time wrecker.

No matter how Mara tried not to think of it, she could picture her mother smirking.

Maybe she should have listened. Her parents knew how to deal with things like this. She should have stayed.

No. Mara sat straight up, suddenly filled with a cold resolve. She wouldn't go back to her parents'. Not after today.

There was only one place she could go.

Who Is Mara Gaines? The Face behind the Time Wrecker Meme

Featured in <u>Generation Y Not</u>

May 23, 2006

It's only been one day since the Time Wrecker Leak, but we're going to go ahead and call it: the world will never be the same. No, not because of the sociopolitical implications of time travel and criminal justice.

We're talking about the *memes*.

Has the internet found a meme that's more versatile than "Rules of the Internet" or the I Can Has Cheezburger cats? It may be too soon to tell, but we're betting the time wrecker meme has staying power. And no, despite what the politically correct pearl-clutchers have said, this meme isn't just a bunch of racists making fun of an Asian woman. It's her expression: that panicked, open-mouthed, deer-in-headlights look that so perfectly relates to all of us in Generation Y.

So: Who is the face behind this ultra-popular time wrecker meme? And how is she dealing with her newfound popularity?

Meet Mara Gaines

Mara Gaines is the only child of Congressman Joel Gaines of Virginia's 8th District and Augusta Gaines, a prominent lawyer in Northern Virginia. And yes, Mara is biracial—the congressman is of European descent, while Mrs. Gaines is the granddaughter of Japanese immigrants.

Mara seemed to be following in the footsteps of her successful parents. Less than a week ago, she graduated summa cum laude from Adams Morgan University and was expected to begin medical school this fall at Georgetown University. She was engaged to marry William B. Sterling, a fellow Adams Morgan University graduate, who was also named on the time wrecker list. The couple was expected to marry this June in a lavish wedding. (Click here to see Mara's wedding details!)

No Stranger to Controversy

Despite her privileged upbringing, Mara has weathered a media firestorm before. Her father, Congressman Joel Gaines, was accused of embezzlement in 1999. (See this article for a complete timeline of the accusations and the congressman's vindication.)

Daddy's Girl

Perhaps it was this difficult time that brought Mara closer to her father. According to a source, Congressman Gaines leaned heavily on his wife and daughter for emotional support during the ordeal.

"Mara and her father are inseparable," said a source close to the family, who asked not to be identified. "She confides in him about everything. If anyone can guide Mara through this difficult time, it's her father."

Time Wrecker Bill

Some might even say that Mara's father is partly to blame for the time wrecker leak. Last week, he introduced House Resolution 6437, a bill that aims to tighten regulations on timeline rectifications. The hacktivists repeatedly referenced "self-centered politicians" in their manifesto, even citing "a new law that would further restrict time wrecking to the privileged few and eliminating the truly disadvantaged."

Lost Love

Ah, l'amour. It seems the time wrecker leak has already taken a toll on Mara's love life. We can confirm that Mara's upcoming wedding to William B. Sterling has been called off. Since Mara was reportedly still wearing her engagement ring, it is likely her fiancé who broke up with her. (Want to know more about engagement and wedding etiquette? Click here to read <u>15 Shocking Wedding Traditions.</u>)

Future Plans

If Mara's father gets his way, HR 6437 will seriously limit how many people can get timeline rectifications. But what about Mara and the 4.5 million people who have already taken advantage of this controversial technology?

We don't know. But rest assured, whatever may become of the real Mara Gaines, the time wrecker meme is here to stay.

Click <u>here</u> for a slideshow of our top twenty time wrecker memes, or click <u>here</u> to submit your own!

Comments:

DW986

Do we seriously have to ask if she was the criminal or the victim? She's the daughter of a lying, embezzling politician and a scheming, nasty lawyer. Criminal behavior must run in that family!!

RedD2go

Seriously, her ex seems like the smartest one here. Can you imagine marrying into this mess? Looks like he dodged a bullet!

Ne1OutThere

Medical school, eh? Maybe she should go into plastic surgery and get some herself while she's at it. That's the only way she's going to have any chance at a normal life after this.

QTpi

I feel so bad for her. Whatever the reason, this woman just broke her engagement and found out she was a time wrecker. Now she's got to deal with the entire world poking into her private life on top of it. Leave her alone!

Lolligaggin

Ehhh . . . if she didn't want to get caught, she shouldn't have done it in the first place. I don't know much about timeline rectifications, but I do know they aren't coerced. She went into this with her eyes wide open.

TurgaTron

Right, right . . . because the concept of privacy is so impossible to understand. Guess I'll expect to see my medical records, video footage of my marriage proposal, and a detailed account of my finances on the internet now. /sarcasm

Lolligaggin

I understand the concept of privacy just fine. What you don't seem to understand is how easily it can be lost. Don't do anything you aren't proud of, is all I'm saying.

....

Chapter Seven

WILL

It was past ten thirty at night before Will pulled into the gravel driveway. He could barely make out the shadowy outline of the double-wide trailer against the night sky. All the lights inside were off, and they were too far out in the country to have streetlights. Will would still know this place anywhere. After all, it had been his home for eighteen years.

Will pulled the key out of the ignition and breathed in the sudden darkness and silence. No headlights. No radio. No air-conditioning. Will felt as if the still, horrible night could swallow him whole.

He wished it would.

He glanced down at his phone again. There was a string of missed calls—none he recognized—and his voice mail was full.

He listened to the first one.

"Hi, this is Cindy from the *Washington Gazette*. We're putting together a story on—"

Delete.

"Hello, I'm trying to reach William B. Sterling. I'm from

the *Nightly News Report—*"

Delete.

"Hi, this message is for William B. Sterling. My name is Lauren from the *Daily Times—*"

Delete.

Will scrolled through again, hoping—just for an instant— that he'd see Mara's cell number among his missed calls. Nothing. No texts, either.

Idiot. Of course she doesn't want to talk to you.

There were a few phone numbers he recognized. Tristan, for example. Will let the voice mail play as the crickets, no longer disturbed by the arrival of his car, started chirping again.

"Hey, Will, just checking in. Saw Mara's picture on the news. This is crazy. How's Mara holding up?"

Will was going to have to call back and explain. Sometime. Not right now.

A light from inside the house turned on and then another. The front door opened, followed by the long, night-shattering creak of the screen door. "Will?" Bonnie Sterling called. "Is that you?"

Will gathered one last deep breath for strength and opened the car door.

◆◆◆◆◆

The next morning, Will woke up in his childhood

bedroom. He remembered where he was before he even opened his eyes. The sheets were pilled and smelled faintly of bleach. The electric fan in the corner whirred and hit his side of the room with a blast of cold air every fifteen seconds. He stretched out his legs before remembering that the twin-size mattress was not quite long enough to fit him.

He hadn't slept here in . . . well, in four years. He and Chris had shared a bedroom until Will went to college. Then Chris had pointed out that there wasn't much room for the second bed and Will had slept on the couch on every visit home.

After Will arrived last night, Chris had retrieved the fold-out cot and mattress from their mother's closet and set it up in his room. Without being asked.

If Chris is being nice to me, I must have really screwed up.

Will opened his eyes all the way, sat up, and swung his legs down to the floor.

Chris slept with one arm slung over his face and a leg out of the covers, grazing the floor. Sleeping was the only time Chris ever seemed to relax. His snoring was loud enough to be heard all through the house. Granted, their trailer didn't have very thick walls to begin with. But snoring that rattled the dishes in the kitchen was still something of an achievement.

Out of habit, Will wondered where Mara was. If she hadn't been at her parents' house, then where was she? Maybe the country club had a bunker or something, a well-appointed room with tight security, designed to house disgraced members of high society until it was safe to return to the public eye.

If the club doesn't have something like that, it should. More likely, Mara had been shuffled off to a friend of a friend. Someone with connections. Someone the Gaines would trust to protect their daughter.

Maybe Mara's saviors would even have a son about her age. Someone that was more *appropriate* for Mara.

Will stomped to the bedroom door and pulled it open so hard it banged against the wall. Chris jerked but resumed snoring. *Oops.* Will tried to be quieter as he walked down the hall to the kitchen.

Becca and their mother were sitting at the kitchen table, fixated on Becca's laptop.

"See, this number shows how many hits an article has," Becca explained. "That's how many times this link has been read."

"Jesus, Mary, and Joseph," Bonnie Sterling said. "Fifty thousand people clicked an article like that?"

At the same time, she and Becca looked up at Will.

"Good morning, son," Bonnie said, smiling wide as Becca quietly closed the laptop. "What would you like for breakfast? Eggs? Cereal?"

"I can get it myself. Thanks, Mom," Will mumbled. He poured half a bowl of oat cereal from a bag and topped it off with milk before he sat down next to his sister. "What were you looking up?"

"Nothing," Bonnie chirped, but Becca looked away. Will's stomach sank.

"I know you're looking up stuff on the time wrecker leak. Anyone would be," Will said. "What are people saying?"

Becca and their mother exchanged a look.

"Please. Just tell me," Will said.

Bonnie bit her lip, and Becca finally nodded.

"You know the picture that showed up in the news yesterday? The one of . . . Mara?" Becca hesitated over her name. "It's a meme now."

Will grunted.

"Do you want to see?" Becca asked. Her hand hovered over her closed laptop.

"Might as well," Will said. "I'll see it eventually, anyway."

Becca cracked the laptop open again and keyed in her password. Her birthdate, Will was pretty sure. He did the same thing. The lock screen disappeared, and the web browser popped up, already open to an image search.

Rows and rows of pictures with Mara's shocked, angry expression stared back at him. Each one had been superimposed with white, blocky text.

When you find out

YOU LITERALLY WRECKED TIME.

When you're living your best life

AND YOUR CRIMINAL RECORD GETS LEAKED.

When you realize

THAT MAN DON'T MATCH HIS DATING PROFILE.

That last one hit Will like a solid punch in the gut. For a moment, he looked down into his cereal, watching the oats float away from his spoon. How long would he have to hold them down until they sank, fat and soggy, to the bottom of his bowl?

"That's enough, now. It does no good to dwell," his mother said. She reached across Becca to touch his hand. "Let's put the computer away for now."

"No, it's okay. I'm fine," Will said and realized in the moment that he was fine. Better than fine. His feelings had shut off entirely. When Will looked back at Becca's computer screen, he felt detached, like he was watching a crime show on TV.

Some of the memes had nothing to do with timeline rectification. Will read them all, pushing the down arrow on Becca's keyboard to scroll.

When you find out

YOUR BOO DOESN'T LIKE NUTELLA.

What do you mean,

Y'ALL DOWNVOTED MY POST??

"Whoever's doing this is nasty," Bonnie declared. "Just being nasty for nasty's sake. I never in my life saw one of these meme things."

"Yes, you have," Becca said. "You like the Cheezburger cat memes."

"What cheeseburger cat?"

"You know, the cat pictures with the cute sayings about what they're probably thinking." Becca put up her hands like kitten paws and widened her big blue eyes. "I can has cheeseburger?"

"Those are memes?" Bonnie asked. "That's different. Everybody likes cats."

And nobody likes time wreckers, Will added silently.

"Is there anything online about . . . me?" he asked, trying to steel himself for the response.

"Not much," Becca said. "Mostly about Mara. I can't believe she made a face like that. She's always so calm."

"It wasn't her fault," Will said reflexively. "She must have been swarmed with reporters. They must have done something to get that reaction."

Becca looked like she wanted to ask Will a question, but a stern look from their mother cut her off.

"Anyway," Bonnie said, a little too loudly, "it looks like

your name hasn't gotten onto much. Seems like people are focusing on some of the celebrities that are on the list."

"Like Deirdre Collins," Becca said. "I can't even imagine what crime she'd be guilty of in any timeline."

"That's enough of that," Bonnie said sharply. "I won't have that kind of talk in my house. In this country, we're innocent until proven guilty, and I don't see one single thing on this hack or data leak or whatever you want to call it that proves anyone is guilty."

"Except the jerks who hacked into the database. That was definitely illegal," Will said, before hurrying to add, "assuming it was an actual hack, and not just a hoax."

No response from Becca or Bonnie. *Nobody thinks this is made up.*

"Well," Bonnie said brightly, "I thought today we could watch a movie or do some work in the garden, if you don't mind, Will. I know you drove a long way, but I'd like some time as a family."

"Is it your day off?" Will asked, surprised. It was after eight on a Wednesday morning, he realized.

"My boss said I could take some time off," Bonnie said tightly. By the look in her eyes, Will wondered if she'd asked for the day or been told to take it.

How would people react to a time wrecker in Deer Hill, North Carolina? Will bet he knew the answer. He was a sinner. Immoral. He'd turned back God's time and turned away from God's purpose.

Maybe he shouldn't have come back.

Will studied his cereal, pressing more and more of the little pieces of oat until they sank under the milk.

"Sure, Mom," Will said. "I'll help you in the garden. Anything you want."

♦♦♦♦♦

Was it actually hotter down here in North Carolina, or had he spent so much time indoors in DC that the weather didn't matter? Probably a little of both. Then again, the physical work of pulling each stubborn weed was enough to make Will break into a sweat. They'd have to stop well before noon, the way the temperature was rising. Will wiped his face with a dirty hand before digging up the next weed.

Chris was working with him, in the sense that Will had started at one end of the garden and his brother was at the very opposite. As far away as his brother could get, really.

It was just the two of them. Becca had hurried off to school after gulping down her breakfast. Will had watched her go, trying to wrap his head around the fact that his baby sister was finishing her last few weeks of high school. When he'd left for college four years ago, Becca was still a kid in his mind. A fourteen-year-old who more often acted like she was ten. Becca had changed so much in the years Will was at school. He'd seen glimpses of it on his visits home, but now Will had to admit that anyone just meeting her might think

Becca was an actual adult.

And I'm back to being a kid.

Will threw a glance at Chris across the garden and was surprised to catch his brother looking at him too.

"Sorry you and Mara broke up," Chris said. He didn't look surprised, Will realized.

Will assumed their mother had coached Chris and Becca before he arrived. Told them the wedding had been postponed, or whatever. But Bonnie Sterling wasn't watching them now. She'd gone inside an hour ago, claiming she needed a shower. Without her there to drive the conversation, Will and Chris were left in this strange brotherly purgatory. Distant. Polite, but just barely.

Will put both hands into the task of pulling up the stubborn weed. "I guess you probably saw it coming," Will said. "A girl like that was never really going to settle for someone like me."

Chris didn't agree with him, but he didn't disagree, either.

"Look, I know you probably don't want to hear this right now," Chris said, "but maybe it's good this happened now instead of later. I'm not saying it doesn't suck, but better to break off an engagement than go through a divorce."

The way our parents did, Will thought, straining until he felt the root start to give. *Not that there was much to their divorce. Dad just walked out and never came back.*

The root snapped, sending Will back on his heels, weed in hands.

"Look sharp," Chris mumbled, just loud enough for Will to hear.

"What?"

"Behind you. Someone's coming." Chris wiped his dirty hands on his jeans and stood up. "Mornin'," he called out.

It was Miss Bitty. Bitty was short for Tabitha, Will knew, but the nickname suited her five-foot frame and tiny brown eyes. Miss Bitty lived in the house directly across from theirs on the gravel road. Most of the homes in the neighborhood were double-wide trailers, like the Sterlings', but Miss Bitty's was a shotgun-style house with a little porch out front. It looked like a dollhouse and Miss Bitty was the doll.

"Good morning, Chris," she said, puffing slightly as she came to a stop by the garden bed. She enfolded Chris in a hug, even though he was dirty, and the embrace left streaks of dirt on Miss Bitty's pink sweatshirt. She turned only slightly to acknowledge Will, who was still standing a good six feet away.

"Morning, Will," Miss Bitty said. Her smile stretched her lips to odd angles. "How nice to see you back home."

Will felt as if he'd been shrunk down from six-foot-three to half Miss Bitty's size. "Yes ma'am."

"I just came to check in on y'all and see if your mama needed anything," Miss Bitty said to Chris. "I can't even imagine what y'all are going through. I just can't imagine. Is your mother home today? I thought I saw her truck."

Will stopped himself from shaking his head. News still

traveled fast in Deer Hill. That much hadn't changed.

"She's home," Chris said. "Probably in the kitchen. I'll walk you up."

Will looked away as Chris held Miss Bitty's elbow and guided her toward the house. Chris was everything their mother had raised her sons to be.

Unlike me.

Will pulled his phone out of his pocket. The voice mail was full again. Nothing from Mara's number. No texts from her, either. The texts that flooded his phone were all from unrecognizable numbers.

time wreckers are going to hell

Criminals belong in JAIL your free pass is up!!!!!!

Who are these people? And why do they think I'm the guilty one? There had to be dozens of William B. Sterlings in the United States. Was it just because of Mara? Because his name was linked to hers, he was getting pulled into the muck?

His phone buzzed again. Another blocked number.

No hiding now jackass we know who you are

Will flipped the phone closed and clenched it in his hand. Was every William B. Sterling getting spammed like this right now? Or was it just him—the one who had a connection to the meme-able Mara Gaines?

The one who used *to have a connection.* Will shoved his cell back in his pocket with unnecessary force.

"Will!"

His head snapped up. It was Miss Bitty running down the hill toward him. Her arms were flailing a little, like a cartoon character.

"Will! It's your mother. Come inside right now!" Miss Bitty's eyes were so wide Will could see the whites all the way around.

"What happened?" Will demanded. He pounded up to the house without waiting for an answer. He was vaguely aware of Miss Bitty behind him, panting, trying to keep up.

In seconds, Will was through the front door, letting the storm door slam behind him the way their mother had told them a thousand times not to do.

Bonnie Sterling was sitting cross-legged on the couch with her face buried in her hands. Her hair was still damp from her shower and hung in tangles around her shoulders. Chris stood behind her, rubbing her shoulders. "It's okay, Mom. It's okay." He didn't so much as glance back at Will, even when the door squeaked a second time, signaling that Miss Bitty had caught up and let herself in too.

"I thought it wasn't true." Bonnie was crying. "I just kept hoping. Maybe it was all some big mistake."

"I know," Chris said. "I know."

"I tried so hard," Bonnie cried into her hands. "I tried to

lead you all on the right path. I tried to be a good mother."

"You are," Chris said. "You're the best mom."

"Then how did I let this happen?" Bonnie leaned forward and started to shake, sobbing. Chris walked around the couch and sat next to her.

Will looked up at the television. The red stripe flashing across the bottom of the screen was impossible to miss. Will felt the heat rising in his chest, his ears ringing. He watched the message cycle past three times, just to be sure he had really read it correctly.

BREAKING: SECOND DATA DUMP IN TIME WRECKER LEAK
New files include time wreckers' birthdates, social security numbers

Behind him, Miss Bitty cleared her throat and walked past, brushing up hard against Will's arm as she did. "Nobody blames you, Bonnie," she said loudly. "Don't you go blaming yourself, either."

Will knew that a good son would go to soothe his mother. Get down on his knees in front of her and take all the blame. Maybe even cry a little too. But Will couldn't move. He stood alone, rooted in place by his own shame.

Second Data Dump in Time Wrecker Leak: New File Poses Increased Security Risk

May 24, 2006

Exactly forty-eight hours after a list of names from the Timeline Rectification database was made public, the so-called hacktivists have released more information and increased their demands for transparency from the government.

At 10:00 A.M. (EST), a second data file was released listing birthdates and social security numbers next to each of the 4.5 million names previously revealed. The end of the file contains a short yet ominous message: "Second warning: end the silence, or we will."

These additional details have many previously unconcerned citizens calling for action. "This is too far. This could ruin lives," stated Dr. Lionel Barker, a professor of sociology at the American College of Lafayette. "Regardless of who on the list may have committed a crime in a previous iteration of their lives, we now have 4.5 million people who have been put at risk for identity theft. The government has a responsibility to protect us from a security breach like this."

Some remain unconvinced that the hackers have the information they claim—or whether the two leaks are indeed linked. Political commentator Ben Graves urged viewers to view the second list with "caution and discretion." In a special morning broadcast, Graves noted, "We should remain wary of sources that will not identify themselves. Even if anecdotal evidence suggests these social security numbers and birthdates are accurate, we still don't have proof of where this information is coming from or who is motivated to release it. For example, could this same list have been compiled after hacking a credit card company's records, or a medical system, or a social services database? Let's just . . . put away the pitchforks for a minute and let the government do its job investigating whether there's any truth to these claims."

However, many of those listed in the leak say that they are already facing serious repercussions. One former employee stated that she found out about the second wave of leaked data from her employer. "He called me into his office and showed me three lines on a printout. He asked if that was my birthday and SSN under my name, and I said yes, thinking he was just updating records or something. He fired me on the spot."

Others have been flooding One Life, One Time help centers, claiming to have been turned out of their family homes. "This is a humanitarian crisis, and it's far from over," warns OLOT president Alicia Barnes.

If you or someone you love has been affected by the Time Wrecker Data Leaks, <u>follow this link</u> for resources and support in your area.

....

Chapter Eight

MARA

So it was true.

Mara pushed off with one foot and let the swinging bench squeak back and forth. Grandmary's sunporch looked like a secret garden this time of year. A hot secret garden. The porch had floor-to-ceiling windows on three sides, but all Mara could see were her grandmother's rosebushes and a peek of her neighbor's backyard.

Mara's laptop was running out of battery power. That was probably a good thing. She took one last look at her name on the list, followed, damningly, by her own birthday and social security number.

Great. Now everyone can steal my identity too. Mara slammed her laptop closed. *As if anyone would want to be me.*

"You're still out here?" Mara jumped, even though there was only kindness in Grandmary's voice. "I'd've thought you'd be back inside by now. This room gets so hot in the afternoon."

Mara eyed the green sweater her grandmother wore over

a long-sleeved shirt and flowing knit pants. Grandmary looked thinner somehow. Almost frail.

"I'm fine out here," Mara said. "Are you all right?"

"Let's at least get a cross breeze going for you," Grandmary said, wrenching open one window with surprising strength and sliding it partway open to reveal the screen. "Get the other side, would you please?"

Mara obediently got to her feet and crossed the room. The locks stuck a little on the windows, and Mara had to brace herself to slide hers open even a few inches. She was rewarded by a small whisper of spring air. Not enough to cool down the sunporch, by a long shot, but it felt briefly cool on Mara's puffy cheeks.

"That's better," Grandmary said. "I was thinking of tuna sandwiches for lunch. What do you think?"

"I'll fix it," Mara offered, but Grandmary held out a hand to stop her.

"You've barely rested since you got here," her grandmother said. "Why don't you sit on the couch for a bit? And take in your computer too. You can charge it over on Grandpap's desk if you like." Grandmary smiled at her fondly. "Your computer probably needs a rest too."

Mara took the laptop and held it to her side, under one arm. Her cheeks went hot. "It's true, Grandmary," she said. "The report I told you about."

"I don't like your reading those kinds of things." Grandmary said. The smile dropped, and she raised one eyebrow at her granddaughter. "There's no need for it."

"I'm a time wrecker," Mara said, trying out the words. "I have to . . . I have to find out what happened and what people know and—"

"You don't need to do any of that right now," Grandmary said. "You've had a shock. It'll make you ill if we aren't careful."

We. Mara let the word wash over her. *Grandmary still loves me. Grandmary would never leave me.*

Mara carried the laptop into Grandmary's living room. The den, Grandpap used to call it. His computer desk was still set up just as he'd left it, complete with the stickers on the sides of the monitor and keyboard. Mara wondered if her grandmother had ever tried to turn on the computer after his death. She guessed not.

This was what true love was supposed to look like. Her grandmother had practically kept up a shrine to her late husband for more than a decade. That was devotion. That was romance. *Not leaving your fiancée's suitcase at her parents' house.*

Mara managed to put down the laptop carefully before she had to swipe away a storm of angry tears. Anger was good. Anger would keep her moving.

In one quick movement, Mara pulled her engagement ring off her finger. She should have done this yesterday. It wasn't hers anymore.

Grandpap and Grandmary used to let her try on this ring

when Mara was just a little girl. It was Grandmary's engagement ring, although she rarely wore it after her finger joints started to swell with arthritis.

"Someday this ring will be yours," Grandpap had told her when Mara would slide it on her thumb and marvel at how heavy the diamond was on her tiny fingers. "When a boy decides he wants to marry you, he's going to have to come through me first. Let me make sure he's good enough for my girl."

"Likely, Mara will have plenty to say on the matter herself," Grandmary would chime in, but she'd be smiling.

Mara had tried it on over the years, noting with pleasure when the ring was too small for her thumb and fit neatly on her index finger. By the time Mara was in high school, it slid comfortably onto her ring finger, although the diamond often spun around the wrong direction. By then, Grandpap had passed away, and Grandmary had given the ring to Mara's father for safekeeping. When Will proposed, seeing the ring in his hand felt like a final confirmation. Even Mara's dad knew that Will was the right man for her.

Mara clenched the ring in her fist now, letting the diamond cut into the soft flesh of her palm.

"Lunch is ready," Grandmary called from the kitchen.

The kitchen table was set with two tuna sandwiches on rye bread with the crusts cut off, and soda to drink. It used to be Mara's favorite meal.

Mara hesitated on the threshold.

"I never said thank you," Mara said. "When I came over last night. You just took me in, and I never even said thank you."

"You did, actually," Grandmary said, gesturing her to join her at the table. "Several times, while I was tucking you into bed. Not that you needed to thank me at all. This is what families do for each other."

Mara slid into her chair, cheeks burning as if she'd been struck. Was Grandmary saying she should have stayed at her parents' house? Did Grandmary know how she'd left?

Possibly reading Mara's discomfort, Grandmary continued. "When your father called yesterday to say you were on your way over, I was so glad. What you need is to get away from this mess for a while." She passed one flowered paper napkin to Mara and took the other for herself.

"Thank you." Mara politely nibbled a corner of the sandwich before putting it back down. So her father had known where Mara would go, even before she'd figured it out herself.

"What did Dad tell you?" Mara asked.

Grandmary looked like she was choosing her words carefully. "Only that they were concerned for your safety and hoped I could put you up for a bit until things died down. You don't have to worry about anything here, Mara. I've known all the neighbors for years. We watch out for each other. No one's going to allow any funny business."

"Thank you," Mara mumbled. Even to her own ears, she sounded ungrateful. *A spoiled rich girl who expected everything handed to her . . . only thought about herself . . . no wonder her fiancé dumped her.*

It happened so quickly, that the words she read online had become her own thoughts.

Grandmary laid a cold hand on Mara's elbow. "Sometimes, families can be . . ." She seemed to cut herself off and let a minute pass before beginning again. "Everything is going to be all right. Even if it doesn't seem like it right now. Everything is going to be all right."

"I don't deserve this," Mara whispered. "I don't deserve any of this." Before she could hesitate, Mara opened her hand and passed the ring to Grandmary. "I should give this back to you. It's yours, anyway."

Grandmary took the ring, but she held it in the palm of her open, wrinkled hand. She reached her other hand over to Mara, who took it. Grandmary's grasp was surprisingly strong.

"I want you to hear this from me, Mara. Whether it's true or not, this timeline rectification business won't change a single thing as far as I'm concerned. You are my granddaughter. I couldn't be any prouder of the woman you are."

"It is true," Mara said. Grandmary didn't let go. "That's what I was trying to tell you earlier. There was a second data leak. It has all our birthdays, our social security numbers—I read it, Grandmary. I had a rectification. I'm a time wrecker."

So was Will. Mara didn't know his social security number, but she'd seen his birthday in the database, written out right next to his name.

"You're Mara," Grandmary said. "You're the same Mara Elizabeth Gaines you've always been."

"You mean you forgive me?"

"There's nothing to forgive. You are not the guilty party here—not for leaking this information or for having a rectification in the first place." Grandmary squeezed her hand one last time and carefully placed the ring on the table. The little *clink* made Mara flinch.

"This ring doesn't belong to me," her grandmother said. "It's yours. When I gave it to your father to hold on to for you, it was a permanent gift."

"I don't deserve it," Mara whispered. "You and Grandpap had such a good marriage."

"Grandpap and I had a real marriage," Grandmary corrected. "Bumps along the way and all. No matter what, you and Will loved each other. That means something. Don't try to tell yourself it doesn't."

Mara picked up the ring and rolled it between her thumb and forefinger. "What am I going to do?" Mara asked. "How am I going to make a life without him in it?"

"Don't worry about the rest of your life right now," said Grandmary. "Let's just worry about the present. There is someone who'd like to visit you if you're up for it."

Mara laid the ring back on the table and withdrew her hands. There was no easy way to say this. "Grandmary, I don't know if I could handle seeing Mom and Dad. I don't mean to put you in the middle of anything, I just . . . I don't think I'm ready yet."

"That wasn't what I was going to say," Grandmary said. "It was your friend Robyn. She had my phone number from a few weeks ago, I suppose, and called to ask if I might know where you were. She's worried about you."

A few weeks ago. Grandmary's talking about the bridal shower. And there they were—more tears streaming down Mara's cheeks. She tried swiping them away with her fists.

Grandmary's hand was on her back, rubbing up and down. "I only mention it because I wasn't sure if I should tell her that you were coming to stay with me, or if you wanted it to be a secret from everyone for now."

"It's okay if Robyn knows I'm here," Mara said, swiping again to unstick her hair from her wet face. "But she doesn't have to visit or anything. She doesn't need to deal with any of this right now."

For that matter, neither does Grandmary.

"We'll let Robyn be the judge of that," Grandmary said. "Go wash your face while I give her a call back."

"Grandmary—"

"Mara. There are people in your life who love you and want to be here for you. It's best that you go ahead and let us."

♦♦♦♦♦

Mara woke up with a start. She'd accepted Grandmary's suggestion to go upstairs after lunch and close her eyes for a bit. Mara was sure she wouldn't really sleep, but it seemed only polite to try.

That must have been hours ago. It was dark outside now, and the whole house seemed still. Maybe her grandmother had gone to sleep too. Without her phone or computer, Mara wasn't sure where to find out what time it was. The little gabled guest bedroom didn't have a clock.

Mara pulled the comforter up over her head and squeezed her dry, swollen eyelids shut. *I don't want this to be my life.* Maybe if she fell back asleep, she'd wake up with things the way they were supposed to be. She'd be in Will's apartment, before the stupid time wrecker leak broke. They'd still be planning their lives together. They'd still be planning their wedding.

Mara flung the comforter off. It was useless to dream about all that now. It was all a lie, anyway, and now everyone knew it.

Will was right to leave her. They'd been married once before, that much was obvious, and they'd both chosen to go back and forget it all. Whatever life they'd built on the truth hadn't been worthwhile for either of them. Why would a marriage between two time wreckers be any better?

Out of habit, she wondered what Will was thinking right now. If he'd left the apartment, he must have gone to crash at Tristan's new place. Or driven all the way back home to North Carolina. Anything to get away from her.

And Mara herself was back in this ivy-wallpapered bedroom at Grandmary's, the same place she'd spent summers and sick days as a kid. Mara even thought of this little angled-ceiling room as her own, in a way. Mara's bedroom at her parents' house had been a museum for their expectations. It was all antique furniture and china dolls, with trophies and awards lined up execution-style on the top of her dresser. While she was away at college, Mara's parents had framed her high school diploma and hung it over her desk. The last time she'd peeked in the closet, her wedding veil was draped between two hangers so it would stay wrinkle-free.

Mara closed her eyes. Her wedding dress. That was one detail her mother hadn't mentioned. It would still be at the bridal shop, waiting for her final fitting. What happened to wedding dresses when the marriage was called off?

Breathe. Mara walked slowly around her room here at Grandmary's, touching each piece of furniture to ground herself. Here was the angled closet where Mara's own clothes had been hung next to the holiday tablecloths. Here was the little bookshelf that held Mara's high school yearbooks alongside Grandmary's collection of *Reader's Digest* condensed books. Here was the dresser, with a row of little origami animals lined up along the top. Mara touched the delicate papers with one finger.

In high school, Mara could fold dozens of origami models. She could even fold dollar bills into turkeys and hearts, a skill that almost made her popular. She'd taught herself origami after reading *Sadako and the Thousand Paper Cranes*. For once, there had been a book Mara had to read in school that had someone who looked like her on the cover.

Back when she and Will were engaged—Mara crossed her thumb over to her bare ring finger—she had even thought about folding cranes for their wedding. Her mother had dismissed that idea immediately. "This is your senior year of college," she'd said. "You don't have enough time to be folding paper birds when you should be studying. If you and William are determined to get married in 2006, you'd better leave the wedding planning to me."

It probably wasn't just the timing that bothered her. Folding a thousand and one cranes for a wedding day was a Japanese American tradition, one Mara had to read about online. Mrs. Gaines had always rolled her eyes whenever Mara asked her questions about Japanese culture. "I don't know, Mara," her mother would reply tartly. "My parents raised me to be American."

Even though they were kept in prison camps during the war? Mara had wanted to ask as she got older, but she didn't dare. She read about it instead. Wondered on her own what it would have been like for her grandparents to be bussed miles away from home. To be asked over and over to prove their loyalty, only to be locked up all the same.

Mara liked to imagine that her Oma and Papa would have done origami with her if they had still been alive. Maybe they would have told Mara about growing up in California and their lives before Manzanar. What their own parents had been like and why they'd emigrated from Japan.

Or maybe they just would have been disappointed in me. Like Mom.

On a hunch, Mara pried open the top drawer of the dresser. She was right—the drawer was still packed with her scrapbooking supplies and leftovers from school assignments. *Grandmary even saved the projects I didn't finish.* The thought made Mara smile. And there they were: dozens of packets of unused origami papers.

Mara removed them and tried to shut the drawer, but it stuck on a couple of red Styrofoam balls. Those were from high school too. Mara remembered building a double helix for science class over spring break one year. She had spent hours painting Styrofoam balls and sticking them together with toothpicks, balancing the whole thing precariously on a cardboard box lid. That would have been the year her father was being investigated and Mara had been shuttled to Grandmary's house more than usual, to "get away for a bit."

Thinking about her father made Mara's stomach hurt.

There had been a time, when Mara was a little girl, when her father would have built that model with her.

Congressman Gaines used to bring Mara to his office and let her twirl in his big, important chair while he stood. Her father would hold a finger to his lips and wink at her when he picked up the phone to join a call. Mara would bite her lip to stifle her giggles, delighted by the feeling of getting away with something. What would the other grown-ups think if they knew Mara was there, spinning so fast that her pigtails stood straight out?

Mara wasn't sure when that ended, exactly. Somewhere along the line, she'd stopped being her father's little buddy and became her mother's mini-me. A strong woman in the making. A powerful woman with a future. And Mara had gone along with it, trying harder each year to hide the fact that she was neither strong nor powerful.

It had been a wonderful lie. It could have been a wonderful life.

Mara sat cross-legged on the bare floor with a pack of metallic gold origami paper. This pack had been opened before, but other than a few papers near the top that curled at the edges, it was still usable. She folded a square of paper into one triangle, and then a second. Funny how it could all come back to her so quickly. Just like riding a bike. After a few mistakes that had to be smoothed out and refolded, Mara had produced one golden crane. Its beak was crooked, and the wings revealed a little of the metallic paper's white underside, but at least it stood on its own.

Mara reached for a fresh square of the origami paper.

Grandmary had been right earlier about staying off the internet. This was exactly the kind of distraction she needed. Mara folded three more cranes, then five. Now they made a straight line across the floor, single file, like they were marching off to war. She was going to have to find something to do with them all.

I'll make a thousand of them. The thought came to Mara suddenly, but once it did, it felt almost right. *No. I'll fold a thousand and one paper cranes, just like I planned.*

By now, turning and creasing the paper was automatic. It only took five minutes to make a crane—sometimes less— but she had to be careful not to leave fingerprints on the glossy paper. The foil showed every mistaken fold too, no matter how she tried to smooth it out.

Isn't that the truth. Some mistakes can't be undone.

Mara pulled on a finished crane's wings to open up the middle and make the bird stand. Too hard. The edge of the crane's delicate wing tore along the crease.

"Damn it," she muttered aloud, and crumpled the model in one hand. It took only seconds to squash it into a small golden ball and flick it across the floor. The others toppled over like dominoes.

Mara winced as she flexed her aching thumb. The whole idea was stupid. A couple who folded a thousand and one cranes were supposed to be granted a happy marriage. What was Mara doing this for? She wasn't a bride anymore. *I'm doing this for me.* The next thought came to Mara as suddenly as if it had always been there, just under the surface, waiting for her to realize it.

When I've folded all one thousand and one cranes, I'm going to heal my broken heart.

That's ridiculous, Mara thought in the next instant. But she reached for a paper square and kept folding anyway.

I Knew Three of the Time Wreckers And I Wish I Knew More

Guest post by Elizabeth Yates for <u>The Inspectator</u> blog

When I realized three of my former classmates were on the time wrecker list, I found myself scanning the database for another name. A name I've tried to make myself forget so many times, only to have it pop up again and again.

I don't know what I was hoping for. I guess that's the thing about loving someone who hurt you. You know how dangerous they can be, but at the same time, you're always hoping they could get better. I guess if I saw his name on the time wrecker list, it would have proved me right on both counts.

I didn't find the name I was looking for. Of course not. To have a timeline rectification, you need to have been convicted of a crime, which means you need to be charged in the first place. But as I scrolled through the list of time wreckers, I did get a little teary. Only 4.5 million out of 300 million people in America. What is it with us and justice? Are we so scared of what the world would look like if we actually made things fair?

I'm just going to say it: the people who are against timeline rectification aren't "suspicious of the data" or "concerned about privacy." They're protecting their privilege.

The thing is, our criminal justice system is heavy on the word *criminal* and light on the *justice*. Be honest: Would you rent an apartment or go on a date or hire someone with a criminal record? That's an automatic no from me. Trust me: I know how dangerous a person can be and never be in the system at all. But that's not really fair, is it?

Which is better: permanently marking someone unemployable, untrustworthy, and undatable, or giving them a chance to truly rehabilitate and start fresh?

Time wreckers, I'll be honest with you: I wish I could have a timeline rectification. If I could go back and live my life over, I would never have dated Stefan.*

We met in 2002, when we were in college at Adams Morgan University. He was the kind of guy everybody has a crush on at least once. You couldn't help but notice Stefan when he walked into a room; he was cute, sure, but mostly he was charming. Everyone's attention naturally focused on Stefan, and I was over the moon when his attention focused on me.

That's not to say that Stefan didn't have his demons. In some ways, I think that's what kept me infatuated with him so early on. There was something about being his confidante: the only one he could open up to about his troubles with his dad, his insecurities with his schoolwork, his fears about the future.

He fooled me into believing that he was only one small step away from perfection. I fooled myself into believing my love could get him there.

I wasn't even angry at him, the first time I sat silent and unmoving on his bed while he destroyed his laptop with a baseball bat. He'd downloaded a virus by accident. We've all done it, but under the pressure of a project deadline and afraid of falling farther behind in class, he lost his cool. That's what I told myself: he was a sensitive person, really, someone who just couldn't handle everyday frustrations. He just needed me to be there for him, reassure him, love him the way only I could, and he wouldn't get so upset.

Everything Stefan did afterward confirmed it for me. He was so remorseful I felt terrible for him. I found myself reassuring Stefan after he turned up with flowers and apologizing that I "had to see him like that." No, of course I wouldn't leave him over something so trivial. I'd have to be crazy to throw in the towel on him, on us, after one little outburst. He was so grateful to have my forgiveness he actually cried. Told me he didn't deserve a girlfriend like me.

He was right about that.

Looking back, I'm scared by how quickly things escalated. Stefan's temper flared more and more, which I saw as a sure sign of the stress he was under. And before long, I had taken my self-imposed job of "helping Stefan" far too seriously.

He never asked me to stop seeing my friends. Of course not. It was just that I could see how stressful it was for him, trying to make small talk with people he didn't really know. So I made the excuses, put off making plans, and slowly withdrew. He didn't tell me not to accept an internship the following semester, either. But Stefan was so upset at the idea of us spending less time together. What if I was too busy to make time for him? What if I met someone else? And so I turned it down, confident that he just needed a little more reassurance right now, a little more support since he was going through so much.

I wish I could say that I realized what was happening the first time he raised his hand to me. But I didn't. I was only angry at myself. Couldn't I see that he just needed to vent? I should have known better than to leap in and offer advice. If only I'd been more thoughtful, more sensitive, he wouldn't have slapped me.

I didn't realize what was happening until my cousin asked me to be a bridesmaid in her wedding. At that point, demurring was reflexive. I knew Stefan wouldn't enjoy attending the reception, where he knew so few people, to say nothing of all the weekends I'd be spending away from him to go dress shopping, plan the shower, and attend the bachelorette party. Would Stefan even be okay with my going to a bachelorette party?

My cousin stopped me in the middle of my string of excuses. "What's really going on?" she asked, and I found myself telling her.

And telling her.

And telling her.

Two weeks later, I broke up with Stefan. And that's when the second stage of my nightmare began.

One of the things that had initially attracted me to Stefan was the way he relentlessly went after everything he wanted. Basketball. Pledging his fraternity. Me. But what was charming and exciting at the beginning of our relationship was terrifying after we broke up.

Stefan refused to accept that it was over. At first, it was just phone calls and presents. Then he would happen to show up wherever I was on campus. After a few days, he kicked down my door, insisting that I had to talk to him. I called the RA and the campus police, who were no help.

"It sounds like he really loves you," they said. "Maybe you should just hear the poor guy out. Don't leave him hanging." Encouraged by their response, Stefan told everyone that we had a fight and I was just being immature.

Funny how my ignoring someone at two in the morning was immature, but him kicking in my door was understandable.

I ended up having to transfer schools to get away from him. Finally, thankfully, he gave up. Some women aren't as lucky. From what I understand, Stefan continued on at Adams Morgan University as if nothing had ever happened. I started over at College Park, telling everyone I had decided to switch to a different major that wasn't offered at my old school. I hit the ground running, spending the next two years rebuilding my GPA. It took me much longer than that to rebuild my self-esteem.

I still wonder what would have happened if I had pressed charges against Stefan—for assault, for destruction of property, for stalking and harassment. But I never tried. Getting laughed off by campus police once was hard enough. Why keep putting myself through that when, let's be honest, the most he'd ever get would be a slap on the wrist?

To the three time wreckers I know, and the many I don't: thank you. You've done more for justice in this country than many people ever will—including myself. You saw a way to move yourselves past the labels of "criminal" or "victim." And if our current justice system makes it so hard to seek justice for fear of ruining someone's future, it only makes sense that we would go back and change the past.

Names changed to protect the innocent. And the not-so innocent.

Chapter Nine

WILL

The house was quiet when Will woke up Thursday morning—almost afternoon, really. His muscles were even more sore today than yesterday. How long did it take to recover from a six-hour drive?

Will slowly stretched, wincing when his feet knocked over the stack of folded clothes balanced precariously at the foot of the bed. Will should have unpacked properly or kept his things in the suitcase. But it felt strange to declare he was moving back here when he had an apartment back in DC and even stranger to act like a day-trip visitor in his family home. So here were his clothes, in limbo. Just like him.

For a fleeting second, Will allowed himself to hope that the silent house meant that the rest of the family was off at work and school. No such luck. If he strained his ears, Will could just hear a murmur of voices from the living room. He checked the clock again—eleven thirty—and hustled into yesterday's jean shorts and a fresh T-shirt.

The voices he'd heard were coming from the TV. *It's a talk show,* Will thought. He recognized the punctuated, back-and-forth banter between a drawling, deep-voiced man and a shrill, almost histrionic woman.

Deirdre Collins. Her talk show was still on the air? Will had barely seen it since he'd been away at college, but it was a familiar sound in his childhood home. Will wasn't sure whether his mother loved or hated *The Deirdre Collins Show,* but either way, Bonnie Sterling had never missed an airing unless she was working.

"Hey, Mom," Will said, rounding the corner. "Sorry I slept in so late."

"Mom's at work," Chris said, barely glancing up. His eyes were focused on Becca's laptop screen, set up on the coffee table in full view of the television. "And Becca's at school, obviously."

"Oh." Will slid down on the quilt-covered couch opposite Chris. "So this is what you do on your days off, huh?" he said, trying to make a joke even while his heart hammered against his ribs. Ridiculous, to be so unnerved by his own brother. His *baby* brother, even though, at twenty years old, Chris didn't look much like a baby anymore. Even on a morning off, Chris was wearing a golf shirt buttoned all the way up to the neck and a pair of khaki shorts with clean trainers.

"No," Chris said. "This is what I do when I find out someone in my own family is a time wrecker."

Onscreen, the studio audience applauded in response to whatever Deirdre Collins had just said. It was the only sound in the Sterlings' home for a long time.

"Listen," Will said finally, "I know you and I don't see eye to eye on a lot of stuff, but this time wrecking thing . . ."

"Is a sin," Chris finished. "The hackers haven't said what crime it is you were involved in the first time around. It doesn't matter. You still know you did wrong by turning back time."

"Timeline rectification isn't a crime," Will shot back.

The tips of Chris's ears turned pink. "I didn't say it was a crime. I said it was a sin."

"Hear that? That right there? That's the kind of thing that made me stop going to church."

"Maybe it's about time you went back."

Here we go again. "No thanks," Will said.

Chris slammed down the laptop screen and stood up. "Then why are you here?"

"Excuse you?" Will sputtered. "Who the hell do you think you are?"

"Just hear me out. I am your brother and I love you. I will always be here for you. If Mara had left you because you were a drug addict, or if you'd cheated on her—"

"Don't you dare."

"I told you to listen. We would have welcomed you home and put you up just the way we are now. And we would have helped you get back on your feet. Rehab, counseling, whatever you needed. Anything at all. But you can't just waltz back in here like none of this is your fault."

Will stood too. "I'm not doing this with you. I didn't do anything wrong."

"Neither did we."

I can always leave. But it was the next thought—and go where?—that made Will turn back around. "You know what? You don't like time wrecking, fine. You don't like me, fine. Stay out of it. This has nothing to do with you."

"This has everything to do with me. Why do you think Mom was home yesterday morning? You think she just called off work for some quality time with her prodigal son?"

Will's white-hot rage suddenly turned to ice. "What happened?"

"She called off so she could scrub the dog crap off your car before you saw it. Whoever it was threw bags of it on our porch too. Surprised you didn't smell anything. Becca and I did."

Will couldn't speak.

"Good thing they didn't set the bags on fire. How fast you think it takes a trailer to burn up? Think we could've gotten everyone out in time?"

"Mom didn't tell me," Will finally managed. "I didn't know."

"She didn't want you to know."

Will was still imagining the living room filling up with foul-smelling smoke. They wouldn't have had time to save anything. The whole trailer would have gone up in minutes.

"I can't believe someone would do that," Will said. "I'd

just gotten here the night before. Were people watching for my car or something?"

"You know Deer Hill's a fishbowl. Everybody knows everything."

"I thought I knew Deer Hill," Will muttered. "I remembered people here being a little more forgiving."

Chris shrugged. "Can't forgive the unrepentant."

Will spun on his heel. "That's it. Forget it. I'll pack up what I brought and get out of here." He stormed down the hall, making each footstep thunder.

"Of course you will," Chris called after him. "Go ahead and run away again."

Will slammed the bedroom door shut, but not before Chris hurled his final accusation.

"You're just like Dad."

◆◆◆◆◆

The fold-out cot squeaked terribly whenever Will rolled on his side to check the time. Half an hour passed. An hour.

Will had been lying facedown on this cot since his argument with Chris. He'd half expected his brother to walk in at some point, demanding that Will get up and get out. It was Chris's room, after all.

But he hadn't. Some time ago, Will had heard Chris walking out the kitchen door and starting his truck. Driving away.

And now Will was alone.

I'm pathetic. Ridiculous. I'm a lazy, stupid worthless lump of . . . Will didn't even have the energy to keep beating himself up. Chris had summed it up, hadn't he? Will was just like their father.

They'd been here in this room the day Dad left. Will was only four years old. He had been playing with Chris while baby Becca slept in a playpen in the corner. The door was shut, but it wasn't much help. Will had made it his job to talk as loudly as possible to cover up the sound of their parents arguing in the kitchen.

They were playing superheroes, Will remembered. Will was always Spider-Man, and Chris, who was only two, was clutching the Superman action figure.

"Spider-Man's gonna rescue the princess. See? She's trapped," Will had said, pointing to Becca, asleep in her playpen.

"Baby," Chris corrected him.

"Pretend, Chris," Will had said, flinching at the sound of something being thrown in the kitchen. A pot? No, there was no clanging sound. Maybe it was a book. Something heavy.

"Okay," Chris said. "Princess."

"Yeah. And Spider-Man's going to save her. See? He shoots out his webs like this"—Will hissed between his teeth to make a satisfying sound effect—"and then he grabs 'em and walks up the building."

"Well, maybe if you'd gotten a damn *job* instead of having another damn *kid* . . ." The rest of his father's words were drowned out by another object being thrown. Will heard the tinkling of glass. Whatever that was, it had broken.

"Superman," Chris had lisped around his pacifier. "Superman fly." He raised the Superman figure as high as he could reach, whizzing it through the air as he swayed on his tiptoes.

"Get out!" their mother screamed. It was so loud that both boys simultaneously stopped playing. "Just get out, you bastard!"

The door had slammed, as it had so many times before. The baby had woken up then, and there was Bonnie, blinking her own eyes when she came in to walk little Becca around the room, talking quietly, reassuring her as she always did. Chris and Will had gone back to playing, soberly, but relieved that the fight was finally over.

But their father never came back.

Now Will was almost the age his father was back then. Will was twenty-two; his dad had been twenty-three or twenty-four the year he walked out on his wife and three kids. No one directly talked to Will about his dad, but he'd heard the whispers well enough when he was growing up. Some people said he just hadn't been ready to settle down. Others blamed alcohol, or stress over money, or plain old bad temper. Most people, for reasons Will couldn't understand, simply blamed Bonnie Sterling for "not doing enough" to keep the marriage together.

Or maybe he was just a loser.

Will's father was exactly the kind of person who would have had a time wreck, Will thought. When his dad had a problem, he ran out and left everyone else to pick up the pieces.

Who do I think I'm kidding, anyway? When Will had proposed to Mara last year, he'd dismissed every suggestion that they were too young. He and Mara were different. They were special. They could make it through anything.

But maybe it was just Will trying to prove that *he* was different, *he* was special, *he* wouldn't repeat all his father's mistakes.

And now here he was. Less than a week after graduating college, just a few days since the hackers broke open the database. Will had run away at the first sign of trouble.

Just like Dad.

♦ ♦ ♦ ♦ ♦

Will was waiting in the driveway when his mother got home from her shift. Becca hadn't come home from school yet. Chris was still gone. He'd probably picked up an extra shift at Lowry's store.

Will's old sedan glimmered in the sunlight. How could he not have noticed it yesterday? No car that had survived the drive from DC to Deer Hill would look this clean. It must have been covered in dirt and backroad dust by the time he pulled in Tuesday night. Will tried to imagine what it looked like the next morning when Bonnie Sterling called out from work.

"What's wrong, baby?" Bonnie Sterling's worried eyes had been on him before she'd even shut her car door. Now she was crunching up the gravel in her wide-heeled sandals, scanning him and the house for damage. "Did something happen?"

"That's what I should have asked you," Will said. "Mom. Why didn't you tell me about the . . . the stuff on my car, and the porch? You should have gotten me up. I would've taken care of it."

"Don't you even think of such a thing," his mother scolded. She pushed her sunglasses up on top of her head and studied Will's face before she pulled him into a hug. "Who told you? You don't need to be worrying about any of that right now."

"Yes, I do," Will said. "I didn't come here so people would start going after you and Chris and Becca. I wouldn't do that to you."

"Don't you go blamin' yourself for someone else's ugliness," Bonnie said firmly. "Now come on in. I pulled a double shift and my feet hurt. Pour me a lemonade, would you?"

Will did as he was told, but he wasn't about to let the subject drop. Once his mother was settled in on the couch with her glass, Will sat across from her and started in again.

"I didn't come here to be a burden," Will said.

"Families take care of each other, honey," Bonnie said. "We help out."

Will sat next to her, so gently he barely dented the couch cushion. "I know a lot of people around here think that time wrecks"—Bonnie flinched at the word—"are wrong. That all of us on that list sinned, no matter what we were taking back. And I just wanted to ask you . . ." No. He was already regretting this. He did not want to ask. "I wanted to ask what you believe."

Bonnie took a long sip of her lemonade, followed by another and another. Will's heart sank a little more each time. Didn't he already know? Why did he have to push to hear her say it?

"I believe in a loving and forgiving God," Bonnie said finally. "I don't think anyone on earth can punish you worse than you're already punishing yourself, and no one should try, either."

"Mom." Will opened his mouth and shut it again. There were no words.

"It's on all of us to acknowledge our own sins. No one else can do it for you," Bonnie said firmly. "Now let's see about dinner. I was thinking tuna noodle casserole. Doesn't that sound nice?"

ONLINE EXCLUSIVE: Deirdre Collins Blames Herself for the Time Wrecker Leak in Emotional Show

The talk show host gets real about the time wrecker leak, her own suspicions, and discovering the truth about herself.

Deirdre Collins, host of the popular daytime talk show *The Deirdre Collins Show*, took to the screen to address her feelings about the timeline rectification data leaks. Earlier this week, she was interviewed on several late-night shows before broadcasting a live, special edition 90-minute show Thursday to discuss her outing as a time wrecker.

"Seeing my name on that list . . . [it] was soul-shattering," said Collins. The seasoned talk show celebrity had to stop and wipe away tears many times during the special edition broadcast. Collins shared, "I've often felt, particularly within the past few years, that there was something 'off' about my life . . . just a feeling that I wasn't living as my most authentic self, that there was a missing piece. At first, I had thought perhaps my soul was trying to lead me in a different direction, or that it might be time for a change in my relationships or my career, but now I see why I've felt so disconnected from my life. I've had a timeline rectification. Who knows what my life was like originally? Who knows what I could have been?"

While most of those named in the time wrecker leak have not reported any awareness that they had a timeline rectification, Collins is adamant that the data leaks simply confirmed her own suspicions that something was amiss. Further, Collins believes she may have the answers as to why the hackers released the list now.

"I do fear that I am in some way responsible," Collins said. "My goal as a host, as a television personality, and as a human being is to create a platform where we can talk openly with each other. I know that if I am feeling these things, if I am sensing this disturbance in our national climate, then other people are too, and I want to give those voices a chance to be heard. And the response to my providing that platform and sharing so much of myself in the public forum is that some people have been trying to shut me down. Some people . . . they see a good thing happening and they have to try to ruin it."

Regardless of whether revealing Collins's past timeline rectification was a factor for the hacktivists, she is definitely here to help the nation heal and rebuild. At the conclusion of the show, Deirdre announced that she had established a charity called Time to Heal, with the specific purpose of providing legal aid and counseling services to all of those affected by the timeline rectification leaks. With some 4 million people now at risk for identity theft and fraud in the wake of the data leaks, news of the charity was warmly received by the studio audience. (Click here to learn more about Time to Heal and access services.)

Some critics of the show are quick to point out that Deirdre's assertions come at a time when her show desperately needs a ratings boost. It's been long speculated that this may be the final season of *The Deirdre Collins Show*. As reality television shows gain more of the spotlight in prime time, talk shows like Deirdre's are becoming a rarity. Some have even gone so far as to suggest that Deirdre was involved in engineering the data leak herself in a desperate attempt to gain notoriety.

Collins firmly denied such rumors. "No, I had no knowledge whatsoever that the leak would happen, or that I would be named [on the list] . . . As much as dealing with this shock has made me want to crawl into a hole, I know that the only way we will find healing and understanding is in having these difficult dialogues and exploring this issue together."

Comments:

Merrilee157

This just in: talk show host makes current event all about herself

JusTrollin

please if she was going to go back in time why wouldn't she have done something about that hair? there's a crime against nature.

RoryNRic4Ever

I think people are just reading too much into it. For whatever reason, at this point in our (rectified) life maps, someone saw an opportunity to hack and leak the database. Look how many people are on that list. There could be a million different variables that came together that made this possible in this 2006 when maybe it wasn't possible in earlier iterations of 2006. Ugh, my head hurts now.

IsntSheLovely

Okay, but if someone's going to go to the trouble of hacking a government database, I hope they were trying to do something more than embarrass a talk show host.

....

Chapter Ten

MARA

The sun was starting to set, washing the living room in a warm, orange glow. Mara's head was pleasantly sleepy. The knots in her shoulders had relaxed, and she sank as much as she could into the stiff chintz cushions of Grandmary's couch.

Mara had never been more grateful to see her friend Robyn. She had arrived just after dinner. Based on her makeup, she must have come straight from work. Everything about Robyn's work makeup was subdued: matte olive foundation, barely rosy lips, a hint of mascara. Her brown curly hair was pulled back into a severe bun at the back of her neck, although little wisps were pulled loosely around her face. Robyn looked so different than she had in college, when all her bath towels were perpetually stained with bleach and purple hair dye.

College. Had it really been only weeks ago?

Robyn was now sprawled opposite Mara on the couch, sipping the remains of her single glass of pinot grigio. Mara had already refilled her own glass twice, and it was looking empty again. Mara reached across the coffee table for the bottle.

"Are you going to have anymore?" Mara asked. "Or can I kill it?"

"It's all yours," Robyn said. "I'd join you if I didn't have to drive home tonight."

Mara topped off her glass and set the empty bottle down harder than she'd meant.

Robyn raised her eyebrows. "You okay over there?"

"Define 'okay.'"

"You know what I mean."

"I wouldn't drive anywhere," Mara said. "But there's nowhere I can really go, anyway."

Robyn managed to smile in a way that was all sympathy, no pity. "You're handling all of this amazingly well. Really. I always said you were one of the strongest people I ever met."

"Yep. So strong my fiancé dumped me and my parents kicked me out. Oh, and the entire world hates my face." The third glass of wine was making Mara's lips feel buzzy. Did it even really matter what she said now?

"I'm so sorry about Will," Robyn said. "I really am. I didn't see him reacting this way at all."

"Yeah." Mara took a too-big gulp from her glass and sneezed. "Sorry."

"Bless you."

Mara tried to piece together the words she needed. Her brain wasn't cooperating. "It's been almost a week. We found out about the leak Monday, and now it's Friday. It happened so fast." She took another sip. "And now I'm here."

Robyn shook her head. "This week has been insane. Surreal. I never in a million years would have guessed . . ." Robyn's voice trailed off, as if she wasn't sure how to finish the sentence.

"I know," Mara said. "I haven't even gone online since Wednesday. Not since the second leak, you know. The one that proved it was us."

Robyn's eyebrows shot up. "Nothing since Wednesday?" Then she seemed to catch herself. "That's smart. Just take a break from it all. Give yourself some time to process."

Mara's heart was hammering. She forced herself to sit up a little more and look directly at her friend. "So I guess there was another leak, huh?"

Robyn hesitated over the answer. "Yes," she said at last. "I feel like I'm always the bearer of bad news with you. I'm so sorry. When I called you on Monday, I thought you knew. Honestly."

"You didn't do anything wrong!" Mara tried to sound reassuring, even though her own head was spinning. "And I can read you like a book, anyway. Hazards of being best friends, right?"

Robyn gave a hollow laugh. "Still. I'm not saying another word about . . . anything. Ever. Gotta do some damage control here."

"You are fine." Mara's mind was spinning in lazy circles.

What was the third data leak about? What did Robyn know now that Mara didn't?

Not tonight. Mara adjusted a throw pillow behind her to keep herself sitting upright. "I'm glad you came over. Thank you. It's so nice to just relax for a change."

"Exactly." Robyn leaned back too and rolled her neck a few times.

"Speaking of, how was your first week on the job?" Mara asked.

"Oh, you know. Exactly like it was before graduation, just full time," Robyn said. "It feels so weird to have the bachelor's degree now. I can't be a full-fledged counselor until I have my master's, so it's just like . . . hooray, I'm closer!" She made a whoop-de-doo circle with one finger.

"At least you're done with your senior project," Mara added. "Maybe you'll actually get some sleep now."

"More like way too much sleep." Robyn stretched. "Yesterday, I just came home from work and crashed on the couch. What about you? Are you . . ." She paused. "Did you make all of these?" Robyn nodded to the origami cranes.

It wasn't the most graceful change of topic, but Mara was more than happy to skip talking about her own sleepless nights. "They're cranes," Mara said. She carefully set down her wine glass and picked up one of the models that were scattered across Grandmary's coffee table. She'd only used about half the pack of gold paper so far. Mara had made ten cranes earlier this evening while she was waiting for Robyn to get here. That brought her count up to forty-two. "I decided to start a project. I'm going to fold a thousand and one."

"That's a lot."

"It's a tradition." Mara pinched the crane's wings, making them spread. "Folding a thousand and one cranes before your wedding is supposed to bring you good luck. Teaches you patience and perseverance and all that." She put the crane back on the table alongside the others. "Obviously, I don't need good luck for my marriage anymore. But in general."

"Do you have to fold all the cranes by yourself, or can people help you?"

"People can help," Mara said. "If I'm remembering right, I think the bride and groom do it together, and the families help."

"Show me how," Robyn said. "Assuming you're sober enough."

Mara stuck her tongue out at her, but truthfully, it was a little hard to force the delicate paper into neat, precise folds. The model she produced for Robyn was passable, even if its wings didn't exactly line up.

Robyn's first crane had to be refolded so many times the paper bird was soft with creases. Mara stopped to take another sip of wine. When she looked up, Robyn was frowning over another square of paper.

"Okay, it's going to take you forever to fold a thousand of

these things," Robyn announced.

"A thousand and one. And it's not like I have anything else to do."

Robyn rolled her eyes. "But you will. I mean, this isn't the rest of your life. It's only for now."

That sounded like something Will would say.

The sun had completely set now. The only lights in the room came from a pair of Grandmary's table lamps, which cast long, strange shadows on the walls. Mara was struck by the *wrongness* of it all. She shouldn't be here. She should be with Will.

Mara felt her chin wobble, and then the first hot tears escaped, dribbling out the corners of her eyes and leaving stinging trails down her cheeks. Robyn put down her attempted crane and moved closer, holding her shoulders while Mara let go and sobbed.

"You're going to get through this," Robyn murmured every so often. "I promise."

"I can't." Once Mara dared to say the words out loud, it became a chant inside her head. *I can't. I can't. I can't.*

"We are going to get you through this," Robyn said. "Me, your grandmother, and a whole lot of other people. People from school have been IM'ing me all week asking how you're doing. They want to know if you're okay."

Mara blew her nose. It would feel better if she could keep crying somehow. But the tears had disappeared, and she was left feeling shaky and numb. "What people?" she asked.

"Lauren, Jade, Katie . . ." Robyn ticked off the names on her fingers. "That's just off the top of my head. And Jessica too, obviously."

"Has Will?"

"No," Robyn said. "No. I would have told you."

"Oh."

"Have you talked to him at all since Tuesday?"

"Nope."

"Maybe you should," Robyn said. "Eventually. Find a way to end things so at least it's not this big question mark."

"I don't even know what I'd say to him if I had the chance," Mara said.

"Was he that shocked by the leak? I know he's kind of religious. Maybe he feels guilty or something," Robyn said, adding quickly: "Not that he should. Not that *anyone* should."

"I don't think that's it," Mara said. "When it happened, Will kept talking about how it wasn't that big a deal and maybe it was all made up." Mara's stomach twisted a little more with each terrible truth she said out loud. "I was the one who panicked."

"I doubt that," Robyn said. "You always have a reason. You don't go flying off the handle."

"It's because I went to talk to my parents," Mara said. "They canceled the wedding, and Mom wanted me to come over the next day and help."

Robyn's eyebrows shot up. "And you *went*?"

"I thought it was the right thing to do," Mara said.

"They're my parents. I thought if I just smoothed things over . . ."

Robyn didn't say anything, but Mara felt defensive. "Will knew where I was going. He knew I was coming back."

"He did?" Robyn asked. "Like how long were you gone?"

"I was a little later than I expected. I tried to call him," Mara said. "My phone broke."

"It broke?" Robyn stared hard at her. "Mara, this could all be a mistake. You've got to get through to him somehow. Email. Go to the apartment. Send a carrier pigeon. Something."

"I tried. I went to the apartment after I found my suitcase at Mom and Dad's house. He was gone. Like, *gone* gone. He probably went back to North Carolina."

"This is crazy," Robyn said, sinking back into the couch cushions. "This is absolutely crazy. This isn't like him at all." She sat up again suddenly. "Wait. How did your phone break?"

"It was an accident," Mara said. "Mom and I were arguing, and she grabbed for it."

"Oh my God, Mara." Robyn stood up and walked across the room. "She broke your phone."

"It was an accident," Mara said again.

Robyn shook her head. "Girl, sometimes your parents . . . they just . . ." She shook her head again. "It's not right."

"It was my fault," Mara said.

"How?" Robyn demanded. "How was it *your* fault?" She

was angry now. Her eyes were boring into Mara. "And don't say you made her mad."

"I did, though."

"Mara," Robyn said. "Is that why you're really here? Tell me the truth."

"They didn't kick me out. They wanted me to stay," Mara said. "Mom had a whole plan. She was going to turn the wedding dinner into a fundraiser for my dad."

"Gross."

"And when I said I wouldn't go, that I was going to find Will, she told me if I left, I couldn't come back." Mara felt her stomach twist yet again. She should have eaten something. Crackers, maybe. But now she was too tired to get up off the couch.

"And then you left and couldn't find Will, either." Robyn shook her head. "That's awful. You could have come to my place too, if you needed it. I know you have Grandmary, but the offer stands."

"Thanks," Mara said. "I didn't call because I wasn't sure if . . . did you and Jessica move in together? Is she living at your place now, or are you at hers?"

"No. I asked, but she turned me down," Robyn said matter-of-factly. "Jessica's still my girlfriend and everything, but it's been a little awkward. That's all."

"Oh my gosh." Mara reached out for her friend, but Robyn waved her off.

"I'm fine. It's nothing like what you're going through,"

Robyn said.

"You've been letting me go on about my stuff and didn't even mention this? I'm still here for you, Robyn. Did Jessica give you a reason? Just not ready to take the next step or what?"

"Basically," Robyn said. "She didn't want us to move in together until I was out to my family."

"So Jessica gave you an ultimatum."

"No. She didn't tell me I had to come out to them or anything. Just . . . she was okay with it when we were in college and only people from school knew. But now it's like . . . Jessica and I've been together two years, and I haven't even told my parents I'm bi."

"It's complicated, though. Your parents . . ." Mara wasn't sure what to say next.

"They wouldn't hurt me or anything. They'd never do that. It's not dangerous for me like it is for some people." Robyn paused. "But they'll be disappointed. They'll hear 'bisexual' and think, *Well, you* can *fall in love with a man. Why don't you just do that?*" Robyn attempted a smile, but her face was twisted in pain. "Well, you know. Families can be difficult sometimes."

"I hear that," Mara said. She wished she could say something for her friend. Do something. But all Mara could think to say was, "I'm sorry."

"Yeah." Robyn gave a forced smile. "Things are going to get better. For both of us."

It took Mara a few minutes to realize that her friend didn't sound very sure at all.

♦♦♦♦♦

Mara needed coffee. Strong coffee—enough to wash out the terrible aftertaste of last night's wine and stop the headache spreading between her temples. She changed out of the sweaty tank top and shorts she'd slept in for a pair of capris and a T-shirt.

It felt a little too normal, picking out her clothes from the closet here at Grandmary's. Like acceptance. Like Mara had somehow agreed to let this be her life now.

Mara padded quietly down the hall, noticing that there were still soft snores coming from Grandmary's bedroom. Her grandmother was always an early riser, and here it was—Mara checked the hall clock—half past nine.

She must be tired. We've all had a hard week.

Mara made her way to the kitchen and plugged in the coffee maker. The water started to gurgle while Mara measured out two scoops of grounds into the filter.

What Robyn had said last night was bothering her. *It could all be a mistake. He didn't know your phone was broken.*

And why hadn't she called him yet? Maybe not from her parents' house. Not right away. There hadn't been a phone at the apartment, either. Will and Mara had planned to just use their cells rather than pay for a landline.

Mara looked up at the old-fashioned phone on the wall in Grandmary's kitchen. *I could have tried once I got here. Heck, I could dial his number right now.*

In a sudden burst of courage, Mara reached out and pressed the receiver to her ear. The dial tone buzzed, daring her to take the next step. She had his cell number memorized. All she had to do was push the buttons.

The coffee maker ground to a stop. Mara hung up the phone and fixed herself a cup of coffee. *I can't call yet. I'm not ready to hear him say out loud that he's done with me.*

Mara took her coffee into the living room, where she and Robyn had sat and talked for hours the night before. Robyn's crane flopped next to the small flock Mara had assembled. She could always do more origami while she gathered her courage. At this rate, it was going to take all one thousand and one to heal enough just to dial a phone.

Baby steps. Mara settled herself at Grandpap's computer desk, where her own laptop had been charging for days now. Good thing Mara had it with her, even if she hadn't been brave enough to go online lately. Grandpap's old desktop computer probably didn't work anymore. Even if it did, she'd probably have to install all the updates Grandmary would have been putting off before she could do anything.

Last night, Robyn had mentioned a third data leak. It was time to see what that was about. Unbidden, her mother's voice popped into her head. *You have to stay informed. You need to know what people are saying if you're going to control the story.*

Was that why it was so hard to call Will now? Was Mara so controlling that he had to leave her like that, without even giving her a vote in how their relationship ended? She had decided on her own to go and placate her parents. Why should she be mad that Will had decided on his own to call it off completely?

Mara opened her laptop. It felt surprisingly cool, having been untouched for so long. Mara powered it on and silently thanked whatever neighbor hadn't locked their Wi-Fi.

There were 1,840,000 hits. Mara gasped out loud when she saw the search results for her own name. That awful picture was a meme now, filling up the image bar like a series of horrible mirrors. Underneath were pages of articles with headlines such as:

Daughter's Sordid Past Inspired Gaines's Time Wrecker Bill

"The Wedding's OFF!" Time Wrecker Mara Gaines Ditches Fiancé Days before Wedding

Online Security: What All of Us Can Learn from the Time Wrecker Scandal

Third Time Wrecker Leak Confirms Dates, Connections

Mara swallowed hard and sank back into Grandpap's chair. While she was sleeping, the rest of the world had been wide awake.

Whoever was leaking these databases wasn't particularly

good at formatting. Mara had to download and open it as a spreadsheet. It took time—time that Mara spent alternately tapping her foot and re-stirring her coffee.

The file was ready. Mara searched for her own name and pulled up the row, now with two new columns.

Name: Mara Gaines Sterling

Crime: October 18, 2002

Rectification: May 11, 2011

Five whole years from now. It was eerie, looking at the date written out in plain type. *No big deal. You were twenty-seven years old in your first life map. The one you went back and changed.*

Mara swallowed and clicked on the rectification date. There were only two other rows that matched hers.

Name: William B. Sterling

Crime: October 18, 2002

Rectification: May 11, 2011

Name: Jason Alexander Mann

Crime: October 18, 2002

Rectification: May 11, 2011

I met Will in 2004. Mara rubbed her eyes, hard, with the knuckles of both fists. *He started talking to me in the dining hall. He asked about my book. I let him borrow it.*

No. In this first life, their real life, Will and Mara must have met in 2002. Mara counted back. Not even halfway through their first semester of college.

And who was Jason Mann? Surely there had to be some memory of him buried deep in the recesses of her brain. What could have happened that involved all three of them? A car accident?

It occurred to Mara that she didn't know what kinds of crimes usually got rectified, anyway.

Not something awful, hopefully. Not murder or rape or . . . but if it wasn't an awful crime, why would she and Will have gone back to undo it?

Mara rubbed her temples now. Those people with One Life, One Time had a point about timeline rectifications, even with all their fearmongering. It was all too much for one person to process.

She and Will had undone their first meeting. They'd gotten to the altar in their first life map and been married for years, but what they'd built wasn't worth keeping.

Or maybe it was worth keeping, and they'd made a terrible mistake. Maybe this Jason Mann was the one at fault. Maybe Mara and Will believed enough in their love that they'd felt safe taking a risk.

If only Mara knew which one it was—that she and Will

found each other again because they belonged together, or if they'd separated again because they didn't. She had to know. There had to be some kind of clue.

And Mara had the whole internet to help her figure it out.

I'm on the Leaked List: Why Don't You Think I Was the Criminal?

Readers React Submission from Jason Mann

On May 22, 2006, I found my name on the leaked Time Wrecker list.

On May 24, 2006, my birthdate and social security confirmed my identity.

On May 26, 2006, I discovered that the original crime—whatever it was—occurred in 2002, when I was just a college freshman. It was rectified in 2011.

That's it. That's all I know, and unless either the hacktivists or the government want to release more data, that's all we're going to know about my life as a time wrecker. That's not stopping anyone from making assumptions, though, and if you ask me, that's the problem.

Naturally, my family and friends assumed my innocence from day one of the data leak. Even when evidence started pouring in that positively identified me on the leak list, even when the dates proved that I was one of three eighteen-year-olds involved in the crime, my loved ones held fast to the idea that surely I had been the victim of it all. Those who even suggested that I was the guilty party rushed to say that I must have been falsely accused. I hate to say it, but I can see how it would be easier for an innocent man to plead guilty and clear their name with a time wreck rather than going through a trial.

The fact remains that I am most likely not as innocent as my mother would like to believe. (Scratch that—I am *definitely* not as innocent as my mother would like to believe.) I can't argue with the facts, limited as they are. I was involved in a crime and I could have been the criminal.

Who knows? Maybe my forgotten past has nothing to do with the decisions I made after graduation. I like to think that it was always in me to serve my community, even when I could have taken a job at my father's company just as easily. Or maybe my decision to work for a nonprofit is nothing more than subconscious penance for my past misdeeds.

I don't know.

And neither do you.

This is the ultimate expression of social privilege: by any standard, the hacked time wrecker list hasn't really affected me. I didn't lose my job, my girlfriend, or my family. I haven't been harassed or stalked—if anything, people think more of me now, not less. Wouldn't it be better to stay silent and safe in the background? Wouldn't it be better, as my mother says, not to borrow trouble?

Or maybe that's exactly why I should speak out.

The time wrecker scandal has just given us another way to shame and abuse the exact same populations that already suffer discrimination in this country. Look at the headlines. As everyone tries to guess who the guilty parties are and what they're guilty of, the biases are disturbingly clear:

Are you poor? You probably committed fraud or theft in a past life map, you lazy freeloader.

Are you famous? You probably got there by paying people off and erasing your past misdeeds, you two-faced fraud.

Are you a woman? You were probably sexually assaulted. Granted, you might not have been the criminal, but honestly, haven't you kind of led men on in the past? Maybe you should just not be a slut.

Are you a racial minority? You must be guilty of whatever crime we dream up.

And, as if that isn't bad enough, people are even going after those who *aren't* on the time wrecker list:

Currently incarcerated? Ugh, aren't you sorry? You can go back and fix that now, you know. You don't have to be a drain on society's resources, living it up in jail.

Injured or disabled? Well, was it because of a crime? No? Well, maybe there's someone you can charge with criminal neglect or medical malpractice even so you could . . . get that fixed.

Have you been robbed? Yeah, right. You probably just staged it for the insurance money. If it really bothered you, you'd have insisted the criminal have a rectification.

Never mind that those assertions don't reflect the truth of who people are, their circumstances, what they value, or even how timeline rectification works. These statements reflect our prejudices. And apparently, that's all the justification some people need.

As much as I hate what the hacktivists did, they did not single-handedly create this scandal. These prejudices, these attitudes, have existed for years and decades and even generations. Isn't it time we stopped finger-pointing and started supporting each other instead?

I can't fix all the social problems facing us today. No one person could single-handedly fix this mess. But I can take a stand, and I stand in solidarity with every other time wrecker.

I was named on the leaked list. And for all you know—for all I know—I was the criminal.

Comments:

Stu B.
This was a brave (and necessary) piece.

Roy Ballenger
In other words, you were marginally inconvenienced by a nationwide sensation and used it to get your fifteen minutes of fame. Shut up. You know nothing about real suffering.

Sasha Langhorne-Craig
Good for you for checking your privilege and shining a light on our societal assumptions. I can only hope more follow your lead.

Peter
Wow. Apparently snowflakes don't even have to be in the spotlight before they start melting.

Chapter Eleven

WILL

Jason Mann wasn't a bad guy. Will read over the opinion piece three times, looking for something to hate. This would be so much easier if Jason sounded just a little bit like a jerk. But he didn't.

In fact, Jason sounded like the kind of guy Mara would like.

Will put the laptop aside and sat back on his cot, which let out a horrifying creak. They couldn't all three be good people, could they? Someone had to be the bad guy. It certainly couldn't be Mara, Will was sure of that. And a terrible sinking feeling in his stomach told Will that it couldn't be Jason, either.

Whatever Will had done in his past life couldn't have been that bad, he told himself. After all, Mara still fell in love with him. Still married him. Which was more than Will could say about his life now.

Will pounded a fist into his pillow and immediately felt stupid. Little kids did stuff like that. Throwing punches whenever they got mad, even if it was just a pillow this time.

Will froze. *This time.*

Maybe all of this was just proof that timeline rectification worked. Whoever had done wrong in 2002 the first time around hadn't done it again. Will and Mara had even met and almost married again in this life map.

Will tried out the words in his mind, turning over each one to see how it felt.

Time wrecks are a good thing.

I'm proud I'm a time wrecker.

We can all be good people.

I'm grateful I got a second chance.

It felt too good to be true.

◆ ◆ ◆ ◆ ◆

ALL I NEED IS A LITTLE BIT OF COFFEE AND A WHOLE LOT OF JESUS. Will eyed the plaque his mother kept by the coffee maker as he poured himself a cup. Will hated coffee. He had probably been the only music major at Adams Morgan who made it through senior year without late-night caffeine breaks.

But this morning required coffee. Jesus too, assuming He was listening. Will offered up a half-hearted prayer just in case.

The problem with running away was that a person could only run so far. Rent was going to come due on his apartment in DC on the first of the month. Landlords didn't care about things like broken engagements or hacked databases. They cared about rent, paid in full and on time.

He could pay over the phone if he had to, although he grated at the idea of paying rent in DC while he slept on a cot two states away. Will had enough savings to cover the whole summer, plus another month. But even if he did live in the apartment he was paying for, where would he work?

In between clearing out his email inbox and reading up on the great and probably innocent Jason Mann, Will had double-checked his dates for new-teacher orientation. Just the idea of going back into a music room—as the teacher this time, not the student—was enough to lift Will's spirits. This was the longest he'd gone without playing piano in years. Maybe that was all Will needed. Put him on a piano bench, and he'd start to feel like himself again.

But then he came across an email he needed, an email he had almost deleted because the subject looked so innocuous. It was from Principal Crosby, who'd offered him the middle school music teacher position last month.

Re: Interview 05/09/06

Dear William,

I regret to inform you that we have rescinded our verbal offer for the position of

ORCHESTRA/BEGINNING INSTRUMENTAL MUSIC TEACHER

for the 2006–2007 school year. After much consideration, we have chosen to go in another direction.

Regards,

Principal Clifford Crosby

Will couldn't really be surprised, could he? Hiring a time wrecker couldn't be a good look for the school system. Not when there were dozens of applicants with verifiable squeaky-clean records. And Will remembered with a sinking heart, he hadn't signed a contract. Those would have been given out at the end of orientation.

Guess I don't need to remember those dates anymore, either.

Will tried telling himself there were other schools. Other jobs. Will remembered stories from his professors about teachers being hired in the district midsemester, or even midyear. Something would turn up.

Assuming any school would take the risk of hiring a time wrecker.

He had to shake these thoughts out of his head. Principal Crosby hadn't said anything about the timeline rectification. It could be anything. Maybe a teacher they'd had before decided to apply and beat him with seniority. Or they'd cut funding and had to make it a part-time position, shared with another school. It could have been anything. But none of those scenarios was going to give him a paycheck.

Will sipped the coffee and grimaced before setting up

Becca's laptop on the kitchen table. He could search the school district's website for jobs and apply online. Although maybe it would be better to do that at the library instead of taking his chances with Becca's internet connection. Will drummed his fingers on the side of the computer and sighed.

"Whatcha up to?" his mom asked, bustling into the kitchen. She was dressed for her second job at Morrie's, where she worked as a waitress on the weekends. Somehow, Will's mother always managed to wash her polos without the shirt getting puckered around the embroidered restaurant logo. The collar wasn't curling up in the back, either.

"Looking for work," Will said. "That job as a music teacher fell through."

"Oh. I'm sorry to hear that," Bonnie said. Unlike Will, she drank her coffee with gusto. "We can find you something here. I don't know if it'll be anything to do with music, but we can come up with something that pays the bills. I'll ask around." She patted Will's shoulder. "Things are going to work out. You'll see."

It occurred to Will that his mother didn't seem at all surprised. Maybe it was a forgone conclusion to everyone except for him. His life in DC was over now. He was back in North Carolina to stay.

Will looked out the kitchen window. The hills that rose behind them suddenly felt like they were penning him into Deer Hill. So what if he'd gone to college? Fallen in love?

Almost gotten married? Will was right back where he started.

♦♦♦♦♦

Will laced up his sneakers extra tight and stretched before breaking into a jog. In high school, he used to go for a run every morning before class. It was more of an excuse for solitude than anything else. When he hadn't made the cross-country team his junior year, he'd stopped and focused his time after school on piano instead. Music was his passion. His ticket to college. It could have been—maybe still would be someday—his profession.

But running was just a hobby. Will could feel how out of shape he was with every footfall. He was wearing the wrong clothes for this. Cargo shorts that flapped and smacked his knees as he ran, a T-shirt that was already collecting sweat between his shoulder blades. It was too close to noon to be out like this. The sun beat down on Will's neck.

Will ran anyway.

It was only about three miles from their house into town. Most of it was a gravel road that twisted twice and pitched up to a steep hill toward the end. Will stayed to the right on this road, running in the indentation where car tires had worn the loose, slippery gravel into a powdery, packed-down surface.

Mara had been horrified the first time Will brought her

home. "There's no way this is a legal road," she'd said, clutching onto the safety bar with both hands. "What if a car is coming the other way? Look at this turn. You'd never know someone was coming until they hit you."

"That's why you honk when you're at the bottom of the hill," Will had explained. "Let people know you're coming."

Mara had closed her eyes briefly, apparently not reassured.

"Then what? There isn't even enough room for two cars to pass each other. This is a path. It's a path that's a car-and-a-half wide."

"So one car pulls over," Will said. "It doesn't happen much. Not a lot of people drive down this way."

Remembering any conversation with Mara hurt, but today it made each bounce on the gravel road extra painful. Will crested the top of the hill and limped over to the side to take a break.

Down below, he could see where the road eventually bisected Main Street. That road was paved at least, but only about a mile long, and the businesses weren't much to speak of. There was Lowry's. Then there was a library. A bank. The barbershop, with its old-timey red and white striped pole out front, was housed in somebody's basement.

"Your hometown is a Hallmark card," Mara had declared. And Deer Hill did look picturesque when Will had looked at it through her eyes. It was the kind of town where everyone had time to stop and get to know you a little better. The opposite of what it was like to grow up in DC, Will supposed.

If he squinted, Will could see the very beginning of South Street where it intersected with Main. Two miles down South Street was the old elementary school where Will had gone. Now the building housed the only church in Deer Hill.

Originally, the Deer Hill Community Bible Church had been intended as a closer option for the Methodists, who had to drive to the next city otherwise. It had come to include some of the Baptists after they lost their sanctuary in a storm. They'd rebuilt an almost identical white clapboard building just outside of town, but it had taken time, and by then, half the Baptist congregation had decided to stay.

Will could remember when he loved going into his elementary school on Sundays too. It was an excuse to play hangman and tic-tac-toe on the big white board in dry erase marker and play tetherball outside after Sunday school. It wasn't until middle school that Will started to be bothered by the questions his church couldn't answer. Every year, it was harder for Will to fold himself up in the tiny school desks and even harder to participate in the lessons.

By the time Will was a teenager, his friends had started choosing a Sunday to walk up during service and confess their faith. Peace washed over their faces, and Will would imagine what it was like to be so sure. Will believed there was a God, or at least there had been, once. Sometimes he even felt like He was still present, especially during some of the songs they played in worship. But he couldn't say that God was his best friend, his rock, his redeemer. The most Will could say was that he liked the idea of a loving and present God. Emphasis on *present.*

If ever there was a time for God to show up for him, this was it. Will hunched over his knees on the grassy hill, even though it was a little easier to breathe now. He closed his eyes just in case that would help God know he was serious.

If you're up there, give me a sign. Will's prayers were a little rusty. Maybe that was why no answer came. He tried again. *I don't know why I had a time wreck. I don't know if it was my fault. But if I was wrong, just tell me and I'll say I'm sorry.*

Still nothing. Will tried not to drag his feet as he turned his back on the little town and trudged down the hill toward home.

✦✦✦✦✦

Will's phone rang when he was only halfway down the road. *It could be Mara. All I had to do was pray and God reconnected us.* Will fished his phone from the pocket of his cargo shorts and was deflated when he saw the caller ID.

It was just Tristan. Will tried to hide the disappointment in his voice when he answered the call.

For his part, Tristan sounded surprised that Will picked up.

"No, I just . . . you haven't been answering your phone

much lately. I was going to leave you a voice mail. But no. I'm glad you answered."

"Oh." Will didn't know how to react to that. "Well. Hi."

"Hey. So, I wasn't sure if you were still in North Carolina or what your plans were, exactly. But if you're going to be around next weekend, I can still meet up with you for pool or go out to a bar or whatever. Whatever you want. Figured I'd offer."

Next weekend. When he and Mara should have been getting married.

Where was Will going to be on the day of the wedding-that-wasn't?

Will closed his eyes and gritted his teeth. *Great.* Right after he asked God for some answers, He'd turned around and sent more questions.

"I don't know," Will said. "It's a mess. It's a huge mess. I need . . . I want to come back to DC, but I need a job."

"I thought you had something lined up already with the school system."

"Fell through. Just trying to cover all my bases, if I can't find another teaching job. Do you know of anything?" Will ran a sweaty hand through his hair. "What about the restaurant where you work? Think they might hire me to fill your spot when you leave?"

"I'll recommend you to Dave, but you know that's just a part-time thing. I don't know if waiting tables is going to cover your whole rent. Remember? If it was a bad month for tips, I could barely cover my half sometimes."

"But if I pick up extra shifts, it could be enough. It's not like I'd have to work around my school schedule." Will chewed on his lip. It would be tight. How many months before he was living paycheck to paycheck? How many more until he was back in Deer Hill permanently, living off his mom until someone agreed to hire him?

No. Will wasn't going to let that happen.

"You can try," Tristan said doubtfully. "Like I said, I'll recommend you to my boss. Dave's cool. He'll probably give you a chance."

"Thanks, man." Will cleared his throat. "And next weekend—yeah, let's do something."

"Good," Tristan said. "It'll be good to see you again."

"If I'm back in town by then, I mean."

"Right," Tristan said. "If."

♦ ♦ ♦ ♦ ♦

Will wasn't surprised that his mother insisted they all go to church the next morning, but he had hoped he'd be able to sneak in the back after the service had already started. Bonnie Sterling had other plans. And so Will found himself lifting and unfolding 110 folding chairs with his brother and sister as the rest of the congregation trickled into the old elementary school multipurpose room. Will concentrated on spacing the chairs evenly along the same line of the scuffed linoleum floor.

Will had expected that his first official outing into Deer Hill would be like seeing Miss Bitty for the first time—only a million times worse, since the entire church would be watching and judging. But it really wasn't that bad. There were a few curious glances, a couple straight-up stares, but most of the congregation went out of their way to smile when they passed by.

Even Chris seemed to be in a better mood than usual. "We've been sitting up by the band," he said, once the last chair was in place. "You don't mind, do you?"

Will did mind. He hadn't even liked sitting up front before he was outed as a time wrecker. But Chris was acting so nice—*normal*, even—that Will followed him anyway.

Despite himself, Will relaxed when the band started to play. Contemporary worship music wasn't normally his thing. But his mother was already raising her arms and swaying a little. Chris and Becca were singing along too. For the first time since Will had arrived, everyone in his family was smiling.

When was the last time Will had felt anything like joy? Immediately, he thought of Mara, and then Will felt himself go again. He was a miserable island in a sea of happy, God-loving Christians.

"Let it out, honey," Bonnie whispered, leaning over and pressing a plastic packet of tissues into his hand. "You don't have to handle all of this alone."

Will smiled back at his mother, but as soon as she looked away, he folded the tissue packet in half and crammed it in his pocket. *I am not going to cry in church. I am not.*

Other people cried in church all the time. More often than not, people let their voices quiver when they asked for prayers—for surgery, for rain, for forgiveness.

Forgiveness.

Someday, I'm going to have to forgive Jason Mann. Just thinking of his name made Will's throat tighten. It made it harder to breathe. It made it easier to think.

I hate Jason. Was it terrible that thinking these words gave Will peace, even while everyone else around him was singing and praising God? Will clenched his fists inside his pockets and recited it to himself anyway. *This must be Jason's fault. It has to be. I hate Jason. He did this to us.*

Ever since the third data leak on Friday, all the talking heads on TV had been speculating on the hacktivists' next move. Would they reveal who was the criminal and who were the victims? Would—as Deirdre Collins put it—*we finally get answers?*

Please. Seeing Jason Mann's name alongside his and Mara's—*that* was an answer on its own.

Wasn't it?

The song ended, and the congregation sat with a collective chair-squeak.

The pastor opened with prayer, theatrically tapping the wireless microphone before he began wandering up and down the makeshift aisle. This was a new guy. The pastor Will had grown up with had moved on to greener pastures, and the pastor who took over for him had just retired. This one, Pastor Evans, had started last February, and the regulars still seemed entranced by him. When he said, "God's peace be with you," they chorused "and also with you!" with enthusiasm.

What would it feel like to have peace right now? No one else in the congregation was a time wrecker. Just Will. Everyone else had been happy to stick it out with the life they had. They'd faced their struggles instead of turning back. So why hadn't he? Was it really that bad, what he and Mara were up against in their old timeline? Or could they have made it through if only they had more faith, or more strength, or more patience?

Wondering what had happened was enough to drive a person crazy. Mara was probably racking her brain, trying to figure it all out. Will guessed she wasn't feeling any peace yet, either.

In the same small, selfish part of his heart that clung on to hating Jason, Will hoped Mara hadn't. At least not yet.

Mara had never talked much about religion. She claimed she was agnostic, but Will had never seen her looking for proof of any God.

"I feel like there are miracles," she'd said once. "We talk about some things in physics that just make it seem like there has to be intelligent design behind it, somewhere.

There has to be something that set it all in motion. A god, maybe, or at least something like one."

"Do you think there's a plan?" Will had asked. He was pushing her, just that once, expecting that she would say no, of course not, there were too many variables or something. But she'd surprised him.

"I think there could be," Mara had said, balancing her pretty chin on both hands. "A lot of scientific discoveries are just realizations, really, that things that seemed random actually behave in a pattern. It's beautiful, thinking that everything in the universe is working toward something. I don't know if it's true. I just like the thought, I guess."

Now Will felt a strong hand on his shoulder. It was the pastor. Was this like grade school when the teacher would walk around the classroom and tap your desk if you weren't paying attention? No, Pastor Evans had already moved on down the aisle, brushing shoulders, making eye contact, asking questions during his sermon, and really pausing for the answers. It was different from how their old pastor used to do things, but no one seemed to mind.

Maybe Will had misjudged Deer Hill. Or maybe Will wasn't the only one who had changed in the four years he'd been away. There used to be a time when people muttered to each other about whether the sermon threatened too much hellfire or not enough. "People don't like change," Bonnie Sterling had always said. But it seemed they could get used to it. Learn to like it even.

Everyone seemed to be leaning forward in their seats now, hanging on to Pastor Evans's every word. He had found his way back to the front of the room and stood there, fingers laced, seeming to contemplate his next words.

"This week has been a hard one in our country," Pastor Evans said. Will's heart started to race. "When we are confronted with someone else's sin, it is so easy for us to think, 'Whew. I'm not perfect, but at least I would never do *that.*'" The congregation laughed a little, and Pastor Evans continued. "Or we might say to ourselves, 'Gosh, I thought I had something to feel bad about in my own life, but look at these guys over here! They're making me look pretty good!'" More laughter. "And it's not a stretch for that to turn into, 'Boy, we gotta take care of those bad people over there doing those bad things. They're the reason we have all these problems in the world today.'" No one was laughing now. "And you know why we do that? Because when we're looking at all the sin that's out *there*"—Pastor Evans made a sweeping motion across the room—"then we distract ourselves from paying attention to the sin that's in *here.*" He pointed to his own heart and dropped his hands.

"This week as I've been watching the news unfold about the timeline rectification scandal, I've been seeing how quickly the mere *suggestion* of past sins is encouraging others to sin openly. I turn on the news and I see gossip. I see pride. I see so much anger and outright hatred. And it makes me ask myself, not only 'How should I act toward those I know have sinned?' but also, 'How would I act if my sin was revealed this way?'"

Will felt as though he couldn't breathe. He couldn't even look up to see if Pastor Evans was staring right at him or if he was right that Chris and Becca were cutting glances his way.

"I feel it is my duty to share with you something I saw on the news just yesterday, something that I'm sure many of you have already seen and heard as well. Early yesterday morning, in Chicago, Illinois, a man named Ramon Bassave was shot and killed just outside his car. Mr. Bassave was only in his early forties. He was a husband and a father of young children—someone very much like you, and you, and you." Pastor Evans was on the move again, gently touching the shoulders of a few men Will thought he recognized. It was hard to tell for sure. His glasses were fogging up. "Mr. Bassave's death is being investigated as a homicide. The police didn't report any leads, but the implication is that he was targeted because his name was on the time wrecker list."

Will could hear his mom pull in a shuddering breath. She didn't let it out. Will reached across Chris, pressing some of the tissues Bonnie had given him earlier back in her hand. Bonnie mouthed a quiet "thank you." But she didn't let go of Will's hand.

"We are warned not to be so invested in judging the sins of our brothers and sisters that we are blind to our own. But see also how hard it is. Just one week ago, how many of us even wondered whether the government had a list of people who had time wrecks? And now, today, a man is dead." Pastor Evans took off his eyeglasses and shook his head. "My challenge to you, brothers and sisters, is that we recommit ourselves to seeing and repenting of our own sins instead of casting stones at each other. If anyone needs to seek repentance now, come forward. God's forgiveness is here for you. He is just waiting for you to repent and receive His greatest gift."

Will's hand was starting to sweat where Bonnie Sterling was still clenching it tightly. This must be it—grace, absolution, whatever he wanted to call it—offered to him on a silver platter. He didn't have to go back to DC. He didn't have to start from scratch, alone. Will could slide right back into life in Deer Hill as if he'd never left. He had a family here, neighbors, a ready-made community that would take him back with open arms.

But first, he would have to repent.

Time Wrecker Murdered:
Grieving Family Blames Cyberbullying

May 27, 2006

CHICAGO, Ill — Police were summoned to the Southeast Plaza parking garage in the early hours of Saturday morning after an anonymous 911 caller reported hearing shots fired. The responding officers immediately located a critically wounded 43-year-old man on the third-level parking deck. Despite lifesaving efforts from first responders, the man passed away en route to the hospital. The victim has been identified as Ramon Leonard Bassave. The case is being investigated as a homicide.

"It's much too early to make any statements about possible suspects or motives," said Chief Deputy Isaacs. "We are conducting a thorough investigation and ask the public to give us time to do our jobs."

Maria-Louise Gravatz, who identified herself as an aunt of Bassave's widow, made a statement to the media from the family's home in Bridgeport.

"Just look at everything that's happened since that time wrecker list was leaked to the press," said Ms. Gravatz, surrounded by three other unnamed members of the family. "Every hour since it first broke, Ramon has been harassed at work, at home . . . and it got worse with every new bit of information that got out. The internet's been the worst. Every single member of our family is getting terrible emails—the kids told us it's called 'cyberbullying.' The whole mess has torn apart our community and our family, and now it's taken his life. We all know it's one of these anti-time wreck people that's done this to him. What I want to know is when these hackers are going to be held accountable for what they've done."

Funeral arrangements will be private. In lieu of flowers, the family has requested donations to the Bassave children's college funds. Donations can be made at any Royal United Bank.

Chapter Twelve

....

MARA

Mara had already memorized the image of Ramon Bassave with his family. There were other pictures in the newspaper articles about his death—vague pictures of the parking garage where he was killed, a picture of his wife's aunt wiping away tears—but the family picture spoke to Mara's soul. Ramon and his smiling wife were sitting on a porch stoop, holding their two young sons. The youngest looked like he was trying to take off his shoe. It was a casual snapshot. Relaxed.

Ramon Bassave was never going to get a second chance at anything, now. It made Mara sick to think about it. He'd been murdered in cold blood. His kids were going to grow up without their father. And no one even seemed to care. By Monday morning, the headlines barely mentioned his family or his life at all. Now it was just things like:

What Crimes Should Be Rectified? A Social Worker Weighs In

Neil Poindexter Suggests Time Wrecking Has Been "A Major

Draw" for Illegal Aliens

PSA: Ramon Bassave Was NOT an Illegal Immigrant. He Was Born in Puerto Rico.

Why was she crying so hard for a man she didn't know and a family she never met? For a moment, Mara wondered if they had known each other in their other lives, their pre-time wreck lives. But it didn't always have to come back to that, did it? It should bother her. It should bother everyone. Bad enough that Ramon Bassave had been killed—why did the news have to erase who he had been?

Mara had to dig for the things that really mattered. Ramon Bassave had been married for ten years. His sons were five and three. He'd been a hotel night manager for five years, where the other employees remembered him as quiet and kind.

I'm going to remember you too, Mara said silently. To herself, to the air, to the universe, to God, maybe. *I'm going to remember who you were. Not just what someone did to you.*

Mara scrolled down to the end of the obituary and clicked on the link for the Bassave kids' college fund. She wouldn't put her name on the donation or anything—who knew how his widow would even feel about her. The original face of time wrecking. But it would be nice to help those kids somehow.

Something was wrong. Mara couldn't access her bank account. Not with her password. Not with her PIN. Not with—

"No," Mara breathed. "No."

How could she have been so stupid? Mara's social security number had been all over the internet since Wednesday. Not to mention her birthday. Anyone could have stolen her identity. And instead of protecting herself, Mara had gone to sleep.

Will wouldn't have forgotten. Will was more careful with money than anyone Mara had ever known. "When you don't have a lot, it's easy to keep track," Will had said once, like it was a joke. Mara had felt the sting of shame anyway.

That's why this was happening now, wasn't it? Mara could afford to go days without checking her bank account. She could run off to her grandmother's and not worry about buying food or paying rent. She'd been irresponsible, and now she wasn't the only one who would pay the price.

It was time to take responsibility. It wasn't just Mara's money in the account. Through college, her parents had paid her *not* to get a job. "School is your work right now," her father had told her. The only money Mara had earned on her own was from her internships and odd jobs she'd picked up here and there. Babysitting a professor's kids over break. Stuff like that.

Mara peeked out the front window to be sure her grandmother was still out gardening. Good. She wouldn't want to hear the call Mara was about to make.

No one answered the Gaines's home phone. Her father's

cell phone number flipped immediately to voice mail. But when Mara called his office—of course he'd be at work on a Monday morning—his secretary patched her straight through.

"Mara," her father said briskly. The sound of his voice sloughed off the thin veneer of Mara's calm.

"Dad," Mara said. "I messed up. I'm so sorry."

"Indeed," her father said.

"I think someone got into my bank account. I can't get in, anyway. I know I should have locked down my accounts when this . . . data leak happened. I knew I was at risk for identity theft and I didn't take precautions. I'm sorry," Mara finished. "When I find work again, I'll repay you what you've lost."

The silence at the other end of the phone was profound. "Is that all?"

Mara wiped her sweaty palms on her shorts. "Yes."

"I see," her father said, so low it was almost a growl. "As it happens, Mara, your mother and I have already taken care of it. You should be thankful that you had a joint account and your mother was able to access it without your cooperation."

"Oh," Mara said. "Yes. That was . . . that was kind of her."

"At the time, she likely would have changed the passwords and PIN to the account as well, for additional security. You'll need to get that information from her directly. I took the liberty of signing up for an identity protection plan and credit monitoring for you when you were in high school. Unfortunately, it seems that was prudent of me."

"Thank you." Mara leaned against the kitchen wall for support. Her knees had turned into water.

"Which brings me to another point," her father continued. "Your mother and I had intended to help you pay for medical school, but given the way you left things with us, I'm afraid I'm not sure of your intentions. Are you still planning to go to school? And if so, perhaps you'd like to think about how you should be acting toward those who are funding this venture."

"I never asked you to pay for med school," Mara said, straightening. "Not once."

"Nor did you decline our offer," her father said. "There are no gifts in this life, Mara. Only transactions. Your current situation is ample proof of that."

And my marriage, Dad? When you offered to pay for our wedding, was it just a transaction *to you?* Somehow, Mara couldn't say the words out loud.

"I'll give you some time to think over what I've said." He hung up.

♦♦♦♦♦

My parents were right.

Mara sat cross-legged on the bed in the little ivy-covered room. Who had she thought she was, walking out on her parents like that? Everything they'd said about her was true. She was irresponsible. Spoiled. Inconsiderate. She was lucky that they put up with a daughter like her.

It was going to have to end sometime. She couldn't keep hiding out at Grandmary's house. Mara certainly wasn't the one who'd paid the highest price for the time wrecker leak now. What would Ramon Bassave do if he had the chances she did? Wouldn't he love to have the problems Mara faced now if it meant he got a second chance at living?

A soft knock on her bedroom door jolted Mara to her feet. *Grandmary must have heard me talking to Dad.* A sick feeling gnawed at the pit of Mara's stomach. *I'm going to have to find a way to make things right with him. If not for my sake or his, then for Grandmary's.*

There was another knock on the door. "Mara? May I come in?"

Mara stumbled and knocked against the dresser on her way to open the door, scattering dozens of her paper cranes as she did. She accidentally stepped on one of them, crushing its wings beyond repair.

I ruin everything I touch.

Grandmary didn't look angry, at least. Not even about the state of the guest room. Grandmary knelt and picked up a handful of paper cranes and put them back on the dresser. "How many of these have you made so far?" she asked.

"A few hundred, I think," Mara said. She tried to keep her voice light and casual, even as her heart hammered away inside her chest. "Last I counted, it was two hundred, but that was yesterday."

"Impressive!"

Or pathetic. "I can't believe you kept all this origami paper."

As soon as she said it, Mara worried that she sounded accusatory rather than grateful. Thankfully, Grandmary seemed to know what she meant.

"This was always your room," Grandmary said. "Whether you were visiting or not." She motioned to the bed, and they sat side by side on the edge of the mattress. "I haven't had much of a chance to talk with your parents since this all came about," Grandmary said. "But if there was ever a question, I hope you know you are welcome to live here with me."

Mara forced herself to meet her eyes. There was no reproach there, which almost made Mara feel worse. "Thank you," she said. "I'm so sorry, Grandmary."

"What on earth for?" She really seemed to be asking. Mara tried to imagine how she could answer.

"For getting you in the middle of all this," Mara said, finally. "I know it's awkward. My crashing here instead of . . . at home."

Grandmary shook her head. "You have always had a home here too, Mara. I'm not in the middle of anything."

"But Dad—"

Grandmary raised both eyebrows. "I've made it my habit never to speak badly of one person to another," she said.

"Particularly when they are both dear to me."

Mara looked down, cheeks burning with shame.

Grandmary's wrinkled hand touched her chin and lifted it until Mara was looking straight into Grandmary's face again. "And because you are dear to me, Mara, I know that you have needed me to be a safe place for you. I hope I always have been. And I hope you know that I always will be."

Mara felt her face crumple and was relieved when Grandmary pulled her in.

"How can you love me right now?" Mara cried. "I've ruined my life. Will's life. I've hurt so many people."

"A life is a very hard thing to ruin," Grandmary said, running a hand through Mara's hair. "Everyone has a past, Mara. Whether we remember it or not. We all have a past."

Mara sat back and wiped her face. For a moment, it felt like her grandmother was going to say something else, but she didn't. Grandmary picked up a square of gold origami paper instead. "May I help?" she asked. "I'm afraid you'll have to teach me the steps a few times, but I've always wanted to give this a try."

Mara pulled the nightstand over to give her grandmother an easier place to work. Mara herself sat on the floor, demonstrating each fold slowly.

"Pass me a stack of that paper, would you, please?" Grandmary asked, after she had produced two slightly cockeyed birds and stood them up smartly beside the rest of Mara's flock.

"Sure," Mara said, peeling off a dozen papers or so. She couldn't help noticing that her grandmother's knuckles were swollen from arthritis. "Do you really want to keep going?"

"Oh, yes," Grandmary said. "This is fun, isn't it? Gives you something to do while you think things over."

"I guess," Mara said.

Grandmary ruefully smiled and began folding a third crane. "You know, Mara, when I got pregnant with your father, Grandpap and I hadn't been seeing each other for very long."

Mara took a minute to catch what her grandmother was saying. "You weren't married yet?"

Grandmary shook her head. "That's one thing that's different between my generation and yours. When I was your age, girls got pregnant before they were married just about as often as they do now, but these days no one seems to raise an eyebrow. It wasn't like that back then. I remember all the panic. 'What will I do? How soon can we get married? What if someone figures out what happened?'" It looked like Grandmary was blushing a little, but her voice stayed steady. "I remember how my mother used to talk about the newly married girls who had babies six months after the wedding. 'Awfully lucky to have an eight-pound baby who's three months early,' she'd say."

Mara stared down at the origami model in her hand, suddenly confused about which step to do next. *They always seemed so perfect.*

"When I told Bernie—your Grandpap, I mean—he was terribly upset. Not angry with me, but at himself. He knew what people would say as well as I did, and he wasn't happy about it. Your grandfather was a proud man. So he says to me, 'Let's say we eloped. We'll have a private ceremony in another town, and we'll tell everyone we got married even earlier than that. That way, they can guess the baby is only a month early, or six weeks early.' And the babies in his family tended to be small, so maybe people would believe us." Grandmary said the next part quietly. "I said no."

"What?" Mara put her half-done crane to the side. "But you just said you'd been panicking too."

Grandmary kept folding hers. "I was, but when I heard it come from him, I couldn't stand it. This wasn't the love I wanted. It wasn't the marriage I wanted. I needed him to love me so much he would shout it from the rooftops. I wanted him to smile and brag that I was his wife, not mumble it and mess with the dates and act embarrassed about it. I wasn't someone to be ashamed of. Well"—she corrected herself— "of course, I *was* pregnant, and I knew people would be ashamed of me for that. But I thought I could survive the whispers and being talked about by other people. It would be hard, but I could survive it. But loving someone who only married me for obligation . . ." She shook her head. "I couldn't have stood that."

Mara tried to imagine her poised, perfect grandmother as a young woman. The same age that Mara was now. "So what happened?"

"Well, as I said, your Grandpap was a proud man. He knew that when I started to show, people would realize it was his baby and blame him for not doing the right thing. So he came back the next day with an engagement ring, begged me to marry him before he left for the oil rig. I was so tempted," Grandmary said. "I wanted to take that ring and figure out the love later. But I still said no. I told him to save the ring and not ask me again until he knew he couldn't live without me."

"Wow," Mara said. She scooted even closer to her grandmother. "That was brave."

Grandmary chuckled a little. "Brave or stupid. Some of both, I think. At any rate, he left for the oil rig, and I stayed home, making plans for what I'd do if he never came back. I had a second cousin in Ohio I was going to go and stay with. Linda, her name was. Of course, I didn't tell her the whole situation over the telephone, but I didn't have to. She knew well enough what I meant. Linda promised me a place to stay and a reference for a secretary job after the baby was born. She was very sweet. She said I wouldn't have to give up the baby if I didn't want to. Her mother lived at the house with her, and she could have watched the baby while Linda and I worked. It wasn't ideal, but it was honest. I had a plan."

"And your parents?" Now Mara felt almost breathless, imagining her grandmother's life over fifty years ago.

"I got terrible morning sickness, just terrible. My mother

figured it out while Bernie was away on the oil rig and told my father. They were so disappointed in me." Even now, Grandmary's eyes shone bright with held-back tears. "My father was in a rage, saying he would find Bernie and make him marry me. He called him all kinds of names for not making things right before he left. And then I had to tell my parents that Bernie had asked and I'd turned him down." Grandmary held her finished crane between her fingers instead of placing it beside the others. "I took the train to Ohio to stay with my second cousin a little early, sick as a dog the whole trip. Linda picked me up from the train station and said, 'Now, Mary, everything is going to be all right. No matter how things look right now. It's going to be all right.' I'll never forget her kindness."

"But Grandpap did marry you."

"Yes, eventually. When he came back from the oil rig, he came to see me at my parents' house and my father gave him a piece of his mind. Then Bernie took the train to Ohio to my cousin's home. He had that ring and he asked me, please, let him do the right thing. And as much as I loved that man, I knew he still didn't love me. This time, it was harder because I was taking advantage of my cousin's hospitality. I worried that she'd tell me to marry him if he asked. Make him support his own child, so to speak. But she said, 'Mary, you're too smart to marry a fool, and if he only wants to marry you out of duty, he's a fool.' So I said no again, and he took the train back to Virginia." Grandmary finally put the crane down and clasped and unclasped her hands.

This is hard for her, Mara realized. *It's only me, and she's still embarrassed to tell her story.*

Grandmary wasn't even meeting Mara's eyes now. "I suppose that could have been the end of it and for many people, it would have. I'd turned him down twice. I'd sent myself away from our town. He could have let me go and started fresh with another girl if he wanted. It would have been awful, but people did that."

"But Grandpap didn't."

"No. He started writing to me." Finally, Grandmary smiled—her first real smile since she'd started telling her story. "The first letter was so strained I'll never forget it. Three lines. 'Dear Mary, I love you. I think about you every day. Please let me come see you again. Bernie.'" She laughed. "I wrote him back and said, 'I love the way you put your arm across my shoulders when we go out driving. What do you love about me?' It went on and on . . . one letter a day for weeks and then months. I was getting closer and closer to the time the baby would come, and here I was starting to wait for his letters like a giggly little schoolgirl. I still loved him, and his letters got longer and longer with all the ways he loved me too. Finally, I wrote Bernie and asked him to come visit me again. We went to the courthouse the day he arrived and got married, just one month to the day before our son was born."

"Wow," Mara said. "Wow." Grandmary's cheeks were still

flushed. Mara looked the other way for a moment, giving her grandmother a moment to collect herself after what she'd just shared. "Does Dad know all this?"

"Oh, we told him ages ago," Grandmary said. "When he was eleven or twelve, I believe. It's hard to tell if it ever really affected him. So far as your father has ever known, his parents were happily married. It's amazing, really. If I could have predicted my own future when I was pregnant, I thought the shame would overshadow me for my whole life. By the time your father was born and we were settled here in Arlington, the pain of it all had already moved out of the foreground."

"And that's why you were so quick to offer me a place to stay," Mara said slowly. "You're paying it forward. You're being like Cousin Linda."

"I'm sure I'd have done it regardless," Grandmary said, smiling down at her granddaughter. "But yes. Everyone needs a Cousin Linda in their lives, at least once."

"Thank you for telling me." Mara reached up and wrapped her hand around her grandmother's. "It means a lot."

"There's one more thing, Mara." Grandmary put a hand in the pocket of her knit pants and pulled out something small. "This ring was never meant to be a prize for two perfect people. Grandpap and I certainly made some terrible decisions, but we made some good ones too." Grandmary opened the drawer of the nightstand and deposited the ring with a little *clink*. "I'm sure this ring means something different to you now, after what happened between you and Will. But it does belong to you. I hope that, in time, you'll be able to see it for what it means to me. You are worth loving, Mara. Exactly the way you are."

Investigative Report:
Explaining Timeline Rectification with
Dr. Aaron Hendrix

By Coretta James

As I take the elevator to meet Dr. Aaron Hendrix, my thoughts are not on time wrecking, or on the data leak, or on this strange, windowless building that houses the Department of Timeline Rectification. My thoughts are, quite literally, on fire.

More specifically, I am recalling the flames that leaped and danced through my grandfather's house one long-ago summer night. I was six years old, wrapped in a thin blanket and held tightly by a police officer. He tried to keep me from looking back at the building where I had, up to that point, spent my entire life.

It had not been a good life. My grandfather was mostly incapacitated, an extremely ill man who was prone to fits of rage and sobbing. My mother was gone, and my father had moved us in under the guise of caring for my grandfather in his old age. In reality, my father was a drug dealer. The fire that erupted in our house that night was arson—the result of a drug deal gone bad.

In 1973, that picture of me, a small child watching my house go up in flames, appeared on the front page of every national newspaper. It was intended to stimulate a national conversation on child welfare, the war on drugs, and criminal justice. It didn't. My father and grandfather died in that fire, as did one of the arsonists. The other three pled out and are still serving time in prison. I bounced from one foster home to the next for twelve years. Thanks, in part, to an anonymous donor "inspired" by my story and numerous scholarships, I went to college, where I double majored in journalism and criminal justice. In my late twenties, I wrote a piece on how my childhood trauma had inspired my career in journalism. That piece won a Pulitzer Prize for Feature Writing.

Who would I have been without that fire? How many years would I have hidden in my bedroom while my father sold drugs out the back door and my grandfather slurred and raged in the front room? If there hadn't been a fire that night, would anyone have rescued me?

I arrive at Dr. Hendrix's office, where I am ushered in by two security guards and the door is immediately closed behind me. I set up my tape recorder, take out my notebook. There are questions I need to ask. Questions I am afraid to have answered.

Was this fire truly the catalyst that forged me into the woman I am today? Or was it all, as Dr. Hendrix would suggest, a tragic and preventable event?

Words such as *tragic* and *preventable* grate on me. I am a survivor, I remind myself. I am an orphan, a foster child, a scholarship student, a breast cancer patient now five years in remission, and a journalist who has covered the front lines of nearly every issue on justice and healthcare in the last decade. Everything in my life has been hard-fought and hard-won.

In my mind, my life began with that fire.

"That crime would not have qualified for a timeline rectification," Dr. Hendrix concurs, as I spell out the particulars of the arson. "We do not allow rectifications that resulted in a death or that involved a minor in any way."

"Are those the only stipulations?" I ask.

Dr. Hendrix chuckles. "Certainly, the criminal must be repentant.

Before we even consider a rectification, convicts must go through a rigorous six-month rehabilitation program. If they can get through that, then we'll start talking to the other people involved."

"And all the victims and witnesses must agree to a rectification," I say.

Dr. Hendrix smiles. "Generally, we don't have a problem ensuring their participation."

"Why would you say that is?"

Dr. Hendrix smiles again and withdraws a pencil and a pad of graph paper from his desk drawer. "Imagine, if you will, that each of us could map the course of our life—so far—on this piece of graph paper. You begin with your birth and continue to have a series of ups and downs as you move across the page." Dr. Hendrix draws a wavy line from the left to the right of the page. "Now, for some of us, there may be a moment—maybe even several moments—that are such an extreme low that it would affect the rest of our lives." He flips to the next page of graph paper and draws another line, suddenly deviating sharply to the bottom of the page. "Suppose this person has robbed a bank, or broke into a house, or committed some other crime. One thing that has been desperately missing within our justice system is the opportunity for them to truly bounce back. Certainly, there are those who do forge a new path, who do emerge from the prison system and become an inspirational speaker, or a religious leader, or even simply a citizen with a new appreciation for their life's work. However, in many cases, the trajectory of their life never recovers." Dr. Hendrix continues the line, hovering near the bottom of the page.

"There are some who would argue this is fair," I suggest. "A reason why we don't commit crimes—because it would have negative consequences for the rest of our lives."

"Some would argue that," Dr. Hendrix agrees. "But realize, this is not the only page in the book." He flips to the next page, and the next, showing that the dark mark he made to show one person's lowest point has left an indent on several other pages. "This person, perhaps, has PTSD from witnessing the crime. Through no fault of his or her own, this person is also now negatively affected by this crime, and their life may not recover to its highest potential. Or this person"—he flips the page again—"perhaps this person was the victim of the crime. Perhaps they were injured or lost their home or business because of this criminal's act. Their lives might not recover, either."

"I would call that life," I say. "None of us is guaranteed a life unaffected by other people's decisions, good or bad. There's something to be said for being able to roll with the punches."

"But some punches should never be delivered," Dr. Hendrix argues. "And that question is really at the core of criminal justice and ethics in our society. Is it better to know who has committed a crime so we can protect the rest of society from them? Or is it better for the crime never to occur at all, whether through prevention or timeline rectification?"

"Perhaps you could explain how a timeline rectification works," I say. "How could it be the equivalent of a crime not occurring in the first place?"

Dr. Hendrix flips back to the original page, with the dark, ugly mark of the crime. "Simply put," he says, "during a timeline rectification, we take the participants to this point in their lives"—he picks up the pencil and places it back on the dot—"and we rewrite it." With a sudden movement, he pushes the pencil straight through the page. What was once the dark mark of the crime is now a tiny, ragged hole. He lifts the pencil up and makes a new line, wavering in the middle of the page at first, and then proceeding to a series of ups and downs. "At this point, the line of this person's life map appears uninterrupted. It is one continuous motion, from life, to death, with many ups and downs in between."

"But this hole," I say, "it's still there. It still happened."

"Did it?" Dr. Hendrix asks, philosophically. "From the perspective of the person on this line, that hole over there doesn't exist. It isn't part of their life map."

"But the other witnesses to the crime," I say. "The victims."

Dr. Hendrix flips the page, showing that what was once an indent is now a small hole in the next person's page, and the next. "It never happened for them, either," he says. "Recall that a timeline rectification doesn't just involve the criminal, but all of his or her victims. When a timeline rectification is approved, they can rewrite their life maps too."

I reach across to the notepad and smooth the small, ragged hole with one finger. "So, this person, who would have had PTSD from witnessing the crime?"

"Never happened," Dr. Hendrix says. "No crime to witness." He redraws the life map on this page, creating a single, uninterrupted line just above the hole.

I flip the page. "And this one?" I ask.

Dr. Hendrix smiles and redraws this line as well.

"Some people are concerned about the regulations surrounding timeline rectifications. Congress just introduced a bill that increased the requirements for participants before approving a rectification. What are your thoughts on that?"

"Oh, that will never pass," Dr. Hendrix says. "HR 6437 is nothing but an attempt to shut us down. Raising the bar until no one can meet the requirements. It's a political stunt."

"And the time wrecker leak? Do you think that's a political stunt too?"

"I'm not at liberty to discuss that."

I rephrase. "The leak listed four-point-five million people," I counter. "With so many rectifications, surely there are concerns about having too great an effect on the course of our world's history."

"Is there a cap on how many lifesaving brain surgeries doctors can perform?" Dr. Hendrix asks. "Is there a limit to how many tumors surgeons can remove, or how many children we can pull back from the edge of the road? What timeline rectification does is just the same. Yes, our society is affected by the fact that we have less crime, fewer criminals incarcerated, fewer crime victims in need of continuing care. We at the Department of Timeline Rectification stand by those positive effects."

I think about Dr. Hendrix's words as I leave the building. What would I do if I were offered the chance to eliminate that one terrible night from my life map? Could removing that experience be as simple, as straightforward, as my decision to remove the malignant lump in my left breast? Can I imagine my life unentwined—unaware, even—of that fiery night?

I look back at the tall, windowless building and wonder if my reservations are due to an appreciation for the path my life has taken, or fear for the life map I could have had.

....

Chapter Thirteen

WILL

Will hovered the cursor over the APPLY NOW button. His résumé had been submitted to the school system's human resources department ages ago, so all he really had to do was fill out a cover letter for each of the open positions. There was an elementary school looking for a part-time music teacher, which wasn't ideal, but it was better than unemployment.

Will eyed the checkmarked box at the end, just above his electronic signature. *"Under penalty of perjury, I certify that all the information I submitted is true and complete to the best of my knowledge."* That was true. As far as he knew, he had no past convictions. So why did he feel like he wasn't telling the truth?

"Um, did you ask to use my computer?" Becca said from behind him. Will jumped. He hadn't even noticed the time, much less that Becca was due home from school. Now she stood fuming in the doorway of Chris's bedroom. With her hands on her hips like that, she reminded Will more of the whiny kid sister he remembered.

"Sorry," Will said. "I didn't know you were home."

"I've been home for half an hour," Becca said. "Geez. Chris and Mom are always on this thing when I'm at school, and now you're doing it too. Seriously, people. Buy your own computer if you want to use one."

"Sorry," Will said again. "I'll log off now."

Becca marched over to his cot and took the laptop from him. "I'll do it for you. What were you looking up, anyway?" Her eyes scanned the website. "Oh. Guess you haven't had any callbacks yet."

"Not yet," Will admitted. "But I just started applying again. There's still plenty of time to find a job for next school year." He said it to convince himself as much as her.

Becca pressed a few keys and shut down the laptop, closing it with a snap. "Good thing this still has battery power. I need it to study."

"You're about to graduate. How hard do you really have to study for finals?"

"Enough to use my own freaking computer. Hey, can you give me a ride to the library?"

"Sure." It was the least he could do. Will dug his car keys out of his pocket. "You can even drive yourself if you want. I'm not going anywhere."

"You really want to hang around the house all afternoon?"

As soon as she said it, Will realized that he didn't. He hadn't eaten much today, either. Now that he was aware of the gnawing in his stomach, it was impossible to ignore.

"Want to get Dairy Queen or something while we're out? My treat."

"Thanks, but . . . I'm kind of meeting someone."

"Ah." Another reason to drive her to the library. Whoever this guy was, Will wanted to check him out.

By the time Will had laced up his shoes, Becca was out the door with her laptop bag and waiting impatiently at the passenger's side door.

"Do you have the deadbolt key?" Will asked.

"Just lock the handle from the inside. It's fine," Becca called. "Come on already."

Will jiggled the handle to reassure himself it was locked—it was—and let the storm door slam shut behind him as he trudged down to the driveway.

Becca raised an eyebrow at Will when he got in the car. "It's not a big deal, you know. We never used to lock the house at all."

"Seriously? After what happened to Ramon Bassave?" Will said. "One lock isn't nearly enough." Will kept his eyes fixed on the gravel road as he started the car and pulled out.

"Sorry," Becca said. "Are you really that worried?"

"I'm more concerned for you guys," Will replied. "I got myself into this mess."

And I've dragged my family down with me. Maybe it had always been that way—Will the screw-up, begging everyone else to help clean up his mess. Will tried to imagine the first life map, the one he and Mara and Jason Mann had abandoned. What could have happened when they were eighteen that they would all want fixed at twenty-seven? Will pictured himself in prison clothes, hoping that Jason and Mara Mann would agree to a timeline rectification. Anything to give a poor convict like Will a second chance.

No, her name had been Mara Gaines Sterling on the list. She loved me. Used to, anyway.

But if I wasn't the one at fault, who else could it be?

Will didn't realize how tightly he was gripping the steering wheel until Becca touched his hand. "I know I probably shouldn't ask—"

"Then don't."

"But have you talked to Mara at all? I know things ended bad between you guys, but maybe if you could just talk—"

"She wouldn't pick up the phone."

"What's that supposed to mean? What happened with you guys?"

Will shrugged, keeping his eyes on the road. "You know."

"No," Becca said. She was being serious, Will realized. "No, I really don't."

He was surprised to discover that he wanted to tell her. Really tell her. Will loosened his grip on the wheel. "When the data leak first happened, Mara's parents decided to postpone the wedding."

"That's what I figured y'all would do," Becca said.

"Really?"

"Now's not exactly a great time to have a wedding," Becca

said. "Who wants to look back on all their wedding pictures and remember ducking from the paparazzi?"

"That's not what marriage is supposed to be like," Will said. "You're not supposed to wait until everything's perfect. You're supposed to be in it together, no matter what."

Becca rolled her eyes. "And they say girls are dramatic. Your whole lives aren't going to revolve around this. It's going to quiet down in a while, and then you won't have to deal with it. Mara should know that. It's not like people are still talking about her dad."

"You just did."

"But not like"—Becca waved her hand—"*everywhere.* It's not still on the news and everything. And nobody really cares anymore."

"Mara cares."

"Well, of course *she* does. You know what I mean. This time wreck thing will probably matter to you guys forever, but not to anyone else, really. I just meant when it's off the news, it'd be a better time for a wedding."

Will silently pulled up to the stop sign and looked both ways before turning onto Main Street. The crunch of gravel disappeared, and the car rode smoother on the asphalt.

"Right. So her parents postponed it." Becca shifted in her seat so that she was facing Will. "Then what happened?"

"She left to help her Mom with a few things . . ." Will hesitated and looked at his sister.

"And?"

"And I got worried about her. She wasn't answering my texts, and some moron had just taken that picture and splashed it all over the internet, so I packed our suitcases in my car and went to find her. I figured we'd get away from DC for a few days, clear our heads."

Becca frowned. "Still not seeing the issue here."

"I was driving around trying to find her. She wasn't at her parents' house, but her dad . . ." The last part came out in a rush: "He told me that if she wasn't calling or trying to find me, I should stop chasing her. He said maybe she was coming to her senses. So I left her suitcase with him and came here."

Becca stared at him so long Will had to take his eyes off the road a few times, just to check whether she had blinked.

"You're a dumbass," Becca pronounced, flopping back in her seat.

"Hey!"

"You are. You're a dumbass, and I can't believe you've been sulking around our house like you're the one who got your heart broken."

"What are you talking about?"

Becca rolled her eyes so hard Will hoped her contacts would get stuck up there. "Well, you should have waited to talk to her instead of her *dad*. Oh my gosh. And now she's probably at her parents' house, all alone." Becca smacked him on the arm, hard. "You're a jerk."

"She. Left. Me." Will bit off each word.

Becca mimicked him. "No. She. Didn't. How can you be this stupid? "

"Fine! I'm an idiot then!" Will snapped back. "Now you know why we shouldn't be together. She's too good for me."

Becca exhaled, loudly. "Do you want my advice?"

"Not really."

"Call her. For all you know, it could just be a misunderstanding. I think you're a jerk, but maybe she still loves you."

Will snorted. "What would I even say? I've left Mara twice—once when we did the time wreck and again last week. Best thing I can do now is let her go."

"Stop," Becca said. "Stop."

Will exhaled. "I wouldn't have told you if I knew you were going to be like this."

"No, I mean *stop*. You missed the turn for the library. Unless you're driving back to DC right now, in which case, you better let me out first."

"Oh." Will pulled into the circular driveway at the bank and turned back onto Main Street. "Sorry."

A short boy with slicked-back dark hair was waiting by the front entrance of the library. Will couldn't miss the way Becca sat up straighter when she saw him and smoothed her long blond hair. Just a friend. *Yeah, right.*

Becca turned to him as he slowed the car to a stop. "Thanks for the ride."

"Thanks for the lecture," Will fired back.

"You should call her," Becca said. "Seriously."

Then she was gone, hooked on the arm of the dark-haired boy. He looked too comfortable standing so close to her. Will watched them disappear into the library before he pulled out of the parking lot.

◆◆◆◆◆

Will rolled down both windows and parked in the shade in front of the bank. There was better cell reception here than there was up by his house. Gave him a good opportunity to clear out his voice mail. It was full, again.

Part of him hoped that one of the messages would be from Mara. The other part was relieved when he didn't see her number on the list. He only listened to a few seconds of each voice mail before deleting, just long enough to be sure it wasn't Mara calling from another phone, but it was plenty.

"Hi, this is Lauren calling again from the *Daily Times* . . ."

"Will, it's Tristan. Just checking on you, man."

"William, this is Angie from One Life, One Time . . ."

One message was just indecipherable screaming. Will jumped when he heard it and looked both ways to see if anyone passing by had heard it too. No, the bank's parking lot was still deserted. Of course it was. Will rolled up both windows anyway and sat in the sweltering heat as he deleted the rest of the messages.

"Jackass."

"Son of a bitch."

"Can you comment—"

"Looking for William Sterling—"

"Time wrecker."

Even after deleting, his mailbox still looked full. There were more voice mails in his saved folder, Will realized. He didn't remember saving any messages. Must have done it by accident. It was crazy, having to clear out his mailbox so often. He'd probably gotten more calls in the last week than he had in his life.

But there was only one call he wanted to make.

"Maybe she still loves you," Becca had said. If only Mara did. Then maybe she'd be ready to hear that he still loved her.

Will's hands shook a little as he pressed number one on his speed dial.

Please pick up, please pick up, please—

"The party you have dialed cannot be reached."

Will held the phone to his ear long after the dial tone had started back up again. Couldn't be reached? Did that mean she was hurt or she was—

No. Mara must have disconnected her number. Duh. If he was getting called and texted around the clock, then Mara must have it way worse.

Will scrolled through his contacts list. Calling Mara's parents was out of the question. He wished he had her grandmother's phone number. Grandmary probably would have talked to him.

That left one possibility.

Robyn's number went straight to voice mail. Will wiped the sweat that had gathered at the base of his neck. Closing the windows had turned the car into a greenhouse.

"Hi, Robyn. I'm probably the last person you want to hear from right now, but please just give me a chance. I can't get a hold of Mara. I understand if she doesn't want to be with me anymore . . . I mean, obviously she doesn't . . . but I just . . . I want to tell her I'm sorry. I should have waited for her to come back. I should have talked to her. I wish . . ." Will puffed out his cheeks, but there was no other way to say it. "I'd do anything to take it back. Please, when you get this message, can you tell her to call me?"

Will hung up fast. It was the most pathetic, lovesick voice mail in history. If Alexander Graham Bell had heard that, he would have decided not to invent the telephone. Robyn would probably play it over and over, laughing with Mara about how ridiculous he was.

No, Robyn and Mara weren't like that. If anything, Robyn would just roll her eyes and delete it.

He hoped she wouldn't.

....

Chapter Fourteen

MARA

"Will called." Robyn sounded breathless.

Mara twirled the coiled phone cable around her arm. She wished Grandmary's kitchen chairs weren't so far away from the wall phone. Mara slid down the wall instead and sat on the tile floor.

"What do you mean Will *called?* He called you?"

"Yes. He left a message. My phone was off 'cause I was at work, which is probably good. If I'd seen him calling me, I swear to God I probably would have ripped his head off. But I guess it's good I heard him out. I don't know."

"Robyn." Mara could barely hear. Her own heartbeat was echoing in her ears. "What did he say?"

"Let me play it for you. Hang on." Robyn was quiet for a minute. "Dang this stupid cell phone. I can't figure out how to play the message while I'm talking to you at the same time." Robyn cursed quietly, and Mara heard several beeps from her keypad. "Okay. Mara? I'm going to call you from the house phone and see if I can play the message for you over the receiver. Does that work?"

"Yes!" Mara almost yelled. "Yes. Please. That would be great."

"Okay. I'm going to hang up and call you right back." The line went dead, and Mara stood up to replace her receiver. This couldn't be happening. But Robyn sounded so sure, and it had to be good news if she wanted to play it for Mara.

Grandmary's kitchen phone rang again, and Mara jumped to answer it.

"It's me," Robyn announced. "Okay. Are you ready for this?"

"Yes!" *As ready as I'll ever be.* Mara cradled the receiver between her ear and shoulder and hugged herself tightly with both arms.

Will's voice. The voice she'd longed to hear for days now, so real and beautiful that Mara pushed the receiver hard against her ear. As if that would make him closer for real.

". . . please just give me a chance . . ." Mara's heart leaped. "I should have waited for her to come back . . . tell her to call me."

Mara closed her eyes. He still loved her. He still wanted to talk to her.

Then why did he leave?

She could imagine, just for a second, that Will was right here with her. Funny how just hearing a voice could do that. She could almost believe that she was back in the apartment and they were talking it through together. Just them. Like it always should have been.

But Will wasn't right here. Mara opened her eyes and studied the faded linoleum of Grandmary's kitchen floor.

"You're so lucky!" Robyn squealed through the phone. "I knew it would all work out. You just had to talk to each other. I can't believe you didn't call him after I left your place on Friday! Or email or something."

"I couldn't do it. I wanted to, but I didn't know what to say."

"Well, call him now! He still loves you, Mara. And whether you meant to or not, you hurt him too."

"How?" Mara demanded. She twisted her fingers in the coiled phone cord. "How did I hurt Will? By telling him exactly where I was going? By protecting him from my crazy freaking parents and handling them myself?"

"Okay, I'm not trying to get in the middle here or anything, but Mara . . . you know how your parents are. You always talk about how they'll never change, but then you turn around and act like they will."

"E-Excuse me?" Mara spluttered.

"Just answer me this. When you went over to help your mom *cancel your wedding*, were you really doing that to protect Will? Or were you protecting yourself?"

"It's not like I wanted to. It's not the easiest thing in the world to deal with my parents," Mara snapped. "You should be able to understand that."

"What?"

"You've been going out with Jessica for two years and won't even tell your parents about her. You won't come out to them at all. So. Look who's talking. Good thing Jess didn't dump you the way Will dumped me."

Too far. Mara wished she could take the words back as soon as she said them. She leaned forward, as if that could erase what she'd done. "Robyn, I'm sorry," she said. "That was way out of line. I shouldn't have said that to you."

"It's fine," Robyn said slowly.

"I had no right," Mara said. "I shouldn't have said that."

"I said it's fine."

"But—"

"Listen, Mara, I have to go," Robyn said. "I'm just passing on the message, okay? Do whatever you want. Call him or don't."

"I'm sorry," Mara said again.

"Talk to you later." Robyn hung up.

♦♦♦♦♦

Mara stayed sitting on the cold kitchen floor for a long time. *How many times am I going to hurt the people who are nice to me?*

No, it was even worse than that. *I hurt the people who are nice to me so I can be nice to the people who hurt me.*

If Mara's mother had called to say she was sorry—well, that would never happen. But if Mara's mother had left her a message. If she'd just acknowledged Mara again.

Then I would already be in my car. On my way over to make things right.

That's how Mara always thought of it. Making things right. But it wasn't right, what she'd done. Will's name had been on the time wrecker list too. Will's wedding had been canceled. Did Mara stay to comfort him? Did she think about what he needed?

No. Mara had gone running straight back to her parents.

For the first time, she let herself imagine what it had been like to be Will that day. Alone in the apartment. Waiting for hours for Mara to come back and not hearing so much as a word.

Will had been right to leave her. Maybe the time wrecker leak was nothing more than the final straw. After all, it had been Will's wedding too. And for the past year, Mara had forced him to let her parents take the driver's seat. Not because it was tradition, but because it was easier to disappoint him than them.

It was easier for me to disappoint Will than my parents.

Mara stood up so fast she hit her head on the wall phone. *Too bad I didn't hit it harder,* she thought ruefully, rubbing the sore spot on her head. If something could just stop her from thinking for a minute, it would be easier than dealing with the reality she'd created.

No, no more of that. Mara squared her shoulders.

The facts were falling into place. Mara's father had some

kind of reason for trying to restrict time wrecks, and it probably had to do with Mara's name being on the list. And if her name was on the list in the first place . . .

It's because Dad wanted it to be.

Mara paced through the kitchen. *If Dad had asked me to go through with a time wreck, I would have done it. I would have convinced Will and Jason to get on board too. The crime had probably been something stupid as well. Something most people wouldn't be allowed to rectify. Like I got in a car accident and he didn't want it on my record anymore. Or maybe we all got busted together at a party, and it got out that the congressman's daughter was drinking underage.*

It made sense. Mara's father used to be in good with the One Life, One Time people. He'd wanted to outlaw timeline rectification for good. But then suddenly, he'd changed. His new bill had been about making time wrecks harder to get, not impossible. Congressman Gaines must have known somehow. Seen the time wrecker list or . . . something.

There was more, Mara was sure of it. In time, the hacktivists or whoever would release the rest of the data. *But I have all the answers I need, don't I?*

It was time to make things right. Try to, anyway. Mara picked up the phone and dialed.

Discussion Thread: Time Wreckers/ Mara Gaines

1moreconspiracy

Good morning, all! Just dropping a link riiiiiiiight here for your listening pleasure:

<u>JILTED TIME WRECKER LEAVES TEARFUL VOICE MAIL FOR EX-FIANCÉ</u>

Kris1157

Boring. Everyone's already heard this!

> **oOoOoCUTIEoOoOo**
>
> Um, not with the audio!!! Thanks

NE1listening

This is the fakest thing I've ever heard or read in my entire life. How many times do you think she rehearsed those tears?

> **Monkeybutts**
>
> Well, obviously they planned this. Wouldn't surprise me if Mara and her "ex" have been talking this whole time and decided to spill the "phone call" to get back in the spotlight.

> **404notfoundyet**
>
> That's just gross. Ramon Bassave literally LOST his LIFE and these two idiots are butthurt that they're not the center of attention anymore.

NE1listening

Ok but seriously! "I'm so sorry. I still love you with all my heart. If only I could take it all back..." UM I THINK YOU DID THAT ALREADY.

1moreconspiracy

Please. "I'm so sorry. For everything. I'm just . . . so, so sorry."
<----This little nugget is how I will be responding to all
internet trolls for the rest of time

Lolololol

    oOoOoCUTIEoOoOo
    Make. It. A. Meme.

        NE1listening
        OMG YESSSSS! That quote on her actual
        nasty face . . . do ittttttttttt

Chapter Fifteen

WILL

She still loves me. Will tried to hold on to that thought as he trudged over the gravel driveway. *She called me back. She still loves me.*

Just wish I'd gotten to hear it before the rest of the internet.

Will let out a long, gusty sigh that must have startled Tristan over the phone.

"How did someone manage to hack your phone, man?" At least Tristan sounded curious, not judgmental. "What'd you do? Use your birthday as your password?"

That was exactly what Will had done. He kicked a rock out of the garden and kept walking. The front yard barely got cell reception, but it was better than inside the house. And it was too hot to walk farther down the road.

"I should've known better," Will said. "I had everything else locked down. My bank stuff, obviously, plus my email, my credit— this is the one stupid thing I forget to double-check."

"Have you called Mara back? Or Robyn? Just explain it

wasn't your fault."

"Not yet." Will kicked another rock. "Mara's going to be furious anyway. Even if most people think it's fake, Mara will know that was her real voice mail." For a moment, Will was tempted to drive his fist into a tree stump but thought better of it. "She's never going to forgive me. Whether she realizes my voice mail was hacked or not. I should have locked it down."

"But Mara loves you. She said so herself. Don't let this become something bigger than it is."

"Loving someone isn't the same as forgiving them," Will said. "Anyway. You said you had something to tell me?"

"It can wait."

"I just want to talk about something else." Will kicked another rock and sent it flying. "Anything else."

"Right. Okay. Well, I have good news and bad news about the job," Tristan said. "I talked to Dave, and he's willing to give you a chance."

"And the bad news?"

"You'll just be busing tables to start."

"Oh. Okay, yeah. I can do that," Will said. *I have a bachelor's degree. I can do a lot more than that.*

"Problem is, he can't give you a lot of hours. Two kids came back for the summer, so Dave doesn't need much in the way of staff, even with me leaving. He told me he could put you on for ten hours, maybe twenty a week."

"Oh." Will ground his toe into the soft soil.

"I know that's not going to be enough," Tristan said. "But it's something."

"Yes. Thank you," Will said, remembering to be grateful. Even ten hours a week was better than nothing. And it would give him time to look for other jobs too.

"There's another thing." Tristan hesitated so long Will checked to be sure he hadn't dropped the call. "I was asking around my church yesterday just to see if anyone knew of any jobs opening up around DC. And the pastor told me that our music director is leaving. She's moving to Cincinnati since her husband got a job out there. I don't know if you'd be interested in something like that, but I was asking around, I heard about this, and I'm just letting you know. It's a possibility."

"Thanks," Will said. *Like I'm qualified to work in a church. The roof would probably cave in on me as soon as I walked in.* "Thanks for looking out for me. They probably want someone with a little more experience."

"I mean, if you're interested at all, the pastor definitely wanted you to come in for an interview. I pulled up one of the videos from your senior concert and played a few minutes of it, and he was pretty impressed."

"Those videos are still online?" Impressed? Someone was impressed with his piano playing? Will had only been out of college for a few weeks, and already it felt like eons since anyone had cared about his music.

"It was right on the music department's website. I didn't

figure you'd mind."

"No, I don't mind." Will's mind was racing. Even if he did get up the courage to interview and got the job and bussed tables on the side, would that be enough to afford a life in DC?

If he couldn't have Mara, was it worth going back to DC?

Will looked up and down the quiet country road where he'd lived almost all his life. Yes. Yes, it was. He sighed again.

"You still there? You're kind of breaking up," Tristan said.

"Sorry. Yeah, I'm still here. I don't know if I'd really interview for it, but thanks."

"No problem. I'll keep asking around too."

"Thanks, man. You have no idea how much I appreciate it."

"One more thing," Tristan said. "You still thinking of being in town on Friday? Where do you want to go? Adams Morgan or somewhere else?"

Friday. That one word pulled Will back to the life that almost was. Friday should have been the wedding rehearsal. Then Will and the guys would have gone back to Adams Morgan to shoot some pool and drink a few beers. Hardly a bachelor's party, Tristan had teased him.

Will kicked another rock and stubbed his toe. He tried to keep his voice light as he answered Tristan.

"Obviously, Adams Morgan," Will said. "And don't even think about going easy on me. We're going to play pool, and

I'm going to kick your butt."

"You keep telling yourself that. See you Friday."

✦✦✦✦✦

"You're really sure you want me to come?" Will asked again.

Bonnie Sterling pressed her lips together in a straight line. "The church is a safe place in times of trouble. This is a time of trouble, so get yourself in that car. We're all going."

Will did as he was told. When they were little, he and Chris and Becca would have fought over who got to ride in the front seat. Now, Chris and Becca were both already buckled into the back seats, leaving Will to ride beside their mother. At least Becca shot him a sympathetic look. Chris acted completely oblivious to Will's presence.

"Here," Bonnie said, tossing a book in his lap. Will caught it just in time. "The chapter for this week is marked. Maybe you can skim over it before we get there."

Will opened the book to the chapter that was marked with a sticky note, but he didn't look down at the words. Reading made him car sick, even for a short drive like this one. In minutes, they had crested the gravel hill Will had barely been able to reach the top of when he was out running.

Without the book to distract him, Will was overly conscious that no one else in the car was talking. Bonnie had nearly lost her voice earlier that afternoon when she'd come tearing home from work.

"What's this I heard about you puttin' some phone call on the internet?" she'd yelled to Will, seconds before the kitchen door slammed behind her. "How am I supposed to hold my head up at work when my own son's making a joke out of a girl like that? No matter what happened between you and Mara, William, there is no excuse. None. You humiliated that girl."

It had taken both Will and Becca half an hour to calm her down and longer still to explain how a phone could be hacked. How someone could possibly have uploaded Mara's voice mail online before Will even listened to it himself. Finally, Bonnie had wiped her red eyes and fixed Will with a stare.

"Well, no matter whose fault it was, you need to take responsibility. That poor girl is only in this situation because of you." She'd stood suddenly and stalked to the doorway. "Our small group meets tonight, and you're comin' with us, William. So help me. If you're going to be under this roof, I'm going to put you on a straight path or . . ." The rest of her rage was incoherent as Bonnie rounded the corner and stormed down the hall.

Becca had turned on him then. "Did you do it?"

"What?"

"Did you?" Becca repeated. "I will keep covering for you with Mom, but you've got to tell me the truth. You have to admit this looks bad, Will. You haven't even talked to Mara in a week, and then suddenly—"

"I would never." For some reason, Becca's suspicion hurt Will even worse. His hands were shaking. "I called her phone number and I couldn't get through, so I left a message with Robyn. Then this morning, I wake up to Mara's voice mail playing all over the internet."

"And did you see it on your phone?" Becca demanded.

"Yes," Will said. "After I heard it online, I checked and found it in my voice mail. But I swear I never heard it before."

Becca stared at him a few seconds longer.

"I would never betray Mara like that. I swear."

Finally, Becca relaxed her shoulders and gave a small conciliatory smile. Will was relieved that at last someone seemed to believe him.

"How am I going to fix this?" Will had asked her. "How am I going to prove it to Mara?"

"For crying out loud, Will," Becca snapped. "Talk to her and straighten it out."

"How am I going to do that? Her phone number doesn't work anymore. I can't call her parents. I don't know her grandmother's phone number, and it's not listed. I called Robyn again, but it cut off before I could leave a message. And after that, it just said the number could not be reached."

"Robyn probably blocked you. I would have too."

"Hey!"

"Well, I would," Becca said bluntly. "Maybe this wasn't exactly your fault, but there's plenty of stuff that was."

Becca's words came back to him now as his mother pulled into the church parking lot. An older couple—Will recognized them a beat too late as Mr. Bill and Miss Cathy—glanced over at their car as they walked in and quickly looked away.

I'm not the bad guy here, Will felt like screaming. But he wasn't the good guy, either. And tonight, Will was sure of it, he was going to be That Guy at Bible study.

I shouldn't be here. I should be driving back to Mara right now. I should do something. Write her an email. Mail her a letter. Something.

Assuming she ever wants to hear from me again.

Will tried not to drag his feet as he followed his family into the church.

◆◆◆◆◆

There were only a dozen people here, if that. The Sterlings' small group met in the back half of the old multipurpose room, where the semicircle of folding chairs looked oddly out of place. One of the cafeteria tables was unfolded and pushed against the side of the wall. The end that was draped with a blue plastic tablecloth was laden with home-baked treats and pitchers of water and lemonade.

The Sterlings had brought brownies, which Becca had

carried in like a peace offering. Will had no appetite, but he took a brownie for his plate anyway. Maybe if he kept his mouth full, no one would talk to him directly.

The book discussion had already begun, plus two or three side conversations. Will didn't listen to any of them. He glanced around the room instead. He had known everyone here since the time he was a child: Miss Martha, the self-appointed organizer of the food pantry; Mr. Matt from the praise ensemble; the other Mr. Matt, who ran a landscape business in town; and of course Mr. Bill and Miss Cathy.

Here came Miss Bitty, puffing in with a plate of her meringue cookies.

"Sorry I'm late," she shrilled. Miss Bitty stopped to hug each person in turn with one arm, using the other to hold her doubled-up paper plate of cookies aloft. She didn't seem to see Will until she'd already hugged Becca beside him. Will half stood, ready to offer a hug, at the same time Miss Bitty said, "Well, I'd better get these cookies to the table!" and turned away.

Awkward. The only empty chair was next to Will. He didn't even offer a wave as Miss Bitty plopped down beside him.

"We had just started the first discussion question at the end of the chapter," Miss Martha said. She was frowning slightly, folding a tiny pink line into her forehead as if it wasn't used to being bent that way. "Though quite honestly, as I was just telling Bonnie, I had a lot of trouble understanding how the author was conveying obedience in this chapter. I felt like there were some areas where the author was making excuses. Like this part where he says"—she ruffled through the pages and removed a slip of purple paper—"here. Page sixty-five, about halfway down. There's this whole paragraph about his obedience to God during his wife's infidelity." Miss Martha frowned deeper. "I have to tell you, I think that he leaned on God not as a guide but as a crutch. You can't just quote Bible passages at people and assume your work is done. You have to believe it. You have to really live the message."

Will looked back down at his lap, suddenly sure that everyone was looking at him. *I tried*, he wanted to say. *I tried and I couldn't.*

Here in this same room, Will had once confessed the faith he didn't really have. It was the day after Will's college acceptance letter came, after his mother had cried for hours. DC was too far away. He couldn't make a career as a musician. What good was a music scholarship if he'd have to study something else to get a job? And who knew what sorts of things could happen to him up north. DC was such a big city. It was too dangerous.

There was only one thing he could do. That's what Will had thought at the time. Bonnie Sterling's eyes had still been puffy and red on Sunday, but she beamed for surprise and joy when Will walked up to the front of the cafeteria-turned-sanctuary at the end of the service.

Will could still feel how self-conscious he was, bowing his head to confess his faith. *It's okay. God understands. I'm sure enough.* Will tried to convince himself the entire time he recited the words of the Apostle's Creed.

"I believe in God the Father Almighty,
Maker of Heaven and Earth..."

But when he said "Amen" and looked up at the congregation, he felt more guilt than peace. Even as he basked in his family's approving smiles, Will still knew he was a liar. And he was pretty sure God, assuming He was looking down at him right then, would know it too.

God still knows I'm a liar. No wonder He hasn't been answering me.

Will couldn't help thinking that this would all be so much easier if he had the faith that his mother and Chris and even Becca seemed to have. They didn't shy away from the questions. They just believed there were answers. Will studied his mother's face as she chimed in to the conversation. "I think he did struggle with obedience," Bonnie said, and it took Will a heart-stopping minute to realize that his mother really was talking about the book and not him. "That was one of my favorite parts, really. I felt like the author was saying he surrendered his marriage to God's will in order to cope with this betrayal. Because although his wife betrayed him, God would never betray either of them. I thought it was beautiful how he said that."

"If that's how he meant it, then I agree, definitely. But that wasn't the sense I got. I felt like he was more avoiding his feelings and avoiding those difficult conversations with his wife." Miss Martha cast glances to her left and right. "Did anyone else feel that? Or was it just me?"

"Sometimes what looks like avoidance is really just a lot of complications." Bonnie sighed. "Y'all know that my husband left eighteen years ago. It was his choice to leave. We would fight and work things out and fight and work things out again and . . ." She drew a deep breath and looked at Becca. "No, it wasn't the marriage I dreamed of. But it was the marriage I had. And it seems like it was so long ago, but I had to ask myself: If he walked back into our lives tomorrow, would I take him back? If God spoke to my heart and told me that in His eyes, I was still married to this man, would I obey Him?"

Will's heart hammered. *No. Please don't. Please say you wouldn't.*

"I honestly don't know," Bonnie continued. "I truly don't."

"I didn't say all that about divorce to bring things up for you, Bonnie," Miss Martha said with a gentle smile. "You know that. Your difficulties aren't the same as these here in the book." Beside him, Will felt Miss Bitty cutting a look his way.

"I know you didn't." Bonnie sniffed a little and dabbed at the corners of her eyes with her paper napkin.

Will could make things better for her. For all of them. Maybe Mara wouldn't forgive him, but the people of Deer Hill would. They'd forgive him for all of it. All he had to do was repent. All he had to say was that he never should have had a time wreck.

No. I can't do it again. He couldn't say he was sorry if he wasn't sure. And Will wasn't.

◆◆◆◆◆

"I thought that was really powerful," Chris said on the ride home.

"It was," Bonnie agreed. "I can't tell you how much it means to me to have y'all there with me. Especially when I'm talking about your father." She signaled before turning onto Main Street. "I hope I've never represented to you children that your father was a bad person. God knows he had some flaws, but if he were ever to choose to seek us out—"

"We know, Mom," Becca said.

Will gripped the edge of the seat so tightly that he felt some of the upholstery give. Oops. He smoothed it back down with one hand.

"Didn't hear much from you tonight, Will," Chris said. Every word was an accusation.

Will didn't bother to turn around. "I hadn't read the chapter," he mumbled.

"I just thought it was a topic you'd have some thoughts

on."

"Chris." Their mother's voice was a warning.

Will whipped around before he could think better of it. Flames leaped in Will's throat and poured out of his mouth. "Really? I would've thought it was exactly what *you* needed to hear," Will heard himself say. "Or do you really think God's leading you to be a sanctimonious pain in the—"

"Enough!" Bonnie commanded. "That'll do from both of you."

Will shot Chris one more glare before he turned back around. The sun had almost fully set now, and long shadows stretched across the road. Even with the air-conditioning on high and the sudden crunch as they turned from pavement onto the gravel road, Will could hear the grasshoppers singing back and forth.

Sudden prickles erupted down the back of Will's neck. He felt like this sometimes in Deer Hill when he couldn't see another car or house in any direction and the world suddenly seemed capable of swallowing him whole. He shivered involuntarily, and Bonnie, misunderstanding, reached over and dialed down the air-conditioning.

They crested the last hill, and Will's stomach disappeared. Bonnie slammed on the brakes, as if somehow that could keep their house from coming into view. But even from here, Will could see the glint of broken glass across the front of the house and the harsh red and black spray paint that stood out against the siding.

"Oh my God." Becca pumped the door handle on her side of the car as if she were really going to leap out, now, when the car was still moving and anything could be waiting for them.

"Mercy," Bonnie whispered.

"Well, there's a big surprise," Chris grumbled. He unbuckled his seat belt and stood up right in the car, balancing himself like a surfer. Bonnie eased to a stop halfway down the road from their house. "Let me go check it out first, Mom."

"Don't you go anywhere," Bonnie said. "Let me think a minute. We should call the police. Go to a neighbor's."

They would have their choice of doors to knock on— every house had its lights on. Will wondered if any of them had seen what happened. *Or maybe they were all in on it.* The thought made him sick.

It was worse the longer Will looked at it. The words that had been spray-painted in black were too difficult to make out, but the words in red were starting to become clear.

TIME WRECKER

GO HOME

BURN IN HELL

GET OUT

Chapter Sixteen

....

MARA

The truth won't set us free. Mara sat on the glider on Grandmary's sunporch, rocking it gently with one foot.

Look at what calling Will had done. Baring her soul just to have it broadcast all over the world. There was a part of Mara—a big part—that hoped this, too, was just some terrible accident. Another hack, maybe.

But there was a bigger part that knew it didn't matter.

For better or for worse, Mara would always be the Time Wrecker now. Not because she'd been hurt the most by the leak. Not because it was her fault. But because the world needed a face and a voice for its enemy, and they'd picked hers.

I deserve to be loved. Mara tried to feel the words Grandmary had told her only a few days ago. But hadn't Grandmary kind of contradicted herself? Sure, she'd pushed Grandpap to truly love her before she married him, all those years ago. Grandmary was honest about that. But she hadn't exactly been open, either. In twenty-two years, even Mara had never known or even guessed that part of Grandmary and Grandpap's story.

And what was wrong with that? Mara pushed off against the floor harder, making the glider swing so fast it creaked. It wasn't anybody's business when her father was born, or in what order her grandparents had gotten married and pregnant. Pregnant and married. But enough people had made it their business back then that Grandmary had gone running off to another state.

Mara pulled up her foot and let the glider swing to a stop.

She almost wished for the swell of shame to come over her now. Or rage. Something. But Mara was horribly blank instead. Hollow. As if she had finally managed to break free from the world that didn't want her anymore, only to discover that she didn't really want to be herself, either.

So, this is what rock bottom feels like.

♦♦♦♦♦

"Mara," Grandmary called. "Mara. Come here now, please."

Something about the way Grandmary called her name made Mara jump off the glider and run into the den to join her. Her grandmother was pushing the buttons under the television screen.

"Do you want the remote?" Mara offered, but Grandmary had found the news channel before Mara even finished her sentence. Usually, her grandmother would have muttered something about remote controls being useless dust-catchers—come to think of it, Mara wasn't even quite sure where it was, anyway. But today, Grandmary was singularly focused on the TV.

"What's going on?" Mara asked. Despite herself, she realized her heart was beating faster. *Not him again. Not after he . . .* She tried to take a deep breath instead. *Stay blank. Stay in control.*

"Nothing, I hope. The local radio said there was a breaking news story, and I heard your father's name," Grandmary said. She sounded breathless, and Mara hurried to put an arm around her grandmother's shoulders. Whatever it was, Grandmary refused to be guided back to the couch. And so they stood, so close Mara could smell the faint scent of her grandmother's perfume mixed with sweat and see the powdery residue of makeup around her hairline.

Don't look for your name in the news. The words came back to Mara automatically. That must have been mostly her parents' rule, not Grandmary's. Hanging on to her grandmother now, Mara couldn't help thinking there was some wisdom in those words. Whatever the breaking news was about, Grandmary didn't seem ready to handle it at all. For that matter, neither was Mara.

A sequence of five notes signaled that the local news program was about to come on. Mara found herself gripping Grandmary's shoulder. The older woman was shaking.

"We're back with breaking news in the Timeline Rectification scandal," said the reporter on-screen. "Former congressional staffer and current congressional candidate Conrad Gibbons has been identified as a 'person of interest' in the data leak. Sources say Conrad Gibbons has turned himself in voluntarily for questioning. Reporter Wayne Klinger is live at the scene now with more information. Wayne?"

The reporter nodded for a few moments before he appeared to hear the question. "Joanna, I'm here outside the FBI building, where Conrad Gibbons went in for questioning just thirty minutes ago. Here's what we know so far: the data leak was a premeditated attempt to undermine Gibbons's political rival, Congressman Joel Gaines, and he did not act alone."

The screen switched to show both frames side by side: Joanna, looking grim at her desk in the newsroom, and Wayne, standing silhouetted against the FBI building. Joanna spoke next. "We've heard rumors that Alicia Barnes will be brought in for questioning as well, given her position as the president of One Life, One Time. Do you have any information on her involvement?"

"Joanna, I haven't seen anything confirming that Ms. Barnes has been called in for questioning, but we will be here reporting as things unfold."

Grandmary looked like she wanted to sit now. "Oh, dear," she said, not quite under her breath. Mara walked her back to the couch, and this time, her grandmother didn't resist. "Oh my heavens," Grandmary said faintly. "And after what happened to that Bassave man. You or your father could be next."

"Let me get you something," Mara said. "Lemonade or . . . or tea or water . . ."

"No thank you, dear." Grandmary's thin hands fluttered between her face and her neck.

The picture on the TV screen blurred, and the reporters' voices were suddenly too loud. Mara blinked and held Grandmary closer.

I can't check out of this one. Grandmary needed her. As shocking as the thought was, that her grandmother could need her instead of the other way around, Mara felt herself rising to the thought.

"It's going to be okay, Grandmary," Mara said. "I promise. We're going to be just fine."

Mara realized, as she spoke, that Will had said the same thing to her only a week ago. The words sounded as hollow as Mara felt.

♦♦♦♦♦

It was Mara who had to answer the house phone when it rang. If her father was surprised to hear her voice, he didn't show it.

"Mara," Congressman Gaines said briskly. "I realize we

ended our last conversation on a bad note, but I need us to put that aside for the moment. Are you and Mother all right?"

"I'm . . ." Mara searched for the right words.

"Your mother and I have had some activity outside our house. I wanted to be sure that you and your grandmother hadn't experienced similar."

"What do you mean, activity?" Mara's mind raced through the possibilities. "What happened?"

"No one is hurt, and we've reported everything to the police," her father said tersely. "They're handling it. Please, just stay out of the public eye for now."

"What about you and Mom? Are you . . . are you safe? Are you still . . . going to have that dinner on Saturday?"

"The dinner has been called off," Congressman Gaines said abruptly. "How is your grandmother? I called earlier to alert her to the situation, and she sounded distressed."

"Grandmary's really upset," Mara said. "I've never seen her shaken up like this."

"Thankfully, you're there to watch over her," Congressman Gaines said.

Was that how they were spinning it now? Was this how her parents would talk about this terrible summer years from now? *One of Joel's political rivals launched an awful campaign against him. The whole thing rattled Mary so terribly that Mara went to spend the summer with her.*

"Dad," Mara began. "About that night. When we were at

my graduation dinner."

You knew, didn't you? That's why you were on your phone instead of paying attention to us. You knew what was going to happen and you could have stopped it. Or warned us. Both.

"I've got a call coming in. I'll have to let you go," her father said. He hung up.

Time Wreckers Fear for Privacy, Safety

ASSOCIATED PRESS — Yesterday's bombshell revelation in the time wrecker leak has left even more Americans afraid for their safety. Since the data leak, the <u>4.5 million time wreckers listed</u> in the initial report experienced increased tension in their families and communities, some with <u>tragic results</u>. These attacks have reportedly increased since Conrad Gibbons came forward as the organizer behind the data leak, purportedly for political gain.

The admission has sent yet another shock wave through the nation, as the organization Gibbons worked for, One Life, One Time, has also been the <u>greatest source of support</u> for time wreckers in the wake of the leak. The president of One Life, One Time, Alicia Barnes, has also been identified as a person of interest in the hack.

"It's betrayal on top of betrayal," according to one individual who was named on the list but asked to remain anonymous. "After I lost my job, One Life, One Time got me free counseling over the phone. Now I find out they were the whole reason there was a leak in the first place. It's sickening."

Others are quick to defend the organization. "Two bad apples don't spoil the whole batch," said another anonymous individual. "One Life, One Time had a good mission. They've done good things. The two people responsible for this mess will answer for it in court. The whole organization isn't to blame."

Of note, HR 6437—the so-called Time Wrecker Bill—was defeated in the House on the same day Gibbons admitted guilt for the data leak. Early supporters of the bill's "common sense approach" to limiting timeline rectifications were outnumbered by those who wanted to take a stronger stand. Those who opposed widespread use of time wrecking are now more likely to support completely ending the rectification program. Others, however, are defending Americans' "right to rectify."

Congressman Gaines, the sponsor of HR 6437, has faced serious personal threats in the wake of Gibbons's confession as well. As the incumbent representative for Virginia's 8th District, he was the target of the data leak, which listed his own daughter as a time wrecker. Yesterday, police were called to the congressman's home after an attempted kidnapping of his wife, attorney Augusta Gaines.

A dinner planned in support of Congressman Gaines's reelection campaign has been canceled out of concern for the family's safety.

The attorney's office says they plan to prosecute all crimes against time wreckers as hate crimes.

Chapter Seventeen

WILL

"It's lookin' better." Miss Bitty stood back. "Can't hardly see it unless you're up close on it now." She smiled at Will. "All it took was a bit of elbow grease."

It had taken *a bit of elbow grease* in the form of two dozen people from the church, who'd spent Wednesday morning helping the Sterlings scrub off the side of their house. It took over an hour of trial and error before they discovered that rubbing alcohol did the best job of removing the red and black spray paint while leaving the tan on the siding. Four people had swept the front steps in shifts, determined to get up every shard of glass. Mr. Bill had come by and replaced the two broken windows. And somewhere in the middle of it all, Becca had left for school and Chris had gone to work. Bonnie had called out. Again.

Mom's going to lose her job. Will hoped against hope that he was wrong. But God, or the universe, or whoever was in charge up there, clearly wasn't interested in cutting them a break.

For now, Bonnie Sterling didn't seem to be worried about

that. As her church friends slowly began packing up and making their excuses to leave, Will's mother hugged and thanked each one.

I want to be like her. Will was so surprised by the thought that he slipped away, around the corner of the house, and watched from a distance. No, this wasn't the life he had wanted. Was it?

Not the small-town part, maybe. But the peace. For a woman whose house had been wrecked, Bonnie looked surprisingly . . . okay. Secure, even when everything around her had practically fallen apart.

Will ducked in the house through the back door. While they'd worked, Will had heard murmurs here and there. No one had said anything to him directly, but he'd caught a few words that piqued his curiosity.

"That family Will was goin' to marry into . . ."

". . . law would've been a step in the right direction. Keep things like this from happening again."

". . . that poor woman just about got killed, it sounded like. Lucky she got away."

The last remark had knocked Will breathless. Someone must have noticed because there hadn't been any more talk about the Gaines family. None that Will could hear, anyway.

Will let the air-conditioning hit him, full blast, now that he was inside and the house was suddenly, startlingly lonesome. Did he dare use Becca's computer again? How mad had she been about it the other day, really?

"There you are." Bonnie Sterling brushed past him on her way to the refrigerator. "I was thinkin' I'd heat up a little of Becca's mac and cheese for us for lunch and toss up a little salad. How does that sound?"

"Fine, Mom."

His tone had given him away, as it always did. Will could feel his mother's piercing look even with his eyes closed. "You okay?"

"I was just thinking . . ." He paused.

Bonnie turned and thrust two forks and knives into his hands. "Set the table while you think, if you don't mind." She stomped back across the kitchen so hard her footsteps rattled the walls.

So his mom already knew what he was going to say. But it had to be said, didn't it? Will laid the silverware down on the edge of the table. "I was thinking about what happened last night. Why it happened. Maybe it would be better for everyone if I just—"

"No." Ordinarily, her raised voice would have been enough to stop him in his tracks. But this was not an ordinary situation.

"Mom, I've only been here a week. This is the second time someone's pulled something like this." Will took a step toward her, but only one. "First it was just my car, but now it's your house. This is affecting you guys. I need to go back and—"

"No." Bonnie shook her head so vehemently that her

sprayed-stiff blond hair trembled a little. "Don't you go anywhere on our account. I won't have it."

"It's my fault, Mom. They're doing this because of me. If I leave, at least nobody will be trying to hurt you anymore."

"Leave and go where, William?" Bonnie slammed the casserole dish of mac and cheese down on the counter. "Go back to Mara? Go back to her stuck-up family and your good-for-nothin' friends? Here you have your family to protect you, your church droppin' everything to come help, and you're talkin' about leaving." She whipped a spatula off the counter and started gesturing with it. "Where do you think you'll find that's so much better? Who do you think is going to love you more?"

"I'm not looking for something better for me. I keep saying it. I'm leaving to protect you."

"And I keep sayin' no," Bonnie hollered. "We only need one martyr around here, and your name ain't Jesus."

"So what should I do?" Will threw his arms up in the air. "Sit here and wait for these people to come back and burn down your house? Hurt Becca?"

"You're going to sit back and let us handle it," Bonnie said. She had stopped yelling at least, but her voice was still high and tight and her eyes were shining. "You're not going to let this sin define your life, William. And we're not going to let anyone else define your life by it, either."

◆ ◆ ◆ ◆ ◆

Dinner at the Sterling home was always served early and hot, even on blistering summer nights like this one. Whenever Bonnie Sterling had an afternoon off, she made a full meal. Meatloaf and mashed potatoes, usually, or grilled chicken and corn on the cob if the weather was nice. On busy nights, which were most nights, the Sterlings ate whatever they could put together in less than twenty minutes. Macaroni and cheese. Pork and beans. Hot dogs warmed in the microwave.

Will surveyed the hall closet-turned-pantry for ideas. A truly home-cooked meal was out—he couldn't stand to heat up the oven when the temperature outside was nearing 100 degrees. He didn't love the idea of tinkering with the grill in all that heat, either. But he had everything needed for his old standby: beef stew over rice. It would be nice to have dinner ready when everyone got home, especially with the news he was going to drop.

It wasn't until he heard the sound of tires in the driveway that Will remembered Becca was vegetarian now. *Rats.* Last time he'd been down for a visit, she'd been on the Atkins diet. Beef stew would have been perfect for her, then. Will quickly found a bag of frozen mixed vegetables and put them in another saucepan to simmer. He needed everything to go right tonight—at least, everything he could control.

Bonnie and Becca trudged in through the door. Bonnie perked up immediately when she saw Will at the stove, carefully portioning out the rice onto four plates. "Well, here's a nice surprise!" she said. "How thoughtful of you. And look, Becca. He's got some veggies going for you too."

"That's nice," Becca said, slinging her backpack off and stuffing it in the corner by the door.

Bonnie fixed a too-bright smile on her oldest son. "Will, this smells wonderful. I should get my recipe cards out and have you give some of those a whirl. It's awfully nice coming home to a home-cooked meal."

Will focused on spooning out the stew with precision. "Chris is going to be home for dinner too, right?" he asked. *Please. I don't want to say this twice.*

"Calm down there, chef," Becca said with a dramatic eyeroll. "He'll get here when he gets here."

"Becca," warned their mother.

Don't start. It'll make tonight even worse. Will tried to catch his sister's eye with no success.

Please come home, Chris.

Thankfully, Will didn't have to wait much longer. The storm door squeaked open, and his brother stomped in.

"What smells?" he demanded.

Will gritted his teeth and set the table. As if it wasn't bad enough that his mother was fluttering around commenting on everything he did—"And you folded the napkins too! Fancy!"—Chris's flat expression was even worse.

Just get through this. Will's heart pounded as they said grace and everyone started to eat. Everyone except for Will.

It was time.

"I really want to thank you guys for all your support this past week. Especially this morning. It's been . . . it's been a really hard time, and I appreciate you all so much."

"That's what families are for, honey," Bonnie said, reaching over to pat Will's hand. Chris and Becca said nothing.

"I know it's been hard on you guys too." Will could tell his mother was about to interrupt, so he rushed through: "And I'm sorry for that. I think it's best if I go back to DC. I've got a few leads on some jobs and . . . it's time. It's just time for me to stand on my own two feet."

Bonnie Sterling froze Will with a long stare before turning to his sister. "And Becca, what are your plans for the week? Are you going to see that boyfriend of yours again?"

"Mom!" Becca cried. "We're just friends!" She shot Will a murderous look.

"All I'm saying is he's a nice young man. It's good to see you doing something besides school and work." Bonnie sighed. "For a while there, I thought you were just going to move into that vet clinic. I still think you're working too much."

"I'm saving for a car," Becca said.

"Perhaps Will can lend you his," Bonnie said pointedly.

"That's going to be hard, once I'm back in DC," Will said. "I can probably start one job on Friday, so I better get back up there soon."

"And Chris, how was your day?" Bonnie asked. "Anything new at work?" She raised her eyebrows at her younger son.

"Yeah," Chris said, looking straight ahead. "Paul quit, so we're short. Need someone to work stocking the warehouse shelves." He glanced over at Will. "My boss asked if you'd be interested."

Will felt as if his tongue were stuck to the roof of his mouth.

Across the table, Chris glowered at him. The job at the warehouse was a favor. Chris had probably had to pull some strings to get his boss to be willing to take him on. He was expecting a yes.

Will laid his knife and fork down on the edge of his plate. "That's a nice offer," he said, measuring his response carefully. "But I already have a lead on another job back in DC. It means a lot to me that I could be home these past few days, but I do need to go back. I think . . . I think it'll be easier on everyone."

"What job?" Bonnie demanded. "What job do you have in DC that's more stable than what you can get at the warehouse?"

"I'd be working at a restaurant," Will said carefully.

Chris rolled his eyes.

"But Tristan's got some leads on a music job too. It's all coming together." That was an exaggeration, Will knew. But his mother didn't have to know it too.

"I know you had your heart set on being a music teacher,

Will," Bonnie said as the silence stretched on. "I even asked Maureen down at the school board, but it's just . . . maybe after things settle down a bit more. Give it a year. I bet something will turn up for you."

"I still have the apartment up in DC."

"Your lease can be broken. I'm sure they'll understand," Bonnie countered.

"But if they don't, I'll have to find a subletter or be on the hook for rent."

"You'll probably just have to pay a fine," Chris scoffed. "I suppose we'll be helping you with that too."

Bonnie's eyebrows shot up, but Will responded first. "I don't need to break the lease and I wouldn't need help paying the fine. I have a job. At least one to get me started. And I'm going back by the end of the week."

Bonnie Sterling's cheeks grew pinker and pinker. Then her lips tightened, her shoulders shuddered, and she began to cry.

"I'm trying so hard to support you," she said, her voice rising and falling. "I just . . . excuse me. I need a minute."

And with that, she jolted back from the table and ran out of the kitchen. Somewhere down the hall—the bathroom, maybe?—a door clicked shut.

"Nice going," Chris said.

"Seriously?" Will snapped. "You were the one getting in my face about this. You were the one telling me to take responsibility."

"I wasn't talking about your stupid apartment lease." Chris threw his napkin on the table and stormed out. After their mother, no doubt. Superhero Chris, swooping in to save the day one more time.

That left Becca, slouching in her seat and eating her steamed veggies with gusto. "This is really good!" she said, mouth full.

"You don't have to pretend." Will sighed. He pushed his own plate aside and buried his head in his arms. He could barely hear the scrape of Becca's chair against the floor. *Great, now she's leaving too.* But instead, Will felt his sister's hand on his shoulder. He looked up.

"Do you really want to go back that bad?" Becca asked. "I didn't think you'd want to. Not for a while, anyway."

"I can't just hide out here. Especially not with how people are going after you guys."

She shrugged. "It's not that bad."

Something in her tone pricked Will's ears. "No one at school is bothering you about me, are they?"

Becca sat down next to him. Will tensed, afraid of what she was about to say. "Not everyone," Becca said at last. "Most people say, like, 'Well, I wouldn't do it, but I can understand the temptation.' That kind of thing."

"But some people say worse."

Becca looked away.

"Becca?"

"Mom said not to tell you."

"I'm a big boy. I don't need you guys to keep secrets from me."

Becca seemed to waver for a moment. "Most people don't really care one way or the other, I don't think. It's just that the people who don't like it—they're the loudest."

Will nodded. "I'm sorry."

"It's not your fault."

"I'm still sorry."

Becca sat down again, pulling her chair closer beside him. "I know I probably shouldn't mention Mara," she started. Will's back stiffened. "But look at what's happening to her. Look what almost happened to her *mom*." Will's face was so hot his ears were about to burn off. *Stop talking, Becca. Stop talking, stop talking, stop—* But Becca pressed on. "If you go back, are you sure the same thing isn't going to happen to you?"

"What happened to Mara's mom? I heard something happened when the people from church were over here this morning. Is she okay? Is Mara okay?"

"Someone tried to kidnap Mrs. Gaines," Becca said. "Right outside Mara's parents' house. Apparently, she was able to fight them off, but . . ."

But what if she hadn't? What if it had been Mara?

"I'm sorry," Becca said. "I shouldn't have brought it up." She stood again and cleared the dishes. Will made no move to help her.

Instead, he quietly walked down the hall to Chris's room.

His mother was there, sitting on his cot.

Don't cave. Will felt his resolve weakening anyway. She just looked so sad. Maybe he could stay. Just another week or two. Give her time to adjust.

No.

"Mom," Will said, as gently as he could. "I know things have been hard for you all with me here. I think it'll be better for everyone once I go back to DC. It'll take the heat off you, and I'll . . ."

"I know," Bonnie said, so softly Will had to strain to hear her. Chris, who had been silently stewing on his own twin bed, looked up in surprise. "You aren't a little boy anymore, Will. As hard as it is for me to let you go, you're a man now. You have a right to make your own decisions."

"Thank you," Will said. "I'll be as safe as I can. I just need to . . . take control of my life again." He moved in for a hug. He hated that he had made his mother cry. Again. Was it too much to hope that this was the last time he'd disappoint her?

"Just one thing," Bonnie said into his shoulder. "Just do this one thing. Promise me you won't go to that protest. I have a bad feelin' about it, Will. Just promise me you won't go."

Deirdre Collins Inspires "Time for Peace" Protests across the Nation

After Deirdre Collins's now-viral interview on *The Late Show*, three words have become a rallying cry for the so-called time wreckers: "Time for peace."

Monday, June 5 will mark two weeks since the first leak of the hacked timeline rectification database. As of this writing, official charges have not yet been brought against admitted hackers Conrad Gibbons and Alicia Barnes, leader of anti-time wreck organization One Life, One Time.

When asked about her feelings on the accused, Collins responded, "For the first week, while the data was slowly being leaked, the focus was on who could be doing this and why they would do such a thing. Now that we have the people responsible— I know they haven't officially been charged, but I think the facts speak for themselves," said Collins to audience applause. "It's time we turn our focus on the victims. We have over four million people who have suffered everything from strained relationships and job loss to assault and murder. No matter what any of us may have done the first time around, we are all victims of this hacking scandal, and it's time we reclaim our narrative."

Collins asked time wreckers, supporters, and allies to wear red on Monday to symbolize their love for each other and for their country.* Since the interview aired, grassroots efforts have sprung up across America to plan walkouts, marches, and even protests on June 5 in defense of time wreckers' rights. Click here to find a Time for Peace event in your area.

*EDITOR'S NOTE: This is a correction from the original article, which erroneously stated that red was to symbolize the blood of Ramon Bassave, whose murder was allegedly motivated by the Time Wrecker leak.

Comments:

Lawrence11

This just in: people who demanded freedom from consequences in one lifeline demand it in the next.

WSB443

Deirdre Collins knows something. Mark my words. You better believe that some of these "time wreckers" got some inside information when this started coming to light.

> **ZipZap**
>
> That's what I've been saying this whole time. She knows she's guilty of whatever crime it was. Why else would she be trying so hard to paint herself as the hero of the downtrodden now? So everyone will rush to her defense and claim she's a changed woman when her crime comes out?
>
> > **WSB443**
> >
> > "The hero of the downtrodden." OMG can I steal that? I need a new screen name.
> >
> > > **ZipZap**
> > >
> > > I'd be honored.

Herekittykitty

Perspective check: roughly 4.5 million people feel their privacy was compromised after a data security breach. Meanwhile, 6.6 billion people have been affected in countless ways by the time wreckers' selfish decisions to mess with time in the first place. Gee, I wonder who deserves sympathy from who . . .

Celadona

*Whom

Herekittykitty

Shut. Up.

....

Chapter Eighteen

MARA

"It's not your fault," Mara said for the eleventh time. "It's really not."

"I basically told you to call him," Robyn said. Her phone connection was breaking up. Or maybe she was crying. Mara wasn't sure. "I played Will's message for you and said I thought you should clear things up. I had no idea he would actually put it online. Of all the stupid, nasty, classless, horrible things a person could do. I hate him. I hate Will and I hate myself for ever believing him. I wish I'd never even told you he called."

"Forget it," Mara said. Standing here in Grandmary's kitchen, twisting her hand through the phone cord the same way she had then, brought back shameful memories of Mara's last conversation with Robyn. "Seriously. I chose to call him. I chose to leave a message. I chose this."

"You didn't choose *this*," Robyn said incredulously. "And then when everything else came out . . . I can't stand it. I can't stand it and I'm not even in your shoes. How are you holding up?"

"I'm fine," Mara said. She let go of the phone cord and watched it spring back.

"You are not."

"But I have to be. I have to figure out a way to move forward. Leave this behind me."

"You don't have to figure it out today," Robyn said. "It's okay to just be sad for a while."

"I'm tired of being sad," Mara said. "I'm tired of waiting to see what other people will do to my life."

"Yeah," Robyn said. "Yeah. We all do."

"What does that mean?" Mara asked. "What's going on with you?"

"Nothing," Robyn said quickly. "It's just overwhelming. All of it."

There was more, Mara was sure. But she let it go. For now.

"Have you heard from your parents at all?" Robyn asked tentatively.

"Dad called yesterday. He didn't tell me anything, of course. But I read about it online."

"I'm not going to ask how much."

"Basically everything." Mara peeked around the corner of the kitchen, just to be sure that Grandmary was still asleep in the recliner. She was. Mara lowered her voice anyway. "The police found zip ties and black trash bags hidden in the front bushes," Mara whispered.

"But maybe . . ." Mara could tell Robyn was searching for

another explanation. Any other explanation.

"It was a kidnapping attempt," Mara said. "And there's a reason that man let Mom fight him off. He realized he had the wrong one."

"Mara. You don't know that."

"Mom is five foot two in heels," Mara said. "If someone wanted to kidnap her, I don't think she could have fought them off. Self-defense classes or not."

"I don't know. Your mom's pretty scrappy."

"I was the target," Mara said. She paced forward, as far as the phone cord would allow. Then she spun around and walked back. "It's the only thing that makes any sense."

"But no one knows where you are," Robyn said. "You're safe."

"For now, anyway. Dad asked the police to keep an eye on Grandmary's house too."

"That's good." Robyn was quiet for a minute. "Do you think it'd be okay to have visitors?"

"Probably. Why?"

"I was thinking I might come over . . . Saturday. So you wouldn't be alone."

Saturday. Her would've-been wedding day. Mara felt sick.

"Not that you're alone with Grandmary there," Robyn said hurriedly. "I don't have to. I just thought if you wanted a friend, I'd be there."

"Sure," Mara said. "Please. It'd be good to see you. Thanks."

"Okay," Robyn said, obviously relieved. "I have some stuff for you. Hopefully it'll cheer you up."

"You don't have to do that."

"But I want to. And um—"

She was hesitating too much. "Is something going on? What is it, Robyn?"

"I really hate to ask, but Jessica wanted to come too. Is that okay?"

So that's what Robyn had been holding back. She and Jessica had patched things up, which was good. But Robyn hadn't wanted to talk to Mara about it, which was bad. *Am I so fragile that my own best friend can't share her happiness with me?*

"I really hate to ask. I'm sorry. I know it's kind of . . ."

Mara forced herself to smile, hoping it would make her voice sound upbeat. "Of course she can. So things are going well between you guys, huh?"

"Yeah," Robyn said. "I guess you could say that."

Mara frowned. So maybe it wasn't all happy news. She started pacing forward again, running her hand along the phone cord as she did. "Come on. If something's bothering you or you just want to talk, you can."

"I came out to my family," Robyn said in a rush. "After the last time we talked."

"Robyn." Mara stopped herself short. "I'm so sorry. I shouldn't have said that to you."

"No, it's not your fault. I just started thinking—if now

isn't a good time, if Jessica isn't a good reason, then when will be the time? What will be the reason?"

"How did they react?" Mara asked, even though she was pretty sure she already knew the answer.

"You know. Dad said he'd always be there for me but asked me to promise not to tell my grandparents. Mom cried." For a minute, it sounded like Robyn was going to cry too.

"Robyn," Mara started to say, but her friend cut her off.

"It's fine. I'm fine. I feel stupid even complaining. I'm a lot luckier than most people. They didn't tell me to leave their house or threaten me."

"But it hurt."

Robyn was definitely crying now. Mara wished she could reach through the phone and comfort her friend. "I'm a disappointment to them. I'm not the daughter they thought they had. I know they love me, but . . . my family wishes I was different."

"I know," Mara said. "It hurts. It just hurts."

"I know you know," Robyn said. Mara could picture her wiping her eyes and straightening her shoulders. "So. Back to the reason I called. What time do you want us to come over on Saturday?"

"Oh. Um." Mara thought for a moment. "Ten, I guess." As if it mattered.

"Then that's when we'll come. Hang in there, Mar. You're going to get through this."

Mara tried to mimic her friend's positivity. "Yeah," she said, with a brightness that didn't even fool herself. "We both are."

♦♦♦♦♦

Grandmary was still snoring softly when Mara got off the phone with Robyn. Mara poured a glass of sweet tea from the fridge and gently set it on the coffee table in case her grandmother wanted a drink when she woke up. Then, not knowing what else to do, she took a tentative seat by Grandpap's desk.

It felt wrong somehow to leave her grandmother unattended, but even worse to sit and watch her sleeping. So Mara folded two cranes from paper squares she'd left downstairs. Then a third and a fourth. Grandmary snored on. Mara wiped off the beads of condensation that had collected on the sides of the glass and pooled on the coaster. At this rate, all the ice would melt and dilute the sweet tea before Grandmary woke up.

Mara tried and failed to resist opening her laptop. *I really shouldn't keep checking.* Mara hovered her cursor over the icon for the internet browser anyway. *Why do I let myself read this stuff?*

Mara clicked open an internet browser and started typing into the search bar: MARA GAINES.

DID YOU MEAN MARA GAINES STERLING? asked the search

engine.

It felt like a punch in the gut. Of course it would pop up that way. That was how she was listed on the database, after all.

Only three days from now, I would've been Mara Gaines Sterling. Mara blew out a breath and searched for "time wrecker" instead.

On the recliner, Grandmary stirred and then sat up, slowly.

"How are you feeling?" Mara asked, twirling around in Grandpap's chair as if she could hide the laptop screen from view. It didn't matter, really. Grandmary probably couldn't see this far without her reading glasses.

"Goodness," Grandmary said. "I didn't mean to fall asleep."

"It's fine," Mara assured her.

"What time is it?"

Mara glanced back at her laptop. "Just past three o'clock."

"In the afternoon?" Grandmary asked, unnecessarily. She used the handle on Grandpap's recliner to push herself upright and carefully stood. "How are you holding up?"

Mara shrugged. "I've been better."

"I would imagine so." Grandmary seemed to be studying her face, searching for something. "Have your parents been in touch with you again?"

"Not today. Robyn called, though. I hope it's okay if she and Jessica come over Saturday." Mara glanced at her grandmother.

"Of course it is."

"Thanks." Mara offered her the tea. Grandmary sipped it and smiled before resting it on the end table.

"I know about what happened to Mom," Mara said tentatively. How much did Grandmary know? She didn't want to be the bearer of bad news.

Grandmary nodded. "I think it's good that you know. I don't like to worry you about what's on the news, but at the same time, you have a right to know what's going on."

So her grandmother did know—and she had been trying to protect Mara as much as Mara had been trying to protect Grandmary. "Yeah," Mara said softly. "I read about it online." She swiveled around again and clicked over to her open browser. The news story about the protest rally was already open. "There's going to be a protest in DC next week," Mara said. "Some of the other time wreckers are organizing."

Grandmary's perfectly arched eyebrows shot straight up. "I hope you're not thinking of going yourself."

"Maybe I should," Mara said. "I can't just wait until all these monsters decide they're tired of hating me. We need to stand up for ourselves."

"There are safer ways to stand up for yourself," Grandmary said.

Mara hated to argue with her grandmother, but something in her wouldn't give up the idea. "I can't stay in hiding forever," she said. "It's not fair. We're the cause of all this. Why should I sit here safe and sound when other people are being hurt and . . . harassed and . . . and killed."

"Who's the cause of all this?" Grandmary asked, and now she seemed all the way awake. Her eyes were bright again, and she held her chin up. Ready to ask the hard questions.

"I am," Mara burst out. "If I hadn't had a time wreck in that other life map, Dad wouldn't have put up that bill. If I hadn't been on the list, no one could have used me to threaten Dad. If it wasn't for me—"

"Stop right there," Grandmary commanded. "I won't have you blaming yourself for this. Not one bit."

"It's just—"

"And I won't have you putting yourself in danger, either. Letting people attack you won't stop them from hurting anyone else."

"I feel so guilty," Mara whispered. "I want to make it all stop."

"No news story lasts forever," Grandmary said. "But Mara, please be thoughtful. Your mother was attacked. This Bassave man was shot and killed. I won't tell you what to do, but please, don't take your own safety for granted."

OPINION: Women Aren't to Blame for Time Wrecking. So Why Are We Blaming Them?

By Tameka Nixon

So last week, a pair of anonymous hacktivists (now revealed to be <u>Conrad Gibbons</u> and <u>Alicia Barnes</u>) leaked a database of private information in an effort to threaten and manipulate members of the United States government.

I just wanted to make sure we were all on the same page here, because when I went to look up the latest developments in the story, all I could find were headlines about Deirdre Collins's net worth and clickbait articles with the details on Mara Gaines's canceled wedding. (Did you know she was planning to tie each guest's table number to a miniature bottle of rosé?)

I wish I was joking.

Why the intense media focus on these two women? Mara Gaines, listed in the data leak as Mara Gaines Sterling, is the daughter of Congressman Joel Gaines, cosponsor of the anti-time wrecking bill and <u>political rival of hacktivist Conrad Gibbons</u>. Within a day of discovering her own name on the leaked list, Mara's face was all over the news. We mercilessly dug up every detail of her life, speculated on her breakup with her fiancé, and debated what she must have done wrong—in her first life map, in her relationship, in seeking a time wreck at all.

Talk show host Deirdre Collins also fell under intense scrutiny after she was identified in the leaked database. Yes, she's a public figure. Yes, she's chosen to speak out on the timeline rectification issue. But does that give us the right to refuse her any shred of a private life?

Making these two women the center of the data leak scandal is distracting us from the real issues at work here. There is something really frightening about the way we turn to social shame instead of community action. We cannot change politics by harassing a congressman's daughter. We cannot control public opinion by threatening celebrities who dare to discuss the issues. We owe it to ourselves to do better.

What the hackers did in releasing this information was illegal, full stop. We should be having discussions on cybersecurity and creating privacy laws and bringing the hackers to justice. We're missing our chance. We're so busy putting someone else's life under a microscope because we want to avoid what introspection would tell us about ourselves. What does it mean to have personal data that is accessible to the government, but not to us? Why are we comfortable with a fundamentally flawed criminal justice system, and how much are we willing to change it?

Perhaps most relevant of all: Why are we so quick to use social shame instead of legal recourse?

Food for thought.

....

Chapter Nineteen

WILL

"You're leaving this morning?"

Will didn't even stop packing to answer Chris. "Yep. If I leave in the next hour, I shouldn't run into too much traffic when I get up near DC."

Chris made no move to help while Will leaned on the top of the suitcase and forced the zipper closed. "I think you're making a huge mistake."

"I know you do." Will hoisted the suitcase off the bed and straightened up. "But I need to get back."

"Right, for your super-important job busing tables. Who cares what Mom or any of the rest of us think," Chris grumbled as Bonnie and Becca came into the room.

"Chris," Bonnie said, putting a hand on his shoulder. "That's enough." She turned to Will. "You'll let us know if you need anything."

Will bent down and kissed his mother on the cheek. "Don't worry about me." As if he could stop her.

They all trailed him out to the car. "Is your cell phone

charged? Do you have enough gas?"

"I'll be fine, Mom. I probably won't have to stop until I get close to Richmond," Will said. "I'll call you when I get there. Thanks for letting me stay here a bit." He made eye contact with each of them, staring hard at Chris until he looked up and met his eye. "I appreciate it. I really do."

"You don't need to thank us for acting like family," his mother said. "You always have a home here."

"I know, Mom," Will said. "And it won't be that long before I'm back. Becca's graduating from high school at the end of the month." He smiled.

Becca pointed a finger at him, pretending to scold. "You better be back for that!"

"I wouldn't miss it for the world," Will said, and meant it.

Will had to hug them all twice before he could get in the car. Even Chris, who kept his back stiff the first time, gave in to a big, back-clapping bear hug on the second round. They waved until he got to the turn at the end of the road, when he waved back before he had to put both hands on the wheel as his tires spun on the gravel. Then they were gone, and his eyes stayed on the road ahead.

♦♦♦♦♦

Will had been on the road for hours, not counting one stop for a bathroom break and a soda and sandwich from the gas station. Now that he was working his way through central Virginia, it took effort not to let the long stretch of road and rolling green hills make him sleepy. Only a few hours left until he got to DC. Will cranked up the air-conditioning and pushed the SEEK button on the radio. It wouldn't be long now.

He was just coming into range for some of his favorite stations. The classic rock station still dipped in and out, but a talk radio was coming through loud and clear. He used to listen to this in the late afternoon when he was studying. It was funny how most of his friends in college had wanted to listen to music while they studied. For Will, who had spent at least an hour a day practicing in the rehearsal rooms, talk radio was less distracting background noise.

The afternoon host wasn't on yet—Dex and Lila's morning show was just wrapping up. Dex was laughing about some kind of incident at a zoo. No one injured, just material for some cheap jokes. Will settled back and turned his attention to accelerating through the upcoming hill.

Something on the radio caught his attention. "And now it's time for the news at eleven," Lila said. "Alicia Barnes, president of the anti-timeline rectification advocacy group One Life, One Time, has confessed to her involvement in the data leak."

Well, of course she did. Will gripped the steering wheel tighter.

The audio clip of a woman's reedy voice came on too loud at first, until someone—Dex, presumably—turned it down.

"Effective immediately, I am stepping aside from my role as president of One Life, One Time in order for the organization's mission to continue without unnecessary distraction. I deeply regret the private conversation I had with Conrad Gibbons and the resulting actions, which have now affected the lives and security of over four million Americans."

How's that for a non-apology. Will almost laughed, until he heard what Dex said next.

"According to Ms. Barnes, Conrad Gibbons initially approached her to ask whether the organization had been donating to Congressman Joel Gaines's reelection campaign, which she confirmed. Later, Gibbons approached her again and asked whether she—that is, the organization—would reconsider their financial support of Congressman Gaines if they had evidence that he or a member of his family had been involved in a time wreck," Dex continued.

Lila gave a long, low whistle. "Wow."

"Right. Now, Ms. Barnes says in her statement that during that private conversation, she was shocked and said—direct quote—'that would change everything.' And according to her, later that day—"

"I thought it was the next day," Lila interrupted.

"Yes, the next day, Ms. Barnes says that she did seek out Gibbons and told him that even if something like that were true, she would have to *consider* whether it impacted their support of the congressman."

"And Alicia Barnes did know that Gibbons was planning to challenge the congressman at the November election." Lila's tone made it obvious what she thought about that.

"I would assume—I mean, Gibbons had already started his campaign," Dex said. "But regardless, according to Barnes, between the time of their first conversation and their second conversation, Gibbons had already coordinated the database hack. So regardless of whether she encouraged him to do it or whether she was part of the actual hacking of the database, she did know that Gibbons was involved."

"And she's just been sitting on that," Lila said. "So I'm thinking she's going to be charged with obstruction of justice for sure. I don't know if there would be maybe a charge for refusing to cooperate in an investigation. Anything else?"

"If you ask me, I think that Alicia Barnes should be brought up on charges as a co-conspirator. I'm not buying this idea that she went back later and, oops, it was too late to do anything. I believe she wanted that leak to happen, and it wasn't until it exploded in the media that she changed her tune."

Sounds about right. Will pushed the power button on the radio and enjoyed the sudden flood of silence that overtook his car.

♦♦♦♦♦

Will had to remind himself to breathe deeply as he approached the Beltway. He couldn't afford to hyperventilate and pass out while he was driving. By the time he was properly in the DC city limits, Will considered pulling over to get a hold of himself.

If I'm this scared, imagine how Mara must feel.

Will squared his shoulders and navigated through the maze of city streets to the apartment building.

To his surprise—or maybe not—there was nothing different about the building at all. What did he expect? Was the whole parking lot supposed to be taped off? Did he think there was going to be a giant sign that said CAUTION: A TIME WRECKER LIVES HERE? Will got out of the car and opened the trunk without drawing so much as a passing glance from a middle-aged woman across the lot.

My name and birthday and social security number have been all over the internet for days now. But no one was waiting to ambush him. No one was desperate to get his picture. He could blend right back in here.

The only thing that was newsworthy about Will had been his connection to Mara. How long would it be until she could blend in again?

The apartment was exactly as Will had left it. It was dark. Refreshingly cold. The vertical blinds clicked and swayed under the air-conditioning vent. Will locked the door behind him and deposited his suitcase on the floor of the living room.

Everything about this room reminded Will of his last moments with Mara. If only he was offered a time wreck now, he would relive that day in a heartbeat. They would keep their phones off and go back to the bedroom to finish what they started, and when they came out that afternoon— or that evening, hell, maybe even the next day—he and Mara would face the world together.

Already that life, that fantasy, felt millions of years away. Could he really imagine going back to the way things were? Will was a different person now than he had been the last time he walked through this door. He felt it as he walked farther into the apartment, flicking on lights, checking the fridge to see if the milk had spoiled (it had) and the bathroom to see if the landlord had fixed that leaky faucet (he hadn't).

No. I can't just move back into my old life. Will was shocked at first by the thought, but it was the truth. Everything felt different because everything *was* different. Maybe this was what people meant by acceptance.

Maybe this was moving on.

♦♦♦♦♦

The last time Will had met up with Tristan, this bar had been crawling with college kids. After finals, the seniors would come here to drown their sorrows or celebrate their success—there was rarely any in-between. Usually, Will and

Tristan downed one beer each before heading back to the pool tables.

But not tonight. Tonight, Will was already two beers in when Tristan showed up. It had taken hours to fall asleep last night and, consequently, Will had slept through his alarm this morning. When he'd awakened at last, there was just enough time to shower and change into a white polo and khaki shorts. Then he'd headed into the restaurant for an orientation tour and to sign a one-page contract. "Any chance you can pick up a shift tomorrow?" Dave had asked. "We can call that your first training day."

"Sure," Will had said, remembering to smile and thank his new boss. He was going to have to do something on his would-be wedding day. Might as well make it useful.

He'd gone straight from the restaurant to the bar to meet Tristan. Will recognized a few of the bartenders, but no one called him by name. Good. Will made it his job to concentrate on his beer until Tristan showed up beside him.

"You okay there?" Tristan asked, by way of greeting.

"I'll be better after tomorrow," Will said. "I'm going to get another beer."

Tristan raised an eyebrow and signaled Louis behind the bar.

"Is working at the restaurant that bad?" Tristan asked.

"Just a crappy day," Will said. "Not the job. Just everything else."

"Right."

Louis passed their two beers across the bar top. Tristan slid one over to Will, along with a bowl of cashews. "How about you eat something too?" Tristan said. Will rolled his eyes and tossed a handful of cashews into his mouth.

"Got any other job leads?" Tristan asked.

"Nada." Will said. "Unless your church is still looking for an organist."

"Music director," Tristan said. "And yes, the pastor asked again if you were going to apply."

"Does he know who I am?" Will asked. "Tell him to do a background check." He frowned. "Wait. It wouldn't be on a background check, right? Tell him to Google my name and see if they still want me."

"They already know all that," Tristan said, frowning slightly. "I told them. They're not going to kick you out for being a time wrecker. I wouldn't go to a church like that."

Will shrugged. "I guess."

"Will," Tristan said. "I wouldn't. I know how people have treated you over this. I wouldn't send you from the pot into the fire."

"I know you wouldn't," Will said. "My thing is . . ." Tristan was staring at him now. He really didn't get it, did he? Might as well come out with the truth. "It's one thing for someone like me to decide to go into a church and sit in the back pew or something. But would they really want me up in the front? Playing the piano? Singing songs that . . ."

That I don't even know I believe.

"I feel like I know what you're saying," Tristan said.

Doubtful.

"I'm going into seminary," Tristan said. "I feel called to be a pastor and I don't even know why. Why me, you know? Why me? I'm not good at public speaking. My family's not really that religious. I wasn't raised with it the way some people are. I feel like I just stumbled into this thing, and now it's my life. I mean I love it, but I don't know how I got here. I don't really know what I'm doing."

"But you feel like you can do it," Will said. "Even if you don't feel like you're qualified yet, you know what you want to do. I don't feel . . . I don't know what I feel."

Desperate. I feel desperate.

Will leaned against the sticky bar top. "You're going to be a great pastor," he told Tristan. "You really are."

"Thanks," Tristan said. "And you're going to find your place. Whether this job works out or something else, or whatever—there's a place for you out there. You don't have to handle all of this alone."

Will stared down at his mug. It was almost midnight. Almost June third.

I don't have to do this alone. But I wish I didn't have to do it without Mara.

We've Changed the Past.
Now Let's Change the Future.

By Reggie Lang, LCPC

Much has been made in recent days about timeline rectification as an agent of healing. It does not escape my attention that the majority of those in the leaked list are young (median age of 32) or that many (although an imperfect measure, I noted roughly 40 percent of those listed share both a last name and rectification date) seem to be linked through family relationships. Married couples, siblings, cousins—regardless of who may have been the criminal and who the victim, we have been presented with a fascinating study of family relationships in turmoil, and how far we will go to protect the ones we love.

In my practice as a family therapist, I've worked with hundreds of such families in crisis. Unsurprisingly, when families first come to my office, they are often focused on returning to "the way things used to be." It takes a great deal of time and effort before all parties shift their priority to healing and moving forward instead of looking to the past.

A key element of the healing process comes in the form of acceptance. We do not accept that the problematic behavior was okay, but we accept that it happened. The wrongdoer accepts that he or she behaved badly and understands that there will be long-term consequences: a lack of trust, perhaps, or future difficulties finding employment. Meanwhile, the wronged party or parties accept that their loved one was capable of harming them and that the relationship they envisioned is no longer possible.

All this healing and acceptance are based on two things: recognizing the problematic behavior for what it was and leaving it in the past. Both factors are necessary for true healing. Simply choosing to "leave the past in the past" without recognizing the harm caused by the transgressor isn't a solution. In reality, refusing to acknowledge the problem simply kicks the can farther down the road, allowing the transgressor to believe he or she was not in the wrong and refusing an appropriate outlet for the wronged party to express their pain. Recognizing the wrongdoing without acknowledging the need to move forward is harmful also. A troubled youth is capable of growth and change, but it will not happen if he or she is constantly shamed for past transgressions. Nor will it help the victims to keep reliving the incident in perpetuity.

In my estimation, timeline rectification is harmful because it undercuts these two basic components of healing. By removing all evidence and memory of the crime itself, we remove these opportunities for those on both sides to learn about each other and about themselves.

I understand that there is a rehabilitation component prior to timeline rectifications, which is designed to ensure that the behavior will not be repeated in the new life map. Perhaps that is true, perhaps not. I am not in a position to determine how effective timeline rectifications are. I could make an educated guess based on the leaked data, but we are not privy to all the data the government has collected on these rectifications.

Nor am I in a position to determine whether timeline rectifications should be legal. I am respected within my field, but I am neither an expert in criminal justice nor a lawmaker.

What I *am* qualified to say is this: we are doing more harm than good by focusing solely on the issue of timeline rectification. Healing, even in perfect circumstances, takes time. Healing from a painful and traumatic discovery, with little hope for answers or chance for redemption, takes even more time. But even these situations are not hopeless. Healing is always possible. Regardless of whether we can change the past, we can always change the future.

I leave you with the same admonition I give the youth in my counseling sessions: "Take responsibility for who you were yesterday. Challenge who you are today. Plan boldly for who you will be tomorrow."

....

Chapter Twenty

MARA

Mara knew what day it was before she opened her eyes on Saturday morning. How could she forget? She knew, too, that the sun was already streaming brightly past the curtains and that there was enough of a breeze to move Grandmary's garden flags and wind chimes.

It was the perfect day for a wedding.

Mara pulled the quilt over her head and squeezed her swollen eyes shut. It had been a long night, and it promised to be an even longer day.

I wish I could just wake up in a new year. Or a new life. Mara burrowed deeper under the covers, ignoring, for now, the stifling heat.

"Mara." Grandmary knocked twice and repeated her name. "Mara. You have company."

I don't want to see them. I don't want to see anyone.

"Take your time. Come down when you're ready."

Mara's eyelids burned again. How much could one person cry?

"Mara?" Grandmary sounded worried. "Are you there?"

And now I've gone and upset my grandmother. As if she hasn't been through enough this week. Mara pulled herself out from under the blankets before she could think about it. "I'll be right down, Grandmary," she said. Her voice sounded like someone else's.

There was no point in taking a shower. Mara pulled her hair back into a sloppy bun and threw on running shorts and a T-shirt. At the last minute, she remembered to put on deodorant. It was only polite.

I'll stay and talk for an hour, tops. Nobody wants to sit and listen to me be miserable any longer than that, anyway. Mara sucked in her breath, exhaled, and walked quickly down the hall.

From the top of the staircase, Mara could see all the way down to Robyn sitting on the navy blue settee in Grandmary's formal living room. When was the last time anyone had sat in there? Normally everyone walked straight back to the kitchen or the den.

Then Mara saw why, and her heart dropped. An enormous brown shipping box was sitting right at her feet. It looked too much like the wedding gifts she'd had to pack up and mail with her mother last week.

"Surprise!" Robyn called out. Mara made her way down the stairs, so slowly that Robyn climbed up and met her halfway. Robyn linked her arm through Mara's and walked her down the rest of the way. "I'm so glad you're up. You're never going to believe this."

Wasn't Jessica going to come too? Mara didn't ask. She allowed herself to be led down to the sitting room and plopped into the wing chair by the window. Grandmary was already moving the box over, alternately pushing it and nudging it forward with her foot.

"Let me help you with that, Mrs. Gaines," Robyn said.

"I told you to call me Mary," Grandmary said, chiding her gently. "And it's not heavy at all, just cumbersome."

"What's this about?" Mara asked. "You didn't have to do anything!"

"Of course we did. Come on. Open it up!" Robyn said.

Who was *we?* Robyn and the absent Jessica, Mara guessed. Grandmary looked as surprised as Mara felt. Her grandmother had settled in the wing chair opposite, perched just on the edge like a curious bird about to take flight.

The top of the box had been held closed by overlapping all four flaps. Mara pried them open to find at least twenty manilla envelopes. More than that—there had to be thirty or even forty.

"Just what you always wanted. An envelope collection," Robyn joked.

For a moment, Mara felt more curiosity than dread. The first envelope was fat but light when Mara picked it up. She loosened the brad at the top and caught a little glimpse of gold paper. "Are these . . . ?"

Robyn sat cross-legged on the floor and grinned. "Remember what I told you? When nobody could reach you on your cell last week, they called me to ask how you were doing."

"Who's they?" Mara asked. *Besides Will.*

"Everyone," Robyn said. "All the people from college who were invited to the wedding, your high school friends I met at your bridal shower. My phone's been ringing like crazy. But everyone who called me wanted to do something for you, and they kept asking me what you needed. So I told people you were trying to make a thousand and one paper cranes, you know, for good luck, and suggested that maybe everyone could pitch in and make a few."

"That's a lot more than a few cranes," Mara said, fighting the tears that stung the back of her eyes.

"It's a heck of a lot more than a few cranes. I told everyone to mail their cranes to me so I could pass them on to you, and honestly I think all the packages drove my mail carrier into early retirement."

"I had no idea." Mara shook the contents loose from the envelope. Ten white paper cranes tumbled into her lap, along with a note on plain notebook paper.

Sorry my folding isn't very good, but I hope these make you smile anyway. I'm here for you whenever you're able to get in touch, okay? Thinking of you!!!

"Is that from Lauren?" Robyn asked. "She called me like eight times last week when she couldn't get a hold of you."

"It is," Mara said. "I can't believe this."

"You haven't seen anything yet!" Robyn fished through the box and handed Mara another large, padded yellow envelope.

Mara's first college roommate had mailed thirty cranes in rainbow colors. Her lab partner from last semester sent twenty-five, all in white. Mara tore open one package after another while Grandmary kept up the tally. Robyn smoothed out the notes and read each one out loud.

I got my mom and sister to help, so there should be seventy-five in here. They're sorry too, about everything. Keep your chin up! Hope this helps get you to a thousand.

Here's my contribution. Just think, only 975 left to go! You're in my prayers through all of this. We're all rooting for you.

Thank goodness for YouTube tutorials, or my stupid ass would still be trying to figure out how to fold these birds!!!! Hehe just kidding—hope I made you laugh at least.

"Oops. Sorry about the language in some of these," Robyn said to Grandmary.

"Goodness, I'm not that easily offended," Mara's grandmother said. "Hand the notes to me when you're done reading them if you don't mind. I think I have a photo album we could use to keep them all together."

Mara slid down from the chair and sat down cross-legged on the floor. She wasn't even halfway through the box, and already she was surrounded by origami cranes in every color. It was beautiful. No, not just beautiful. Magic.

"You must be up to a thousand and one already," Robyn said. "Plus the ones you'd already folded."

"We have four hundred and seventy-one so far," Mara announced.

Grandmary and Robyn both turned to stare at her.

"It's creepy how you can do that in your head," Robyn said.

"Not creepy," Mara said. "It's just math." She scooped up a handful of the cranes and let them flutter through her fingers. "I can't believe you did this for me. Thank you."

"Everyone wanted to help," Robyn said. "Not a lot we can do in person or online, really, but we all love you, Mara. You're not alone in any of this."

"Why don't I go look for that photo album," Grandmary said. "I think it's actually up in your room, Mara."

"Okay," Mara said. "Thanks."

By unspoken agreement, Mara and Robyn stopped opening the envelopes as Grandmary walked upstairs. *She needs this too*, Mara thought. Her grandmother still didn't seem quite herself. After the news had blown up with Conrad Gibbons and her father's campaign, Mara had noticed Grandmary's face was always a bit pinched and her shoulders drawn tight. This morning, at least, Robyn had brought a little respite to both of them.

"So how are you holding up?" Robyn asked. "Really."

"I'm fine! Better than fine. This is amazing," Mara said, but Robyn waved her aside.

"I didn't mean about any of this. I meant—have you heard anything else from . . . anyone?"

"Like Will? No."

"Good. I'm glad he hasn't bothered you anymore. Hopefully he'll realize someday—" Robyn cut herself off abruptly. "Sorry. Not helpful. But whenever you're ready to talk crap about him, I'll be there."

Mara started to open another envelope and put it down. "I don't know. I can't make myself hate him. I mean I do, but then I can't hang on to it. I just feel so sad."

"Yeah," Robyn said. "Yeah. I know."

Mara got back to work on the envelope in her hands. "My parents canceled their dinner for today," she said, keeping her voice flat. Matter-of-fact.

"Well, I sure hope so." Robyn snorted. "I know you're worried about them after what happened to your mom. Anyone would be. But that was low, what they did."

"It was," Mara agreed. "I haven't talked to them lately, either."

"It'll take time to get through this one," Robyn said. "Not saying things will ever be the same again. Or that they should be."

Mara slid her eyes over to her friend. "How are things

with your parents? And Jessica? If you don't mind me asking."

"Oh! Right, I was supposed to tell you when I came in. Jess sends her love and hugs and packed up some cranes for you—I think they're in the little envelope over there," Robyn said. "She decided not to come today because she wasn't sure how you'd feel. She didn't want to intrude, if you haven't really been seeing people."

"Oh my gosh, tell Jess she shouldn't have worried about that," Mara said, squashing the secret part of her that was relieved. Jessica was a friend, but not a close enough friend to cry in front of. "I'm glad things are better between you guys."

"Well." Robyn shrugged.

"Things are better now, right? Now that your parents know?"

"I guess."

Mara shook the cranes off her lap and looked directly at her friend. "You guess? What do you mean?"

"I guess . . ." Robyn's voice broke. She pinched her lips tight for a few seconds before trying to speak again. "I had built it all up in my head, like once I was out to everybody, even my family, it'd be done. No more secrets. No more hiding. No more wondering how people would react if they knew. But it's not."

"Wait, so everyone in your family knows now? I thought you just came out to your parents."

"Oh, no, the whole family knows. My grandma, aunts, uncles, all twenty-three of my cousins . . . no one in my family can keep their mouths shut about anything. Except me, apparently." Robyn let out a small, humorless laugh.

"What happened then? Was your grandma really upset?" Mara leaned forward, ready to offer a hug, but Robyn was staring down at the floor.

"She took it better than Dad, honestly. But she never really liked me, so I'm not sure I had far to fall."

"Geez, Robyn. That's awful."

"No, what's awful is—" Robyn shook her head and looked up. They could hear Grandmary's footsteps coming toward the stairs. Robyn smiled with forced brightness and changed the subject. "So how many cranes are we up to?"

✦✦✦✦✦

"Nine hundred and eighty-five," Mara said, setting the last crane down on Grandmary's kitchen table. Grandmary was leafing through the photo album, stopping to reread some of the notes.

It was late afternoon now. Robyn had left hours ago with the beginnings of a headache. "Take care of yourself," Mara had said. "Call me if you need anything. Anything at all."

Robyn had smiled and nodded, but Mara wasn't sure she would. Her heart ached for her friend.

"It was nice of Robyn to think of doing this," Mara said

aloud. "I had no idea."

"That's incredible," Grandmary said. "You have a great many friends, Mara. This is a testament to how many people love you."

"I'm lucky," Mara said, and surprised herself by meaning it.

Grandmary smiled. "What are you going to do with the cranes?"

"I'd always planned to string them and hang them up somehow. I hadn't thought much about it. I thought I had weeks and weeks until I'd be at this point."

If she and Will had gotten married their way—if Mara hadn't let her mother take over the planning—she would have finished a thousand and one cranes months ago. They would have hung the delicate strands on a makeshift altar. In a park somewhere, maybe, or a bed and breakfast. If Will and Mara had planned it, the ceremony would have been simple but beautiful. Mara could picture the paper birds fluttering behind them as she and Will said their vows.

She looked at the clock. Six thirty. If they'd had their wedding her parents' way, they could have been saying their vows in the country club right now.

If only Mom hadn't taken over. Even in her own head, Mara corrected herself. *If only I hadn't let Mom take over.*

Grandmary was kind enough to break the silence. "Why don't we go ahead and string them now," she said. "I'm sure I have needles and thread around here somewhere."

"You sew, Grandmary?" Mara swallowed hard and tried with everything in her to lighten the mood.

"Not since that play you had in elementary school. Remember that? You were a little fairy, and I made you a tutu. After I sewed all that tulle onto an elastic waistband for you, I swore I'd never stitch another thing, and I haven't." Grandmary laughed.

"I remember that. I loved that costume."

"Then it was well worth the sacrifice. Let me go see if I can find something for your birds."

Mara took advantage of the time her grandmother was out of the room to let a few hot tears roll down her cheeks. Then she blew her nose and pinched her lips together tight. Too many people had worked too hard for Mara to indulge in self-pity now. She squared her shoulders and sat up before Grandmary returned, holding a paper packet of sewing needles and a spool of white thread.

"This ought to do the trick," Grandmary said, seating herself at the table. "What are we doing? Fifty strings of twenty? A hundred strings of ten?"

"Let's start with twenty and see how that looks." Mara measured off enough thread to reach from her wrist to her elbow and cut it. It was nice to have something to do with her hands. "And I still have to fold the last sixteen cranes."

"One thing at a time," Grandmary said, piercing a set of yellow and red cranes on her needle and pushing them, one by one, down the string. "I love this paper. Do you remember who mailed these to you?"

"I think those are from Kiera," Mara said. "I don't know her that well, really. She was in my study group for psychology junior year." She picked up one of the cheerful cranes and added it to her string. "It was nice of her to do this for me."

"It seems a lot of people have been thinking of you," Grandmary said. "I'm glad to see it. You're very loved."

But not by Will, Mara wanted to say. *Not by the person I love the most.*

There was a thought. If only breaking someone's heart was a crime. Then she and Will could have another time wreck and take back every awful thing they'd done. She and Will could start over.

Tears were building behind her eyes again. Mara wiped her nose with the back of her wrist and kept working.

Thankfully, Grandmary changed the subject. "Have you decided what you'll do about school?"

"Not yet," Mara said. "I might defer to another semester, or I might just drop out. I feel like, if my own life's this much of a mess, I have no business being a doctor. I don't want to be involved in someone else's life-or-death situations."

"I'm sure you won't be handling anything dire in your first semester," Grandmary said. "Your confidence has taken a hit, I'm sure, but perhaps getting started with something new will help you rebuild."

Mara strung three more cranes. "I guess so."

"Is it an issue of funding?" Grandmary asked gently.

Mara flinched. "Partly. I didn't want to drag you into it."

"I put the pieces together," Grandmary said. "I know my son and I know he can be hard on you. He's very much like his father."

Mara's ears burned. There was nothing she could say to that. Not to Grandmary.

"He'll come around," her grandmother continued. "Right now, we're all in shock, and people tend to say things they don't mean. Give him some time. Your father won't go back on his promises to you."

I don't want my parents' help anymore. I'd rather pay back loans until I retire than go through this with them again. Mara kept her eyes focused on her string of cranes, terrified that Grandmary would guess her thoughts.

"I haven't even left the house yet," Mara said instead. "It feels strange to plan for my future while I'm still basically hiding."

"Well, that will probably change before long," Grandmary said. "Start small. Take a trip out with Robyn, maybe. It seems like she could use a friend too."

"Yeah." Mara slid an eye over at her grandmother. "I guess you put those pieces together too."

"Only that she was having some difficulties with her family." Grandmary lifted her finished string of cranes and laid them gently over the back of a chair. "I wasn't trying to listen in."

"Robyn's parents . . ." Mara trailed off for a minute, searching for the right words. "They're a lot like mine."

Grandmary frowned. "How so?"

"I mean." Mara hesitated. How could she put this? "They're disappointed in her."

"I'm sure that's not true," Grandmary said.

"Not that they should be. It's tough."

"Well, I know a thing or two about weathering a parent's disappointment," Grandmary said kindly. "It's part of growing up. Learning to do what's best for you even when it deviates from your parents' plan."

"I wish I'd figured that out earlier," Mara said. "Years ago. I didn't think about it at the time, but looking back, I took advantage of Will. I was always trying to smooth things over with Mom and the wedding, and I was trying to manage how things would play out in the news, but I wasn't trying to reassure Will. I just kind of expected him to always be there, always understand." The tears escaped at last. They rolled hot and fast down her cheeks before she could wipe them away. "I should have been a partner to him."

Grandmary put down her needle and put a hand over Mara's. "And that," Grandmary said, "is part of marriage. Every couple learns those lessons, though not nearly as drastically as you've had to. I'm sure that in time he'll understand that you didn't mean to take advantage. Maybe not right now, but eventually. Will is young too."

Eventually is too late. I'll never get another chance with him.

•••••

The day was almost over. Each excruciating hour seemed to drag on even longer, mocking Mara with should've-beens. She and Will would be at a hotel now. They hadn't planned a big honeymoon right away; it was more important to save the money. But they would have spent their wedding night in a nice hotel room, at least.

Mara would give anything to be there now. But here she was, sitting in her grandmother's den on her would've-been wedding night. She looked up at the strings of cranes floating over the mantle and tried to feel happy.

I just have to fold five more cranes. Mara held a white square of origami paper in her hands and tried to convince her fingers to fold the model. *Just five more.*

And then what? She was stupid to think she could fix a broken heart this easily.

"I've been thinking about something Robyn said to you when she was here." Grandmary sat in Grandpap's recliner, dwarfed by the giant chair. Her feet barely reached the floor. "So many people have tried to reach out and couldn't get a hold of you. I know how important it is to protect yourself at a time like this, but you should be able to have a support system too."

"I do," Mara said, looking up at the strings of cranes that hung over the mantle. "I really do."

Grandmary pulled a small blue cell phone out of her pocket and leaned forward to lay it on the coffee table. "I'd like you to have this. I don't use it, and there's no sense paying for it every month if it's just going to sit in my drawer. It doesn't do email or the internet or anything like that, but it could be a lifeline. And when you are ready to go out into the world again, it can keep you safe."

"Do you think I should?" Mara asked, doubtfully, before catching herself. "I mean, thank you."

"You're welcome," Grandmary said. "Think of this as a first step. I wouldn't go parading down Main Street just yet, but it would do you good to have some more connections with the outside world."

"I guess so," Mara said. "I'll have to leave the house someday."

"And when the time is right, you'll know," Grandmary said. "All I ask is that you make sure your parents have the number."

Mara froze.

"They're going through a tough time now too," her grandmother said. "They might not show it in the best way, but I know your parents are under a lot of strain. They just want to do right by you, Mara."

"I know." Mara avoided Grandmary's eyes. "Thanks."

Mara turned the phone over and over in her hand, long after Grandmary had left the room. The weight of it was comforting. It felt like freedom.

What was she going to do with it?

The safe choice would be to keep it tucked close by her side. Always charged. Always ready to call the police at the first sign of trouble.

The braver choice would be to use it to speak up. Not just for herself, but for every time wrecker who would never be able to find a safe place again.

Mom told me I had to control the story. What if I decide to write my own?

Mara tapped a familiar number into the phone and laboriously pressed each button to send a text.

Mara: Its M

Mara: new #

Mara: u doing nething mon?

Robyn: Besides work? Lol

Robyn: I can be free if you need me.

Mara took her time pressing each key to spell out the next message.

Mara: Want to go to a protest with me?

It was only ten seconds before Robyn texted back.

Robyn: I'm in.

Congressman Gaines Now Running Unopposed for November Reelection

June 3, 2006

ALEXANDRIA, VA — Only days after political challenger Conrad Gibbons was called in for questioning for his alleged role in the data leak scandal, he officially suspended his bid for the 8th District's congressional seat. The incumbent, Congressman Joel Gaines, now runs unopposed.

The news doubtless comes as a relief to the embattled congressman. HR 6437, the bill he sponsored that would have dramatically increased restrictions on timeline rectifications, was defeated in the House this week. Allegedly, HR 6437 was the catalyst for Gibbons's hacking and subsequent leaks from the timeline rectification database.

Alicia Barnes, founder of One Life, One Time, has also admitted knowledge of the hack and faces charges of obstruction of justice. She has resigned from her position with the organization. No official charges have been brought against Gibbons or Barnes at this time.

Congressman Gaines did not directly reference the data leak or the defeated bill in his most recent statement to the press. Acknowledging that he will now run unopposed in November, Gaines said, "It's an honor for me to serve the people of Virginia's Eighth District. As we move forward, I remain committed to strengthening the ties within our local community and in our great nation."

Chapter Twenty-One

WILL

Tristan's church was so different from the community church back in Deer Hill. It had a building, for starters—something that was always intended to be a church instead of a made-over elementary school. Will looked up at the saints immortalized in stained-glass windows and thought twice about going in.

I don't belong here. Whether anyone here recognized him as a time wrecker or not, Will was wearing wrinkled khakis and a black T-shirt that had seen better days. His suit hadn't been cleaned since graduation, and he'd realized after his shift last night that he had nothing else to wear to an interview.

He wished he hadn't come. Will felt like the tall, skinny misfit he'd been in high school, standing in front of the Deer Hill Community Church and confessing faith he didn't have to please his mother. Now he was back. The stained-glass saints stared down at him as Will walked up the steps and into the vestibule.

Someone said hello. Someone else pressed a white paper

bulletin into his hand. Will gave a quick mumble and found a seat in the back, trying hard to be forgettable.

He wasn't sure whether it was better or worse that Tristan wouldn't be here today. Better, because at least Will knew he wasn't in a church just to please his friend. Worse, because it reminded Will that he hadn't come to please God, either.

As soon as the opening notes sounded on the organ, Will looked up. The tall, arched ceiling pulled the sound straight to the heavens. It was a beautiful organ, installed to the right of the pulpit. A baby grand sat off to the side, angled a little so it would fit in the corner. The two large instruments were balanced on the left side of the pulpit by two rows of pews for the choir.

The choir stood in unison at a nod from the organist, and soon their voices were the melody while the organ notes played under them. It was gorgeous. Transcendent. This was a place that was made for music.

Will's fingers twitched, eager to be the one playing that magnificent instrument up on the stage.

Altar, Will reminded himself. Altar, not stage. Hymn, not performance. Congregation, not audience.

This isn't my place. This is theirs.

Will slouched down in the pew. There had to be at least two hundred people packed in here, ready to sit, stand, kneel, and pray at all the right times. And he was an outsider.

Will would meet the pastor after the service as he promised. He could do that. But he wouldn't take a job here, even if it was offered. It wouldn't be fair. He'd already taken enough things that weren't his. Were never his.

♦♦♦♦♦

Will didn't have to worry about finding the pastor after the service. The pastor found him.

"You must be William Sterling. I'm Pastor Eli," he said, balancing a paper plate of miniature donuts in one hand and pumping Will's hand with the other. A little line of powdered sugar and cinnamon dusted the edge of his black mustache. "Tristan said you'd be coming. I'm glad. Can we get you something to eat? Our fellowship hall is being renovated, but we have some lemonade and donuts here by the entrance."

Will could see that. He had drifted down the aisle after the postlude, following the tail end of the crowd that was slowly working its way back to the vestibule. Then a cluster of children had gathered around a folding table sandwiched between the coatrack and the front door, making it almost impossible for people to squeeze past.

"No, I'm fine, thanks," Will said. "It's nice to meet you."

"The pleasure's all mine," Pastor Eli said, popping another donut in his mouth. "Let's wait for most of this crowd to clear out of here before we get started."

"Sure," Will said, but just then, someone touched the pastor's arm and leaned in with a prayer request, and a mother came to shoo her child away from the snack table, and the entry was a flurry of noise and confusion. Will backed farther out of the way.

Nobody else was still in the sanctuary except for a balding man who was inspecting each pew, picking up stray bulletins and putting hymnals back in the racks. He left through a door behind the altar that Will hadn't noticed before.

Will walked down the aisle alone, keeping his hands clasped behind his back. The sun shone through the biggest stained-glass window above the altar, casting patches of colored light over the blue carpet runner. Will could feel it deep within him the closer he got to the front of the church—the holiness of it. He was afraid to walk any farther in case he breathed wrong and ruined something.

"Gorgeous instrument, right?" a voice behind him said. Will jumped. It was Pastor Eli, who had apparently finished his donuts and wiped off his mustache too. "This organ here was donated in 1900, and the baby grand behind it was a gift from a family in the nineties. It replaced an old upright we had there."

"They both sounded amazing," Will said.

"Why don't you give it a try?" Pastor Eli asked. "Normally I'd start by asking some questions about your experience, what brings you to apply, blah blah blah. But Tristan already filled us in on your experience, and I was able to find your résumé online. Very impressive, by the way." Will nodded his thanks while the pastor continued. "Why don't you start on the organ? Take your time. Our current director says one of the pedals sticks a bit, so go ahead and warm up. See what you think."

Will's typical audition piece was written for piano, but it would sound majestic on the organ. He twirled the organ seat up. The current music director couldn't have been more than five-foot-five. Will would have had his knees around his chin sitting on a stool that low.

Right hand on the upper keyboard, left hand on the lower. Will warmed up slowly, conscious of how his tentative first notes blasted loudly into the sanctuary. The organ was in tune. He had an ear for that type of thing. The left pedal did stick a bit, but it wasn't hard to compensate. He hit another wrong note and tried not to flinch as it bellowed up from the organ.

He was keenly aware of the pastor settling into a pew about halfway back. Will tried to focus only on the keys, and then the sound of the notes swelling around him. And so Will segued into "A Mighty Fortress Is Our God," a song he was not surprised to realize he knew by heart, a song that was worthy of this kind of instrument.

"Magnificent," said a voice to Will's right, just as the last notes were drifting away, floating up to the arched ceiling. It was the man who had been neatening up the pews earlier, coming back through the hidden door. Peering behind him, Will could see that it was a kind of vestry. A long, full mirror reflected Will's own image back to him, and he turned away.

"Where'd you learn to play like that?" the man asked. He looked down the aisle at Pastor Eli. "This going to be our new music director? He's got my vote!"

Will could feel color creeping up through his face and burning the tips of his ears. "I went to Adams Morgan," he said. "Just graduated."

"Well, they did a good job with you. Hope to hear you playing here again," the man said, clapping a hand on his shoulder as he passed. Will pretended not to notice as the man raised his eyebrows at Pastor Eli and the pastor nodded ever so slightly back.

Maybe he knows who I am, Will thought suddenly. *Maybe that's why they want me. To prove that this is a church for reformed sinners. They're going to put me up on an altar to show that even time wreckers can repent.* He pulled his hands off the keyboard and folded them in his lap.

"That's one of our deacons," Pastor Eli said, after the man had gone into the vestibule. "Can't carry a tune himself, but he has a great appreciation for music." Will gave a nervous laugh, and Pastor Eli raised an eyebrow. "Are you all right, William?"

"Yes," Will lied automatically. The pastor stood and walked slowly up the aisle and sat down in the pew right next to the organ.

"Pause the interview for the moment," Pastor Eli said. "No one has to pretend to be okay in this place. Tristan did tell us about your fiancée. I'm so sorry. What a shock that must have been."

"It was," Will said. "It really was." He had to say it, so he let it all out in a rush. "I don't know why I might have had a rectification. I really don't. And I can't—I don't feel like I could say I'm sorry for doing it. I don't know what happened back then, but I figure we must have had a good reason. I don't know if . . ." The pastor was frowning at him slightly, and Will wasn't sure whether to keep going. "If this is a church that thinks time wrecking is wrong, I probably don't belong here. I think there are good reasons for it. I don't think I could repent if I'm not sure it was a sin."

"I see," the pastor said. "So you're wondering if that's a condition of employment."

"Right," Will said. "I'm not exactly the greatest Christian there is. You probably don't want someone like me up here."

Pastor Eli laughed a little. "I say the same thing to God every Sunday morning."

Will gave a polite laugh and looked away.

"But in all seriousness," the pastor said. "It is not our church's policy to hire only Christians or only people of our denomination for staff positions. The assistant pastor and I obviously have to be called by the council and have been ordained and so on, so for us, that is a requirement. But we do not, for example, require the nursery staff to be members of the church, or the music staff, either. All we require is that the candidate is able and willing to work toward our mission. Now for you, I can see how it could be a requirement in order to feel comfortable playing here."

"Music is a conversation," Will said. "It's not just hitting the right notes. If I'm not sure about the message, are people going to feel it in the song? If it was playing at a concert hall, I wouldn't worry about it, but at a worship service, it doesn't feel right."

"I respect that," Pastor Eli said. Now that he was sitting so close, his eyes were level with Will's, and he didn't look away. "When I was listening to you play just now, I did feel a connection to the song. It happens to be one of my favorite hymns, but I didn't think you were just playing the notes, either."

Will nodded. That was something.

"Would you mind telling me what you were feeling when you played it?"

"I was thinking about the words while I was playing," Will said. "And I was just thinking about . . . how I want it to be true, I guess. I want to feel like there's a place I can go where nothing could get to me the way it does."

"But it's a struggle for you," Pastor Eli said. "You don't feel like there is a place like that for you."

"Right."

"You asked me a question a few minutes ago, and I missed the chance to answer it," the pastor said. "You asked if this church thinks of timeline rectification as a sin. Our denomination hasn't taken an official stance for or against timeline rectifications. That doesn't mean we never will. It has been an ongoing conversation, particularly in the past few weeks, and I'm certain the question will come up at our annual conference. Whether we will put anything to a vote remains to be seen." Pastor Eli must have seen Will's eyes glazing over, because he hurried on. "But the point is that within this church, you will find a wide range of opinions on this topic and many others, just like you will anywhere else."

"Oh."

"Our church has stood in this location for over one hundred years," Pastor Eli said. "We are a very diverse community. Lots of people in DC are transplants—myself included—and we bring our experiences from other states and other countries with us. We disagree on politics. We disagree on social issues. We all struggle with living out our faith in a very complicated world. But the point is that we share that struggle with each other."

Will nodded.

"We've had people come to our congregation from all stages of their faith journey. Some people have been coming to this church since they were babies and some pass through just out of curiosity. We believe there is value in sharing your journey with others even if you're not sure where you're starting from or where you want to go. Not because other people can provide the answers, necessarily, but because they can walk with you." Pastor Eli clapped a hand on his shoulder. "So. Now that I've said far more than you probably ever wanted to know, why don't you play something else? On the piano if you don't mind."

Will hesitated. Was this still an interview?

Apparently it was, because Pastor Eli was already walking back down the aisle, settling in another one of the middle pews. "I like to hear applicants on both instruments," he said. "No holds barred. Play whatever you like."

Will moved down to the baby grand. The pedals were easier to use on the piano, but the music didn't soar the same way. Everything he played now, even warm-up scales, sounded more contemplative. Like a meditation.

Will felt as if he was listening to the piano, to the church, to the sudden stillness that had settled over the sanctuary. He loved it when this happened. Will wasn't so much a musician as another instrument. Just the hands that drew the song out of the piano and let it go.

He recognized the first chords of the intro as he played them. It was from an album Tristan had bought and played a few times back when he was still deciding to go to seminary. *Michael W. Smith*, Will thought. The song was just called "Breathe." That was what Will was doing now. Just breathing. Listening.

"Beautiful," Pastor Eli said, after the last notes faded away. He walked toward the front again and stood next to the piano bench, so Will stood too. "Thank you for coming in today. It was an honor to hear you play."

Will laughed a little. "I don't know about that. It's a wonderful . . ." He couldn't find a way to finish the thought. "Thank you for the opportunity," he said, instead.

"Everything I've heard today tells me that you are an extremely well-qualified candidate to lead our music department," the pastor said. "The next step is for all our candidates to play before our church council. They will deliberate and extend the offer to the candidate they choose. Would you consider coming back for that, William?"

Will blinked. "I figured I bombed the interview."

"Not at all. It was a pleasure to get to know more about you. And regardless of how the next phase of the interview plays out—pardon the pun—you are always welcome here."

"Thank you." Will looked up at the stained-glass windows, into the eyes of the saints who maybe weren't judging him after all. "And please call me Will."

♦♦♦♦♦

Walking back into his apartment was easier, somehow. Will took off his church clothes—what had passed for church clothes—and changed into shorts and a T-shirt. He still had energy. That was different. Ever since he'd come back to DC, all Will had wanted to do was sleep between work shifts. Now he felt as if he could throw a load of clothes into the washer. Unpack his travel bag and put his shaving kit and shampoo in the medicine cabinet.

This was life now. Will didn't love it, but he could survive it.

The mail that had piled up on the coffee table needed to be sorted through. He didn't bother opening half of it. One postcard screamed TIME FOR PEACE! in large white letters. That must be the protest his mother had been talking about, the one that Deirdre Collins started. The people on the front of the postcard were all dressed in red shirts. They'd been badly photo-edited onto a background of the National Mall, with the Washington Monument looming in the background. Will flipped the card back and forth before tossing it, Frisbee-style, toward the trash can. He missed.

What would really happen if someone like him showed up at a protest like that? Will could be recognized. Or—better? Worse?—maybe no one would know who he was.

Back in Deer Hill, being the only time wrecker was like living under a microscope. But up in DC, only the important time wreckers really mattered. Okay, it was going to be hard finding work; Will was working on that. But nobody was out looking for him. He could go to a bar or a church or bus tables at a restaurant, and no one threatened him.

Will imagined, just for an instant, that Mara was here too. Today could have been the day after their wedding—the first day of their honeymoon. Would they be able to come and go without being followed? Not likely. They wouldn't just be screening their calls or sifting through their mail. More likely, they'd be listening for passing cars and footsteps outside the door. Keeping the phone half-dialed for the police.

How long would it go on? How long before the stress of it all tore them apart?

The last time Will and Mara had sat in this room, she'd tried to tell him. Will remembered the desperate feeling that had clawed in his chest as she stood right there and listed all the things about to go wrong. Mara was just being pessimistic, he thought. Jaded. She didn't believe in people anymore. She didn't believe in him.

That wasn't what she was trying to say. Now a different kind of desperation was rising in his chest. He hadn't listened to her, and now he sat here safe and sound while she hid from would-be kidnappers and death threats and who knew what else.

The realization hit him full force. He and Mara could have shared this part of their lives, even if the wedding was on hold. He could have listened.

He sank into the desk chair in the living room. Pastor Eli's words from earlier that morning came back to him now: *There is value in sharing the journey.*

Plucking the postcard back out of the trash, he sighed. It was going to take a lot more than a rally on the National Mall to make peace out of this mess. But it could be a start.

Will held the postcard in both hands and let himself hope.

Marching for My Mother

By Imani Watson

I was ten years old when my mother went to jail.

The shame of her conviction followed me everywhere that year. I saw it in my teachers' eyes, heard it in my classmate's brutal whispers, and felt it every time red-and-blue lights flashed outside my building. My mother's name became a warning in my family, a reminder of how quickly one choice could destroy a woman.

I wasn't allowed to visit her for years. My aunt thought it would be damaging, seeing my mother like that. I hate to admit that my first visit to see Mom was more traumatic than I let on. I remember touching that thick Plexiglass screen, trying to line up my fingertips to match hers.

"Baby," she said to me, not even trying to hide her tears, "don't you ever do what I did. It's not worth the risk."

Had my mother really known what she was risking? Mom was working two jobs (one as a fast-food worker and another as a night custodian) when one of her friends offered her a "business deal." She wouldn't be a supplier—just the middleman between a cocaine dealer and buyers. And she was a single mom working two jobs, staring down an opportunity to make thousands of dollars simply by helping a friend.

That "friend" was caught in a sting operation in the mid-nineties. By turning over the names of everyone she'd worked with, Mom's friend reduced her own sentence to eight years. My mother, who had no new information to barter, was hit with a number of charges that "enhanced" her original crime. Not only was Mom convicted of possession with intent to distribute, but she was described as a "leader in a drug ring," her testimony was deemed an obstruction of justice, and her so-called business deal was now a "drug conspiracy."

My mother's name has appeared on a list of convicts begging for clemency and has been rejected. Her name has also appeared on a list of inmates who completed their GEDs, inmates who've completed social programs and reading challenges and who knows how many drug rehabilitation programs.

But her name wasn't in the hacked Time Wrecker list.

I know that my mother would take that chance, if only it was offered. Has Mom wished she could take back that decision to get involved with her friend's "business deal"? Every second of every day. She fits all the parameters to be approved for a timeline rectification too. Her crime did not result in a death. It did not involve a minor. It happened in 2001, just as timeline rectifications became legal. She is repentant, rehabilitated, and ready to contribute to society, if only she can get that chance.

She will never get that chance.

I'm not a fool. I know that more will come out; it was never about Conrad Gibbons or Alicia Barnes or any kind of politics. This was always about shame, and shame will do more to keep people down than facts ever could.

Mom and I are preparing ourselves for how we'll feel when the news comes out about which crimes were offered a rectification. Because even though the hackers have been stopped, the information is out there. The can of worms has been opened, and people are going to want the rest of the story. I don't need to see the list of race and age and sex to know who in this country gets twice the opportunity to work half as hard. But I know it's there. And I know it's going to come out.

"You can't let this eat at you," my mother tells me, the last time I talked to her about it through that phone, studied her eyes through that thick Plexiglass wall. She looks soft, accepting. "I did wrong and I'm being punished for it. You can control your actions, child, but you can't control the consequences."

Her words hold a warning, one that's been repeated to me every day of my life, by my aunt and my teachers and my neighbors. In this world, I wear a target. I'm not expected to do well. I'm not expected to succeed. There's a hungry world out there, waiting for me to prove that I'm not good enough, not smart enough, not deserving of even the tiny place they've carved for me in their big white world. There are people who will take my first wrong step and hold it out as evidence that I was bound to screw up all along.

I cannot accept this injustice as fact the way my mother has. She calls it a product of my age; I call it a product of my hope. I want there to be a world that sees Mom as a woman who made one terrible decision, not as a throwaway felon. She's not a perfect person and she did deserve to be caught and punished for what she did. But she also deserves a second chance. I believe she's earned it.

Now we just need a world who wants to give it to her.

So, yes, I will be marching on Monday, but not on behalf of the time wreckers. I'm going to be marching on behalf of all those who wish they could be on that list, who have been denied, time and again, the chance to rebuild their lives.

I'm going to be marching for my mother. She has taken risk after risk to try to provide for her family, to try to make it in an often cruel and unfair world. If she wants to risk a timeline rectification, if she is willing to put it all on the line for the chance to undo her crime, I think she should get the chance. And so should every other repentant criminal who's waiting right now for an opportunity that may never come.

The road to justice is long and hard and full of obstacles. I am here for the journey. I hope you are too.

....

Chapter Twenty-Two

MARA

Was the Metro station always this loud, or had the past few weeks made Mara hyperaware of every tiny detail of the world outside? Beside her, Robyn didn't seem to flinch as the escalator brought them deeper into the noise and heat by the platform. Mara hunched her shoulders and pulled the brim of her newsboy cap low over her face.

"Stop messing with your hair," Robyn whispered under her breath.

"I can't help it," Mara whispered back. "I'm so nervous."

"And everyone can tell. Stop. You're not doing anything wrong. Probably half the people here are going to the same place."

Mara adjusted her brim again and peeked up at the blinking sign. Four minutes until their train was due to arrive. Not too long. Good. She cast a sideways glance down either end of the platform. At midmorning, there were the usual clumps of tourists squinting at their maps and shifting heavy backpacks from one shoulder to the other. Halfway down the platform, a group of protestors stood in a semicircle, chests puffed out under the "Time Wrecker" emblem on their red T-shirts. Some of the younger ones were rolling and unrolling their poster board signs.

Behind her, Mara thought she saw another, smaller group—just three people, but one was wearing red from head-to-toe. The other two wore shirts that had WHICH ONE OF US IS THE TIME WRECKER? and arrows that pointed to each other. The group of three stood tall and looked passersby straight in the eye, silently daring them to a challenge. One of them, the tall boy in the middle, caught Mara's gaze and held it for a second too long. Mara turned away, hoping she hadn't been recognized.

When she looked back, the boy was still watching her.

Mara crossed her arms and looked down. Why couldn't she be like the other protestors? They looked so sure of what they were doing, so committed to defending their cause. Would Mara even be here if her name hadn't been on the list?

No. Definitely not.

"You could probably take the second shirt off now," Robyn said. "Looks like everyone's going to the same place." Robyn was already wearing a red T-shirt with TIME FOR PEACE emblazoned across the front and back in permanent marker.

"I figured I'd wait until we were actually at the protest," Mara whispered back. "Don't you think?"

Robyn shrugged. "If it makes you feel better. It's

practically a hundred degrees outside. Come on. Do you really want to be wearing two shirts on a day like this?"

Mara glanced up and down the platform again. "It's not so bad. I'll keep it on a little longer." The digital sign above the tracks counted down. Two minutes until the next train. The lights by the track started to blink.

"Hey," Robyn said. "You sure you want to do this?"

"Can't back out now," Mara said. "I mean. You already took the day off work."

"I took the day off to support you. If this is still what you want to do, we'll go. If you'd rather just get coffee and talk, that's fine."

The rumble on the platform echoed against the domed concrete ceiling. Mara could see the light of the oncoming train in the tunnel.

"No," Mara said. "I'm in. Let's do this."

♦♦♦♦♦

Mara had taken the Metro to Federal Center more times than she could count. It was a decent walk to the Air and Space Museum—one of her favorites—and beyond that, the Capitol and the National Mall. Coming from Arlington, the ride was only a little over twenty minutes. Each time the train stopped and the doors opened to let more people on, Mara counted how many people looked like they were going to the protest too. So far, there weren't many.

Why did Deirdre Collins have to choose red shirts for today? Hasn't she ever seen Star Trek? Everyone knows the red shirts are the first to go.

If Robyn was feeling nervous, Mara couldn't tell. As the train drew closer to their stop, Robyn busied herself with reorganizing her backpack. She'd come prepared: sunscreen, two frozen water bottles and two thawed, and plastic baggies with granola bars and fruit snacks. No matter how Robyn rearranged, the zipper couldn't completely close. Two tubes of rolled-up poster board poked out the side.

"What did you write on our signs?" Mara whispered.

"You'll see when we get there," Robyn replied in a normal voice. "Stop worrying. We're going to be fine."

"Right."

They were in the heart of DC now. Half the people on their train car rose to their feet as the Metro came to a long, shuddering halt. Mara pretended to study the train route posted on the opposite wall of the train as passengers filed off and a new line of passengers filed in.

Four in red shirts. Five. Six. Two families, one with a stroller. Another red shirt.

The picture on the last T-shirt took Mara's breath away. It was silkscreened with her photo from the paper. Underneath, in white letters, the shirt read FREE MARA.

"Awkward," Robyn singsong whispered. Mara didn't laugh. She could hardly breathe. The passenger passed them without noticing, the warning chime dinged, and the train lurched forward to the next station.

"I mean, at least now you know someone else that's supportive," Robyn said. She was still smiling, but her eyes were studying Mara's face. "Are you sure you're okay?"

"I'm fine," Mara said. "I'll be fine."

"Good. Because ours is the next stop."

The platform at Federal Center was already crowded when Mara and Robyn got off. "Which direction are we supposed to go?" Mara asked. "Smithsonian or Independence Avenue?"

"You have to ask?" Robyn pointed to the swarm of protestors that were headed toward the Independence Avenue exit. "We're supposed to meet by the Capitol building. By eleven, we start marching down the mall."

"Supposed to?"

Robyn shrugged. "You really haven't been to a protest before, have you?"

"I never needed to." Mara felt terrible as soon as she said it. She had never needed to, but Robyn had. Mara remembered Robyn leaving for the day to march in a Pride parade in college and printing out cards to hand out on the Day of Silence every April.

Why didn't I go with her?

Immediately, Mara's mind flooded with excuses. *She never asked me. I wasn't sure if I should. It would have been weird for me to show up because I'm not gay. I always listened to her when she wanted to talk. That's something, isn't it?*

It was, but it wasn't enough.

Mara reached out and pulled on her friend's elbow. "Thank you."

"You can go ahead and stop thanking me for taking off work today," Robyn said. "Seriously. I'd rather swim with piranhas than go in today, so this is a serious upgrade."

"No, what I meant was . . . thank you for showing me how to be a good friend. And I'm sorry you had to show me."

Robyn looked to the side before answering. "You worry too much," she said. "Ready to see your poster? Because this is go time."

Go time at a protest felt a lot more like *wait time*. Even when they emerged onto the sunlit sidewalk, the crowd was so intense that Mara and Robyn could barely get through. Still more people were pouring out of the exit behind them.

"This is crazy," Mara said, raising her voice so Robyn could hear her over the din.

"Awesome, right?" Robyn grinned. She whipped out the two posters from her backpack and ceremoniously unrolled them. The one she handed to Mara read, TIME FOR PEACE. The other, which Robyn kept for herself, read, EVERYONE DESERVES A SECOND CHANCE.

Now that they were here, Mara felt like she stood out more in her big blue T-shirt. She eased one arm out, then the other, and pulled it off to reveal her own red shirt. Last night, she'd written TIME WRECKER across the front. Only now, here in the heart of DC, she didn't feel like she was the only one.

The crowd still wasn't moving. Robyn stood on her toes and then pointed Mara to the right. "Try to elbow your way through. We're getting squished."

The shock of being around people again—being around so *many* people—made Mara equal parts claustrophobic and excited. Protestors were packed shoulder to shoulder as far as she could see down Independence Avenue. The energy was contagious. Mara got swiped with the edge of a poster. She leaned forward to see what it said. REMEMBER RAMON BASSAVE was scribbled in thick permanent marker letters.

He should be here too. Mara felt a wave of grief for a man she'd never met—probably never would have met. Ramon Bassave had lived in Chicago. Would he even have flown to DC for the protest if he'd been given the chance?

Never mind if he would have or not. He deserved the chance.

"They're moving," someone said next to her. The news rolled quickly from one person to the next. The march was beginning. Robyn used her elbows to clear a space and propelled Mara farther into the crowd.

The protestors might have started marching a few blocks ahead, but progress was limited to the tiniest, jostling steps here. In the distance, Mara could hear someone talking through a megaphone and a vague, rhythmic murmur of the chanting marchers up ahead.

"You're smiling," Robyn said. "About time."

Mara did feel happy, she realized. She hadn't felt this

good since . . . well, since before the data leak. But how could she not catch on to the enthusiasm of the other protestors? These people she'd never met wanted the world to be safe for her. And they wanted the world to be a safe place for Ramon Bassave, and Deirdre Collins, and Will.

We aren't alone.

The crowd was really moving now. Mara could take normal-size steps, and then the row of people ahead spread out even more. Now she could see the protestors to either side of her and Robyn. She could even make out the uniformed police officers standing guard, and—her heart sank—the counter-protestors standing behind them. The anti-time wreckers must have decided on yellow shirts for today.

For once, Mara didn't want to turn away. She read their signs as she marched past.

ONCE A CRIMINAL, ALWAYS A CRIMINAL
INNOCENT UNTIL PROVEN GUILTY—NOT AFTER!
TIME MARCHES ON

It wasn't anything that Mara hadn't read online a million times before. She wondered if any of the people who were here had left a comment on the articles about her. Recaptioned her picture as a meme. Would they be so willing to do it now, to her face?

A middle-aged woman screamed "Time wreckers!" as they

passed. The force behind her words was pure venom.

Yes, Mara decided. They probably would call her a criminal to her face, and worse. She picked up her pace and held her sign higher—first even with her chest, and then up over her head. For a moment, she even wanted to pull off her hat and whip off her sunglasses too. Why should she have to hide?

I don't. I don't have to hide anymore.

They were closing in on the end of the second block. Now Mara could make out the words to the chant that had started up ahead: "Time for peace! Time for peace!" It caught on quickly. Mara felt her ear going numb as the teenage boy behind her screamed it. A few others punched the air to accent each syllable.

"Time for peace!" Mara cried out. She could feel that she was yelling, but the crowd around her was so loud she couldn't hear her own voice. "Time for peace!"

I belong here. Every step made Mara feel taller and stronger. She was connected to this street, this crowd marching beside her; she was even connected to the people standing behind the police barricade, rallying against the time wreckers. It didn't matter. They could scream all they wanted. Nobody could make her disappear. Nobody could take her place in the world.

Smoke. Mara's eyes and nose filled with it before she realized what happened, before her palms were torn and bleeding from catching her fall. Someone had slammed into her from behind, pushing her knees-first into the road. Her sign was somewhere. Mara couldn't see it. She couldn't see Robyn. There was only shouting and then a confusion of sneakers and signs and backpacks hitting the ground.

"Get down! Get down!" a man screamed, inches from Mara's ear.

A shot rang out.

Breaking News:
Violence at Time for Peace Protest

June 7, 2006

WASHINGTON, DC — A peaceful protest in support of timeline rectifiers' rights erupted in violence today just blocks from Capitol Hill. Timeline rectifiers named on the leaked list have reportedly faced harassment, job loss, and even death. Today they came together with one goal: peace.

The protestors, who witnesses say numbered in the hundreds, had marched only three blocks before the violence began. A combination of pepper spray, smoke bombs, and gunshots were fired by counter-protestors before police were able to contain the situation. Three arrests have been made, although no names have been released at this time. No deaths have been reported. However, fourteen of the protestors were injured, some with life-threatening injuries. More news as it develops.

Chapter Twenty-Three

WILL

Mara wouldn't be there. Will tried to calm himself as he gripped the steering wheel. Not after everything she'd been through, she wouldn't risk going to a protest, of all things.

Yes, she would.

Will wanted to drive downtown with every fiber of his being. He pictured himself tearing through the crowds like the hero of some action movie, spotting Mara through the debris and scooping her up in his arms. Saving her.

No, that wasn't what Mara needed. She didn't want a hero. She wanted a partner. Or she had, anyway.

Something told Will that Mara wasn't at Robyn's place, or her parents', either. And so he found himself driving into Arlington, checking the map for directions even as his heart kept pounding in his throat. This was the right thing to do. The right place to be. He could feel it.

He didn't see any sign of Mara's car at her grandmother's house. He parked on the street anyway and walked, two stepping-stones at a time, up to the front stoop. Will held the bouquet of peonies against his chest, trying to support the top-heavy blooms without squishing them. One last, deep breath. And then he knocked on Grandmary's front door.

The footsteps approaching the door didn't sound like Mara's. She had always been light on her feet. These footsteps were slow, heavy. Like whoever it was, was dragging herself to open the door, leaning to pull it open.

Grandmary.

It was the first time Will had seen her since the graduation dinner. Mara's grandmother wore loose gray knit pants that skimmed the tops of her bare feet and a long-sleeved purple tunic, even though it was at least ninety degrees outside. Her hair wasn't done up in her usual French knot, either. Whitish-gray waves hung on either side of her face and stuck to her neck in sweaty clumps.

"Will," Grandmary said. "I knew you'd come." Her lopsided smile was warm and welcoming. For a minute, Will thought she might reach out and hug him, but Grandmary held tight to the door instead.

"Is Mara here?" Will asked.

"She and Robyn are out at that protest," Grandmary said. "That's Mara. She knows what she wants to do." Her eyes regarded Will softly. "She knows who she wants too."

She didn't know. Will could tell and decided just as quickly that he wouldn't be the one to tell Grandmary about the violence that had erupted at the protest. He would just make his excuses and drive as fast as he could back to DC.

"You two are a good match for each other." Grandmary leaned away from the doorframe and gestured him in. "Why don't you come with me to the kitchen? I'd like to sit down."

There was nothing Will could do but follow her into the house. To do anything else would give away that something was wrong.

Please let Mara be okay. Please, please, please . . .

Will closed the door behind him and nudged off his shoes. There was something strange with the way Mara's grandmother was walking; she wasn't limping, exactly, but she seemed unsteady.

Grandmary's getting old, Will suddenly realized. She had always seemed so strong to him, too much a force of nature to be constrained by things like age or health. Like Mara.

Even strong people break down sometimes.

Will pulled out a chair for her at the kitchen table and sat across from her. There were traces of Mara everywhere. Her sandals were tucked into the corner of the kitchen. A few stray hair elastics and earrings mingled with the spare change in a wooden bowl at the center of the table. Will thought he could even smell the faint traces of Mara's strawberry shampoo lingering in the air.

To his right, he could see straight into a living room. Grandmary used it as a kind of den, Will guessed—a room where she could kick back in the enormous recliner or use the desktop computer. Grandmary probably hadn't been the last one to use the computer desk, though. Piles of paper covered every inch of the desktop, a sure sign that Mara had been there. She used to study the same way. Will had a sudden memory of Mara sitting cross-legged in the center of her dorm room floor, with textbooks and notebooks arranged in a circle around her. He missed her so badly.

"What are those?" Will asked, pointing to the cranes strung over the mantle.

"Mara's friends put those together for her," Grandmary said. "A thousand and one paper cranes."

Mara wanted to do that for our wedding. Will swallowed and put his eyes back on the bouquet of peonies that hung their heavy heads against the paper wrapping. "I'm glad she had people helping her through it. She deserves . . ." He swallowed again. "Mara deserves the best."

"So do you," Grandmary said. She looked at him straight on, until even Will couldn't doubt that she'd meant it.

"Thanks," Will said, feeling the heat rise to his ears. "But I already had it." He looked around. "Do you mind if I put these in a vase?"

Grandmary nodded. "Cabinet under the sink."

Will chose the nicest vase he could find clustered under the pipes. A porcelain vase with little roses down the side. He filled it halfway with water, trying not to think about how this was probably the last thing he would ever do for Mara.

He had followed his instincts today. Trusted his gut. Listened to the Holy Spirit, some might say. Or maybe he had followed some buried-deep memory of their first life map. Will would never know. But he did know that whatever it was had sent him in the exact opposite direction of where Mara was. This had to be some kind of answer.

Will hoped it wasn't.

He brought the vase to the center of the kitchen table and carefully arranged the peonies inside. "I don't blame you for going home to North Carolina," Grandmary said softly. "You and Mara aren't the first couple to get your signals crossed." Grandmary rested her head in her hands and put both elbows on the table.

"Mrs. Gaines?" Will asked.

"Mary. Please."

It took Will a full minute to realize she was asking him to call her by her first name. It was hard to hear her. Will had never heard Mara's grandmother slouch or mumble, but she was doing both now. One of her elbows was starting to slip from the edge of the table. Will reached out and guided it back. She didn't resist.

"The course of true love never did run smooth," Grandmary mumbled. "You have to choose whether to walk away or whether to fight for it. Not just today, but every day. Every determination."

"Mary? Can you look up for me?"

Grandmary looked up slowly, leaning heavily on one hand. Will's mind raced. He dimly remembered something from Mara's flash cards, when he'd quizzed her last semester for one of her pre-med classes. Grandmary's right side seemed weak . . . almost drooping, he guessed, but it was hard to tell. Mara's textbook had only come with exaggerated line drawings. But Grandmary was talking, so that was a good sign, right? Was she coherent?

"Well?" Grandmary asked. "Do you know what you're going to do?"

"Yes," said Will. "I'm going to call you an ambulance, Mary. I think you've had a stroke."

....

Chapter Twenty-Four

MARA

No matter how many of the proffered wet wipes Mara used, she couldn't get the blood off her hands. There was some under her fingernails, even. Was it her own blood? She had scraped her palms when she fell. It probably was her blood. Most of it.

But what about that man?

Mara had locked her elbows the way she was supposed to. Counted as she did chest compressions, stopped and listened for a pulse. She hadn't found one, but maybe she'd just been too nervous. Mara didn't even know the man's name. He'd collapsed next to her, and her college EMS training had kicked in.

Mara had barely noticed when the paramedics arrived. They had pushed her out of the way and taken over CPR. Someone had handed her the pack of wipes. Someone else had checked her pupils and asked her questions until she swatted them away.

Mara's hands were shaking, she realized. Her whole body was shaking.

Strange. Just minutes ago, Mara had been pushing against the man's chest, blowing air into his mouth, watching for any sign of life. The rest of the world had faded around her as she listened for a pulse and counted chest compressions. Now she was back on the edge of the crowd as the paramedics prepared to load the man into the ambulance. Mara would never see him again, she realized. She didn't even know his name.

One of the paramedics broke off from the circle again and approached her. "You did the right thing. Have you performed CPR before?"

"No," Mara said. "I mean, yes. I practiced. I was on the emergency response team at college."

"Do you know him?"

Mara looked past the paramedic. She could barely catch a glimpse of the man on the gurney. His face was ashen, his leg wound still blooming red under the cotton pressed to his thigh. But he was wearing an oxygen mask now. That had to be a good sign.

"No," Mara said. "I don't know him."

He shook his head. "It's a good thing for him that you were there. Big mess. Lucky you thought on your feet."

Mara didn't know how to respond.

Next to her, Robyn put an arm around her. How long had she been standing there? Mara didn't know. "You sure you don't need to go to the hospital?"

"I'm sure." Mara took more deep breaths, wishing she

could exhale the scent of smoke and blood from her memory. "I just want to go home."

"I'll take you."

Robyn started to guide her to the Metro station and stopped. "Oh, no."

The entrance to the station was crammed. It would be impossible to get as far as the turnstiles, much less to the platform to catch a train. They were the lucky ones, Mara realized. The Metro was jammed, but at least they weren't leaving in an ambulance.

"Okay," Robyn said. "Okay. Let's go this way."

It was a mess of noise and confusion working their way back past the paramedics and ambulances. Some people were still screaming. Lots were crying. Mara linked her arm through Robyn's and followed her as she jerked this way and that, using her elbows to push her way through.

The police were blowing whistles and pointing to barricades in the street. Cars that had just turned were honking, and one pulled a very illegal U-turn.

"Let's go the other way," Mara said, pulling her friend in the opposite direction. Robyn followed, and now it was Mara elbowing their way through the crowd.

"If we can get far enough away from Independence Avenue, someone can come pick us up," said Robyn suddenly.

"Who's going to pick us up?" Mara raised her voice over the din.

"I'll call someone." Robyn said. "Once I can hear myself think."

Jessica, Mara guessed. Jess was working on the Adams Morgan University campus this summer, so she might be nearby.

Would Will have come to her rescue, if they were still together? For that matter, would Will have come with her to the protest today? He might have, although he probably would have tried to talk her out of it. Mara could imagine his reaction so vividly it hurt. *If it's important to you, we can do it,* he'd have said. *But are you going because you want to, or because you think you should?*

He knew her so well. Will had always been able to see straight through Mara, and he loved her anyway. She'd thought she knew him too, but had she really taken the time to look?

Or did I just assume I knew better than him? On the wedding, on the data leak . . . maybe even on the time wreck.

They could still hear ambulance sirens and police whistles, but most of the scene was behind them now. "Wait up," Robyn said suddenly. "Wait."

"What's wrong?" Mara started to ask, but Robyn was already sprinting for the boxwood hedge that lined a marbled half-wall. Mara ran after her. She caught up just in time to hold back Robyn's hair as her friend threw up into the bushes.

"Sorry," Robyn mumbled, before she gagged and threw

up again.

Mara waved a pair of nosy onlookers past and patted her friend's back with her free hand. She alternated between saying "It's okay" and "I've got you" until Robyn finally sat back. Mara looked into her red-rimmed eyes and patted her back one more time.

"Careful," Robyn said. "Apparently, I'm explosive."

"It's stress," Mara said. "It's just stress."

"It hit me all at once. Like, completely out of nowhere." Robyn put an uneasy hand on her stomach again.

"It's super common," Mara said. "Especially considering what just happened."

"How are you so okay right now?" Robyn asked. "How is it . . . I just panicked and couldn't think of anything but getting out of there, and you're just . . . you saved a man's life, chatted with some first responders, held my hair back while I barfed. How are you not falling apart right now?"

"I don't know," Mara said slowly. "I guess it hasn't hit me yet. It just— I have to block it out while I do what I have to do." She shook her head. "Kinda makes me feel like a robot."

"Nah, not a robot," Robyn said. "That's why you're going to be a great doctor."

Mara had to blink for a minute. "Thanks," she said, smiling. "I never thought about it like that."

"You should." Robyn smiled back. "I think we're far enough away from the barricade now. Gonna call for a ride."

"Okay," Mara said absently. While Robyn dialed and

talked quietly into her phone, Mara looked off in the distance: at the people walking past, at the busy street, at the outline of the Washington Monument blocks away.

I still have a future. Mara could feel it now. She could still go to medical school in the fall. She would still be a doctor. Not to make her parents proud or to make up for all the mistakes she might have made in the past. Because it was right for her. Mara was a healer.

Robyn was off the phone now. "You sure you're okay?" Mara asked.

Her friend offered a wan smile. "Yeah. You?"

"Yeah," Mara said. "I really am."

"Good." Robyn's eyes were searching the street when suddenly, they widened. "There he is," she said. "Quick!"

"There who is?" Mara asked, at the same time that a dark green sedan pulled up beside them and honked.

It was Frank, Robyn's father. He rolled down the window and glowered. "Get in."

Robyn and Mara slid across the back seat and buckled up. She was still sweating and pale, Mara noticed, but a bit of color had come back to her cheeks.

"Thank you for picking us up, Dad," Robyn said, in a voice Mara didn't recognize.

"Let me focus on getting through this madhouse first," Frank snapped. "You can apologize for your stupidity when we're past Dupont Circle."

Mara tried not to obviously brace herself as Robyn's

father swerved and honked at the panicked pedestrians darting across the road. Every so often, he would hit the brakes and let out a string of curses, punctuated with declarations like "That's why you don't jaywalk through downtown DC, idiot!"

Frank slammed on the horn and the brakes at the same time, and Mara held on to the handle for dear life.

"I hate Dupont Circle," Frank announced. "I hate this entire city. Who the hell builds roads like the spokes of a friggin' wagon wheel and then slaps another grid of streets on top of that? It's the most backward, asinine, obnoxious—" He was interrupted by a coughing fit. Smoker's lung, Mara guessed. He was probably going to want another cigarette after this.

"Now. What the hell were you two thinking, getting mixed up in this? Mara, I thought at least you had more sense." Frank's eyes shot laser beams into the rearview mirror before he snapped his attention back to the road just in time. He leaned on the horn and pushed it three more times for good measure. "Crazy drivers."

Robyn's hand had snaked over to the safety handle over her door.

"I don't know what you girls were trying to prove, rallying or protesting or whatever you thought you were doing out there. There's a difference between standing up for yourself and tempting fate. A man was murdered over this. People have been chased out of their homes, out of their jobs. Think of what happened to your mother, Mara. Think about that."

"That's why we went today," Robyn said, leaning forward to plead their case. "We can't let them terrorize the time wreckers. We can't just—"

"Then write your representative," Frank said. "Put an editorial in the paper. Call the police if you're being threatened. But don't go parading through DC—"

"It wasn't a parade," Robyn interrupted.

"—with a friggin' target on your back. Remember what I told you when you went off to college, Robyn? *Some people are bears.*"

"Dad. Please."

"No, you're going to hear this, both of you. I said some people are bears. You have a point you want to make; most people will listen. You have a reasonable point; most people will even agree with you. But no matter how smart and polite and reasonable you think you are, you can't argue with a bear. It's going to eat you no matter what you say. And do you know why?"

"Dad."

"Do you know why?"

"Dad. *Please.*"

"Because it's a friggin' bear, that's why. That's what bears do. They eat tasty people and they don't feel bad about it." Frank hit his turn signal with unnecessary force. "You two went out today and tried to argue with the bears, and look what happened. You could've been hurt. You could've been killed." He swerved around a slow-moving car and almost missed the exit. "Who's calling? Robyn, if it's your mother—"

"That's me. My phone," Mara said. She fished it out of her pocket.

"Who is it?" Robyn asked.

Mara frowned down at the screen. "It's my dad." Mara had emailed her parents her new cell phone number, like Grandmary had asked. But she hadn't expected either of them to call.

"You better answer it," Frank said from the driver's seat. "If he's figured out that you were in the middle of all that—"

Mara answered with shaking fingers. She plugged her other ear with one finger before she realized it wasn't necessary. Her father's voice carried over the line loud and clear.

"Mara. Your mother and I are at the hospital. Where are you?"

"I'm not hurt, Dad. I'm sorry. I didn't mean to worry you—"

The congressman cut her off. "Your grandmother is in the hospital. She's had a stroke."

The world was spinning again. Mara clutched both arms to her chest.

"I don't care where you are, but you need to get to the hospital quickly. Things don't look good."

◆◆◆◆◆

Once, when Mara was only nine or ten years old, she'd been sent home from school with a fever. It was Grandmary who brought her home and tucked her into bed. She'd read some of Andersen's fairytales while Mara drifted in and out of sleep. Mara could remember the lilt of Grandmary's voice as she read "The Little Match Girl," "The Snow Queen," and her favorite, "The Nightingale."

Now Mara sat by the side of Grandmary's hospital bed, holding her strong left hand and waiting for her grandmother to open her eyes. She'd been conscious when the ambulance arrived, Congressman Gaines had said, but just half an hour before Mara finally made it to the hospital, Grandmary had slipped into unconsciousness. Four hours later, the monitors in the ICU were still the only sounds in the room.

Mara's parents hadn't said anything about the protest when she'd arrived, even though she was still wearing her handmade time wrecker T-shirt. Congressman Gaines had briefed her on Grandmary's condition out in the waiting room, and then she and her father and mother had taken turns cycling in to stand by Grandmary's bed. There were only two visitors allowed in the ICU at a time.

Mara wasn't hungry, but she'd filled up on candy bars and soda from the vending machine when it was her turn to sit alone in the waiting room. Now her parents were in the cafeteria, getting a proper lunch or dinner—Mara wasn't sure what time it was, exactly—while Mara kept up the bedside vigil. The steady hiss of oxygen flowing from the nasal cannula and the beep of the heart rate monitor made a kind of terrible chant, one that Mara punctuated with her own guilty thoughts.

I'm sorry, I'm sorry, I'm sorry.

I shouldn't have left you.

Mara wondered if someone was sitting like this with the man who'd been shot at the protest. They wouldn't have transported him all the way out here, to Arlington. He'd probably been taken to Georgetown or George Washington University Hospital. Wherever he was, Mara hoped that he had someone holding his hand now. Someone worrying over him. Even if he'd been a time wrecker, he deserved to be alive and well now. They all did.

Mara had the sudden urge to wash her hands and arms again. How long would it be until she could scrub the scent of blood and smoke from her skin? From her memory?

Never. There were some memories that could never be erased, no matter how hard she tried. The sight of that man collapsing next to her was seared in her mind's eye.

◆◆◆◆◆

"Mary Gaines is a lucky woman," the doctor said. "She'll be here in the ICU a while longer, but we're out of the woods. She certainly gave us a scare." He shook their hands before leaving: first Mara's father, then her mother, and finally Mara herself. "These aneurysms can happen at any time. She's a tough old bird, but still, it's good you got her here as soon as you did."

Mara could see her father recoil at hearing Grandmary called a "tough old bird." He cornered the doctor in the hallway before he could leave, asking pointed questions about rehabilitation and therapy.

That left Mara standing alone with her mother in the nearly barren waiting room.

"It wasn't your fault," Mrs. Gaines said, holding both of Mara's hands in both of hers. "I want to make sure you know that."

Mara nodded woodenly.

"Sometimes these brain aneurysms are brought on by stress, but there's no way of knowing that's what happened here."

Mara nodded again. She wanted to get up, stare out the window, but her mother's hands were clamped around hers.

"I just don't want you to blame yourself. No matter where you were, no matter what you were doing, this isn't your fault." Mrs. Gaines leaned in closer and dropped her voice to a whisper. "And your father does not need to know any more about what you were doing today."

"I know," Mara said, irritated, but Mrs. Gaines didn't break her gaze. "Okay. I understand."

Her mother held her hands a few seconds longer before

finally releasing them.

Mara stood back, taking in every detail of this woman who looked so much like her and still felt like a stranger. No wonder the would-be kidnapper had mistaken Mrs. Gaines for Mara. They were the same height now, the same slim build. Mrs. Gaines's dark hair had barely begun to gray. For a moment, Mara let herself imagine those moments of panic her mother had gone through. Someone had jumped out from behind a tree, right in their own front yard. Tried to take her to . . . Mara couldn't bring herself to think of it.

I'm so glad they didn't. I'm glad Mom is okay.

"You and your grandmother have always had a special bond," Mrs. Gaines said. There was a touch of wistfulness in her voice. "I wish you'd had the chance to know my parents too. They would have been proud of you."

"They would?" Mara asked. Her heart swelled at the praise and was immediately thirsty for more. *What about you? Will you ever be proud of me?*

But her mother only gave her upper arm a squeeze, in a move that might have been comforting or might have been a reminder to behave. It was hard to tell.

Congressman Gaines was coming back to them now as the doctor hastened away down the hall. Mara stepped forward to meet him and wrapped a tentative arm around him. She was surprised when he hugged her back.

"Grandmary gave us a scare today," her father said, in a voice Mara didn't recognize. "We're very lucky. Your grandmother is a good woman. Strong. Stronger than most."

Stronger than me.

As if he could read her thoughts, the congressman continued, "You've always reminded me of her. Ever since you were a little girl, you were ready to take the world by storm."

No, I'm not. Grandmary was strong. I'm scared and I'm lost and I don't want to take the world by storm. I want the world to stop storming me.

"I wish I was more like her," Mara said instead.

"There are things I would change, if I could turn back time." Mara flinched, waiting for the reproach, but her father seemed serious. "Your grandmother isn't a perfect woman, but she's always been ready and able to fix her mistakes. That's a good deal braver than many people ever are. I've certainly never been good at it."

Not now. Please. I just want to think about Grandmary. Not any of . . . this.

"I'd like to pay for your medical school," her father said. Mrs. Gaines looked up at him with surprise, but the congressman continued unfazed. "I hope you will decide to go when the fall semester starts. Becoming a doctor may be challenging, but I've always felt . . ." He stopped. "It's right for you. You're a healer."

Mara tried to savor the words, but they fell flat on her empty heart. "I appreciate it," she said. "I do, but I think it's best if I pay my own way. Thank you."

The congressman nodded. She expected him to argue, but he said only, "Your grandmother would likely say the same thing in your position. Please know we're always here for you if you need help. Financial or otherwise."

"Thank you."

"And Mara . . ." Was it possible that Congressman Joel Gaines looked embarrassed? "I'd like to apologize for my role in what happened between you and William. I may have been out of line in what I said to him. If you two choose to reconcile your differences in the future, you'll have my blessing. Particularly after his actions today, your mother and I are deeply indebted to him."

Mara had been so intent on keeping her face composed that she almost missed the last part of his little speech. "What was that? What did Will do today?"

"He called the ambulance for your grandmother," Congressman Gaines said, surprised she didn't know. He frowned at his wife, but now it was Mrs. Gaines's face that remained impassive.

"Where's Will now? Did he come to the hospital?" Mara's heart was beating hard.

"I haven't seen him," her father said. "Your mother said that after the ambulance arrived, he went back home."

◆◆◆◆◆

Home. Mara pulled the shoulder strap of the seat belt taut and then released it, letting it zing against her hand as it snapped back into place. She hadn't been in her mother's SUV since that terrible Tuesday. Now she was strapped into the back seat, looking back and forth between her mother's silhouette in the driver's seat and her father's in the passenger's seat. Mrs. Gaines was clutching the steering wheel with her hands precisely at ten and two. Based on the glow emanating from his side of the dark car, Congressman Gaines was checking his BlackBerry.

Mara's raw nerves were beginning to give way to a horrible tiredness. She could sleep for days. No, of course Mara wouldn't be able to do that. Visiting hours would start up again at eleven tomorrow. The long weeks and months of Grandmary's recovery—*if she recovered*, her brain added before she could stop it—stretched out in front of her.

"I'm sure you'll want to get a change of clothes for tonight. We'll drive you to Grandmary's to get your things," Mrs. Gaines said.

"I'll walk in with you while your mother waits in the car," Congressman Gaines offered, without looking up.

The newly rebellious part of Mara wanted to insist that she would be fine, that she should stay in Grandmary's house overnight to watch over things, but the terrible, all-consuming exhaustion had taken over.

"Thank you," Mara said, and closed her eyes.

It was good that Grandmary's house was so close to the hospital. Ten minutes, really. Thank goodness she didn't live farther, or else . . . Mara stuffed that thought down too. The little house was dark when they pulled up. Of course. Even though they had just left Grandmary at the hospital, a tiny part of Mara's heart crumbled at seeing the house without her.

Mara forced herself to think of something else, anything else. As her father helped her out of the car and walked her across the stepping-stones, Mara made a mental list of everything she'd need to do tonight. The world had kept turning, even after the data leak, and it would keep on turning, with or without Mara. She was going to have to keep up.

Memories of smoke and gunshots hit Mara full force. Her father caught her arm. "Are you all right? Did you trip?"

"No," Mara said. "No. I'm fine. Really."

Congressman Gaines looked at her through narrowed eyes. "I know where you were today," he said. "Thank you for not bringing it up to your mother."

She didn't want me to bring it up to you. Mara stifled a sigh. *Classic Mom and Dad.*

Congressman Gaines escorted her to the front door and watched her unlock it. Once she was safely across the threshold, he offered her another one-armed hug.

"I'll wait here," he said. "I'm sure you want to go upstairs and change."

Mara leaned against her father and pretended, just for a moment, that he'd said *I love you* instead.

There were a few scuffs and muddy marks on Grandmary's floor—probably from where the paramedics had arrived and brought in the gurney. Mara added mopping to her mental to-do list. Grandmary wouldn't want to come home to a messy house.

It was going to be a long time before Grandmary came back home. Would she be in a rehabilitation center, Mara wondered? Or would she be able to come home with nursing assistance? Mara's parents would pay for it, she was sure, but when would Grandmary be well enough to leave twenty-four-hour care?

Mara continued down the hall. Out of the corner of her eye, she caught the glint of some of the golden origami cranes, reflecting the kitchen lights as she turned them on. The other white and colorful cranes swayed from side to side.

Folding a thousand and one cranes was supposed to heal my broken heart. Looks like they just made things worse.

She barely noticed the peonies on the kitchen table until she caught their heady scent. Grandmary must have been gardening before her stroke. Was that how Will had found her?

No. Mara frowned at the bouquet that filled the white vase in the middle of the table. These were several shades lighter than Grandmary's pink peonies—so pale they were almost white. They were all in bloom too. Greenhouse flowers, she thought. The kind you had to buy at a floristry.

Will. Will had brought her peonies, and she hadn't been here. Grandmary had a stroke, and Mara hadn't been here. Mara held the cold porcelain vase in both hands and breathed in the flower's perfume.

I have to find him.

Mara gently set down the vase and ran up to the staircase. She climbed the steps two at a time and hurried down the hall to her room. What do you wear to go and find your ex-fiancé? Not a blood-stained protest T-shirt. That was for sure. Mara pulled it off and shoved her shaking arms into a summery pink top. Peeled off her sweaty shorts and socks and pulled on clean capris and sandals.

After a second thought, she opened her nightstand drawer and closed her fingers around Grandmary's ring. Her ring. Mara slipped it onto her pinky finger and pounded her way back downstairs.

"Dad?" Mara called. Her father opened the door and was beside her immediately. "Dad," Mara said, and her hands were shaking so hard she had to grip the ring like a talisman. "Earlier when you said you had a role in what happened between me and Will. Did you say something to him?"

Congressman Gaines shifted his weight and crossed his arms. "William came to the house looking for you the day you were running errands with your mother."

"What did you say to him?"

"William and I had a conversation." The congressman looked away from Mara for a second, but only a second.

Then his face rearranged itself into its usual expression. Noble. Impassive. Cold. "I may have given him the wrong impression and I've apologized for that."

His tone held a note of finality. Mara backed away.

"I won't be going back to the house with you and Mom tonight," Mara said. She bit off each word, watching to see if they hit their mark.

They didn't. Her father sighed. "Mara, it's getting late."

"It's not too late," Mara said, staring her father square in the eyes. "I have an apology to make too."

Congressman Gaines looked like he was about to say something, but he didn't. Mara pulled her car keys off the hook and threw the long strap of her purse over one shoulder.

"Do you know where you're going?" her father asked. "Are you sure about what you're doing?"

"Positive." If all of this had taught her one thing, it was that there was only one place, one person, that felt like home.

....

Chapter Twenty-Five

WILL

Mara wasn't at any of the hospitals. Most of the shooting victims were taken to the George Washington University Hospital. One had been transferred to Georgetown. This much Will had been able to find out. There was no record of Mara Elizabeth Gaines at either one, but maybe they were keeping her registration private. Hospitals did that, didn't they? Or maybe she didn't have any ID on her. Maybe she was listed as a Jane Doe, waiting, alone and scared.

Or maybe she's fine, Will reminded himself. She's fine and she's better off without you.

Rumor had it the Metro was a disaster. Delays for miles. Will had driven straight into the city and parked, stupidly, right on the Adams Morgan University campus. It wasn't nearly close enough to Independence Avenue, but it was the only place he could think of to find a parking spot. Will had walked, jogged, and ran for miles to reach the intersection where the shooting had broken out. But it was late afternoon now, and other than a few strings of caution tape and a cluster of police officers talking, there was no evidence of what had happened earlier. For the most part, passersby walked around the roped-off area as casually as if it marked construction or wet concrete.

It was terrible, witnessing how quickly the world started moving on again.

Will trekked up and down the sidewalk. What had he been hoping to find, exactly? Did he really think that if Mara needed help, she'd still be here hours later? Or that if she didn't, he'd find her strolling alongside the road, looking for him?

It was a fool's errand, but it was still hard for Will to turn back and start the long, slow walk back to Adams Morgan. Will had a stitch in his side now. He even thought about hopping on the Metro for one stop or calling a taxi, but that would be more hassle and money than it was worth. Will reached his car before sunset and drove back to the apartment building before dark.

As soon as Will collapsed on the couch, he knew he wasn't getting up. Adrenaline had kept him going ever since he left Mara's parents at the hospital, but the full force of his defeat was starting to hit him. Well, so what if he did fall asleep here? Will's next shift at the restaurant wasn't for days. He could sleep off the next eighteen hours, if he wanted, and Will felt himself about to do just that. He turned on the television to keep himself company and drifted in and out to the sounds of game show hosts and commercials.

Will was startled awake by a knock on the apartment door. He jolted forward and sat straight up. Had he turned the TV off on his own? When did it get dark? Either he'd slept longer than he'd thought, or this was a dream.

Another knock. Then a familiar voice calling through the door. "Will."

If this is a dream, I don't want to wake up. Will practically vaulted to open the door, and there she was. Sweaty strands of hair had escaped Mara's messy ponytail, and her face was pink and splotchy. She must have been crying. Will could tell. But she was here now, here and real, looking up at him with a hundred questions in her eyes.

"You came back." It was magnetic. Immediate. Will reached out and pulled her in toward him.

"I'm sorry," Mara said breathlessly, and then the door slammed behind her and she was pressed up against him, folded up inside his waiting arms. She kept saying it, even with her face buried in his chest. "I'm sorry. I'm sorry. I'm so sorry."

"No, I am," Will said. "Mara. It wasn't me who did that. My voice mail got hacked. I would never do that to you."

Mara held him tighter. "I should have known. I should have called you again. I should have—"

"No more should-haves," Will said. "No more." He looked down and found her face was tilted up, waiting for him.

He kissed her. Long and hard and slow. Two weeks'

worth of kisses wrapped up in this one. Two lifetimes' worth.

"I meant every word I said," Mara murmured. "Over the phone. I love you. I always have and I always will. And I'm so, so sorry. I had the chance to handle everything with you and I just . . . I just decided to do everything my own way."

She was starting to cry again. Will kissed her before he could start too.

"I let myself play comparisons. I convinced myself I wasn't enough for you," Will said.

"It sounds like my dad did that. But not just him. I made you feel that way," Mara said. "You were always more than enough."

"But I shouldn't have decided you were better off without me."

"I think we're better together," Mara said. "I know I'm better when I'm with you."

"We were married before," Will said, and he made himself pull back. "We were married before and we risked it all. What if we never find out why? What if we find out and we don't like what we hear?"

"I don't know." Mara gripped his arms. "I'm honestly not sure which would be worse."

"I know. I know."

"But I do know this." Mara stepped back too and looked him full in the face. "The worst thing in all of this was being apart from you."

"So why did we choose it?" Will asked. "Not just this time, but in our other lifetime. Our first one."

"I guess we didn't know how lucky we were. The first time or . . . this time."

Will moved closer again. "Either way you look at it," he said, "we have a second chance. We could try again. If you want."

"Will Sterling." Mara reached up and guided his chin down, until his eyes were level with hers. "I would be so lucky to have any second chance with you."

It felt exactly like coming home.

OPINION: Alicia Barnes's Confession Gives Us Few Answers, More Questions

By Portia Hamlin

Perhaps the most concerning part of Ms. Barnes's public confession last Wednesday is this statement: "I want America to heal. I have confessed, and now this needs to be over."

On the surface, this hardly seems more alarming than the rest of Ms. Barnes's confession. Certainly, none of us is sleeping well with the knowledge that someone could so easily release top-tier classified information for political gain. Those who were named on the list will likely never sleep well again, knowing how quickly and disastrously they can be vilified for crimes they do not remember.

No, Ms. Barnes, your confession may be complete and sincere, but America cannot heal just yet. We need more than a resolution of what happened to cause the data leak. We need to decide how we will move forward. In the wake of the time wrecker scandal, America faces a new challenge: How will we regulate a technology that was designed for justice but can, obviously, be used for even greater injustice?

Empirically, timeline rectification works, *as long as procedures are followed to the letter.* In the internet age, can we expect anything to be kept confidential? Can we justify using this technology if the ethics depend on privacy—the one thing Americans clearly cannot count on?

No, Ms. Barnes, the scandal is not over. Your political stunt has shone a bright light on the injustice of modern justice, just the way you intended. Now Americans need to grapple with how hard they are willing to fight for justice . . . or, more accurately, how much injustice they will tolerate.

The spotlight is on the issue, and the entire world is watching. Let's hope we make the right call.

ACKNOWLEDGMENTS

What happened to Mara and Will?

Before I published *Every Last Minute*, the first book in the Time Wrecker Trilogy, I already knew how their timeline rectification would turn out. But would the risk be worth it? This was the question I found myself struggling with; not only as I wrote draft after draft of the second book in the trilogy, but in my own life as well.

As it happened, my writing process for this book was rudely interrupted by foot surgery and even more rudely interrupted by a long, complicated recovery. When I was finally able to get back to writing, I brought the whole messy business of healing with me and poured it into Mara and Will's story. The time away made me more conscious of how complicated the time wrecker leak would be for Mara and Will and what it would look like for each of them to grow through it. It also brought a renewed appreciation for how many people help us during the messier parts of our lives.

I want to thank my friends who encouraged me to keep writing and share the rest of Mara and Will's story. Sarah, Allison, Kim, Len, Bob, Gary, Jo Anne, Deb, Peter, Renea, and Mindy—I am extremely grateful for your support and encouragement.

Many thanks are also due to the Writerly Whatnots, to

the Curiouser Author Network, and to the beta readers who read over the final draft. Sarah, Peter, and Renea: I am indebted to each of you for your help scouting for plot holes and asking the tough questions about time travel.

One of the highlights of my experience in publishing Book One of the Time Wrecker Trilogy was working with Monica Haynes of The Thatchery and Shayla Raquel. I am so grateful for the opportunity to work with them again! Monica always captures the essence of a story in her gorgeous designs. Her book covers are truly works of art! Shayla went above and beyond as an editor, patiently working with me to correct everything from punctuation and grammar to fine-tuning the characterization, emotion, and plot. I'm so thankful to both of them for making *Any Second Chance* ready to send out into the world.

And finally, the greatest thanks are due to my husband, Andy. Our love story is still my favorite.

Ellen Smith is a freelance education writer and speculative fiction author. When she isn't busy writing, Ellen can be found reading, dabbling in various crafts, and generally avoiding housework. No matter what she is doing, Ellen is always wondering, "What if?" Ellen lives with her family near Washington, DC.

REVIEW ANY SECOND CHANCE

Did you enjoy *Any Second Chance?* Please take a moment to
leave a review!

Connect with the Author
Mara and Will's story continues in Book 3 of the Time
Wrecker Trilogy: *All Kinds of Time.* Keep in touch to stay
updated on the next book in the series!

Facebook: https://www.facebook.com/ESWrites/
Instagram: https://www.instagram.com/ellensmithwrites/
Twitter: https://twitter.com/EllenSmithWrite
Website: www.ellensmithwrites.com